Words Of Cheer For The Tempted, The Toiling, And The Sorrowing

by

T. S. Arthur

Words Of Cheer For The Tempted, The Toiling, And The Sorrowing
by T. S. Arthur

Copyright © 2023

All Rights reserved.

No part of this publication may be reproduced, stored in a retrieval system, or transmitted in any form or by any means, electronic, mechanical, photocopying or Otherwise, without the written permission of the publisher.
The author/editor asserts the moral right to be identified as the author/editor of this work.

ISBN: 978-93-59950-09-9

Published by

DOUBLE 9 BOOKS

2/13-B, Ansari Road
Daryaganj, New Delhi – 110002
info@double9books.com
www.double9books.com
Tel. 011-40042856

This book is under public domain

ABOUT THE AUTHOR

Timothy Shay Arthur, or T. S. Arthur was born on June 6, 1809, and died on March 6, 1885. S. Arthur was a well-known American author in the 1800s. Many people know him for the 1854 book Ten Nights in a Bar-Room and What I Saw There, which was a temperance story. It helped make Americans dislike alcohol. When he wrote his stories with care and compassion, he shared beliefs and ideas that were common in American "respectable middle class" life. A story of his called "An Angel in Disguise" shows how much he believed in the healing and changing power of love. He also wrote dozens of stories for Godey's Lady's Book, which was the most famous American monthly magazine before the Civil War. For many years, he published and edited his own magazine, Arthur's Home Magazine, which was modeled after Godey's. Arthur did a lot to explain and spread the values, beliefs, and habits that made up proper middle-class life in America. He is almost lost today. While a child, Arthur lived in Fort Montgomery, New York. He was born in Newburgh, New York. By 1820, Arthur's miller father had moved to Baltimore, Maryland, and Arthur went to school there for a short time.

CONTENTS

PREFACE	9
AUNT MARY	10
THE DEAD	20
DO YOU SUFFER MORE THAN YOUR NEIGHBOUR?	22
WE ARE LED BY A WAY THAT WE KNOW NOT	26
THE IVY IN THE DUNGEON	29
THE GARDEN OF EDEN	31
HAVE A FLOWER IN YOUR ROOM	35
WEALTH	38
HOW TO BE HAPPY	40
REBECCA	47
LIFE A TREADMILL	49
ARTHUR LELAND	53
THE SCARLET POPPY	58
NUMBER TWELVE	64
TO AN ABSENTEE	68
THE WHITE DOVE	69
HESTER	81
THISTLE-DOWN	82
THE LITTLE CHILDREN	94
WHAT IS NOBLE?	99
THE ANEMONE HEPATICA	100

THE FAMILY OF MICHAEL AROUT	101
BABY IS DEAD	111
THE TREASURED RINGLET	113
HUMAN LONGINGS FOR PEACE AND REST	115
"BE STRONG"	119
THE NEGLECTED ONE	120
THE HOURS OF LIFE	129
MINISTERING ANGELS	140
OURS, LOVED, AND "GONE BEFORE"	141
OUTWARD MINISTERINGS	151
BODILY DEFORMITY, SPIRITUAL BEAUTY	153
THE DEAD CHILD	155
WATER	157
BEAUTIFUL, HAPPY, AND BELOVED	159
"EVERY CLOUD HAS A SILVER LINING"	160
AN ANGEL OF PATIENCE	162
THE GRANDFATHER'S ADVICE	163
A HYMN OF PRAISE	173
AN ANGEL IN EVERY HOUSE	174
ANNIE	176
MOTHER	177
GREAT PRINCIPLES AND SMALL DUTIES	179
"OF SUCH IS THE KINGDOM OF HEAVEN"	181
THE OLD VILLAGE CHURCH	183
"THE WORD IS NIGH THEE"	188
AUNT RACHEL	189
COMETH A BLESSING DOWN	192
THE DARKENED PATHWAY	193

LOOK ON THIS PICTURE	200
THE POWER OF KINDNESS	202
SPEAK KINDLY	204
HAVE PATIENCE	206
DO THEY MISS ME?	213

PREFACE

AS we pass on our way through the world, we find our paths now smooth and flowery, and now rugged and difficult to travel. The sky, bathed in golden sunshine to-day, is black with storms to-morrow! This is the history of every one. And it is also the life-experience of all, that when the way is rough and the sky dark, the poor heart sinks and trembles, and the eye of faith cannot see the bright sun smiling in the heavens beyond the veil of clouds. But, for all this fear and doubt, the rugged path winds steadily upwards, and the broad sky is glittering in light.

Let the toiling, the tempted, and the sorrowing ever keep this in mind. Let them have faith in Him who feedeth the young lions, and clothes the fields with verdure—who bindeth up the broken heart, and giveth joy to the mourners. There are Words of Cheer in the air! Listen! and their melody will bring peace to the spirit, and their truths strength to the heart.

AUNT MARY

A LADY sat alone in her own apartment one clear evening, when the silver stars were out, and the moon shone pure as the spirit of peace upon the rebellious earth. How lovely was every outward thing! How beautiful is God's creation! The window curtains were drawn close, and the only light in the cheerful room, was given by a night-lamp that was burning on the mantel-piece. The occupant, who perhaps had numbered about thirty-five years, was sitting by a small table in the centre of the room, her head leaning upon one slender hand; the other lay upon the open page of a book in which she had endeavoured to interest herself. But the effort had been vain; other and stronger feelings had overpowered her; there was an expression of suffering upon the gentle face, over which the tears rained heavily. For a brief moment she raised her soft blue eyes upward with an appealing look, then sunk her head upon the table before her, murmuring,

"Father! forgive me! it is good for me. Give me strength to bear everything. Pour thy love into my heart, for I am desolate—if I could but be useful to one human being—if I could make one person happier, I should be content. But no! I am desolate—desolate. Whose heart clings to mine with the strong tendrils of affection? Who ever turns to me for a smile? Oh! this world is so cold—so cold!"

And that sensitive being wept passionately, and pressed her hand upon her bosom as if to still its own yearnings.

Mary Clinton had met with many sorrows; she was the youngest of a large family; she had been the caressed darling in her early days, for her sweetness won every heart to love. She had dwelt in the warm breath of affection, it was her usual sunshine, and she gave it no thought while it blessed her; a cold word or look was an unfamiliar thing. A most gladhearted being she was once! But death came in a terrible form, folded her loved ones in his icy arms and bore them to another world. A kind father, a tender mother, a brother and sister, were laid in the grave, in one short month, by the cholera. One brother was yet left, and she was taken to his home, for he was a wealthy merchant. But there seemed a coldness in his splendid house, a coldness in his wife's heart. Sick in body and in mind, the bereft one resolved to travel South, and visit among her relations, hoping to awaken her interest in life, which had lain dormant through grief. She went to that sunny region, and while there, became acquainted with a man of fine intellect and fascinating manners, who won her affections, and afterwards proved unworthy of her. Again the beauty of her life was darkened, and with a weary heart she wore out the tedious years of her joyless existence. She was an angel of charity to the poor and suffering. She grew lovelier through sorrow. A desire to see her brother, her nearest and dearest relative, called her North again, and when our story opens she was in the bosom of his home, a member of his family. He loved her deeply, yet she felt like an alien—his wife had not welcomed her as a sister should. Mary Clinton's heart went out toward's Alice, her eldest niece, a beautiful and loving creature just springing into womanhood. But the fair girl was gay and thoughtless, flattered and caressed by everybody. She knew sadness only by the name. She had no dream that she could impart a deep joy, by giving forth her young heart's love to the desolate stranger.

The hour had grown late, very late, and Mary Clinton still leaned her head upon the table buried in thoughts, when the bounding step of Alice outside the door aroused her from her revery. She listened, almost hoping to see her friendly face peeping in, but wearied with the enjoyment of the evening, the fair young belle hastened on to her chamber, and her aunt heard the door close. Rising from her seat at the table, Miss Clinton approached a window, and threw back the curtains that the midnight air might steal coolingly over her brow. Her eye fell upon the rich bracelet that clasped her arm, a gift of her brother, and then with a sad smile, she surveyed the pure dress of delicate white she wore. "Ah!" she sighed, "I am robed for a scene of gayety, but how sad the heart that beats beneath this boddice! How glad I was to escape from the company; loneliness in the crowd is so sad a feeling." At that moment the door of her room opened, and Alice came laughing in, her glowing face all bright and careless.

"Oh! Aunt Mary," she exclaimed, "do help me! I cannot unclasp my necklace, and my patience has all oozed out at the tips of my fingers. There! you have unfastened it already. Well! I believe I never will be good for anything!" And Alice laughed as heartily, as if the idea was charming. "When did you leave the parlours, Aunt Mary? I never missed you at all. Father said you left early, when I met him just now on the stairs."

"I did leave early," replied Miss Clinton. "I chanced to feel like being entirely alone, so I sought my own apartment."

"Have you been reading, aunt? I should think you would feel lonely!"

"I read very little," was the reply, in a sad tone. No remark was made on her loneliness.

"It seems so strange to me, Aunt Mary, that you are so fond of being alone. I like company so much," said Alice, looking in her quiet face. "But I must go," she added; she paused a moment, then pressed an affectionate kiss upon her aunt's cheek, and whispered a soft "good night." Miss Clinton cast both arms around her, and drew her to her heart, with an eagerness that surprised Alice. Twice she kissed her, then hastily released her as if her feeling had gone forth before she was aware of it. Alice stood still before her a moment, and her careless eyes took a deeply searching expression as they dwelt upon the countenance before her. Something like sadness passed over her face, and her voice was deeper in its tone, as she repeated, "Good night, dear Aunt Mary!" With a slow step she left the apartment, mentally contrasting her own position with that of her aunt. Circumstances around her and the society with which she mingled, tended to drown reflection, and call into play only the brighter and gayer feelings, that flutter on the surface of our being. She had never known the luxury of devoting an hour to genuine meditation on the world within—or the great world without. The earth was to her a garden of joy; she lived upon it only to enjoy herself. Like many selfish people, Alice's mother made an idol of her beautiful child, because she was a part of herself; and Mrs. Clinton was not one to perform a mother's duty faithfully in instilling right views of life into her daughter's mind. Thus, with a depth of feeling, and rich gifts of mind, Alice fluttered on her way like a light-winged butterfly, her soul's pure wells of tender thought unknown to her. How many millions pass through a whole long life, with the deepest and holiest secrets of their being still unlocked by their heedless hands! How few see aught to live for, but the outward sunshine of prosperity, which is an idle sunshine, compared with the ever-strengthening light that may grow in the spirit! How strong, how great, how beautiful may life be, when smiled upon by our Creator! how weak, how abject, how trampled upon, when turned away from his face!

With better and more quiet emotions, Mary Clinton retired to rest. "I can love others, if I am not beloved," she murmured, and the dove of peace fluttered its white wing over her. Her resigned prayer was, "Lord, into thy hands I commit my spirit." Tears of earnest humility had washed away all bitterness from the wrung heart of that lovely being. How beautiful was the angel smile that played over her face, in her pure dreams!

A few weeks after, Alice entered her aunt's apartment one drizzling, damp, foggy, uncomfortable day. "Such miserable weather!" she exclaimed, throwing herself idly into an arm-chair; "I believe I have got the *blues* for once in my life. I don't know what to do with myself; it makes me perfectly melancholy to look out of the window, and nothing in the house wears a cheerful aspect. Mother has a headache; when I proposed reading to her, she very politely asked me if I would not let her remain alone. She says I always want to sing, read, or talk incessantly if she wishes to be quiet. I can't ding on the piano, for it is heard from attic to basement. I don't want to read alone, for I have such a desire to be sociable—now, Aunt Mary, you have a catalogue of my troubles, can't you relieve me, for I am really miserable, if I don't look so!" Alice broke into a laugh, although it did not bubble right up from her merry heart as usual.

"If your attention was fully engaged, you would not mind the weather so much," remarked Aunt Mary, with a quiet smile. "You are not in a mood to enjoy a book just now, so what *will* you do, my dear?"

"Mend stockings, or turn my room upside down, and then arrange it neatly," said Alice in a speculative tone. "There is nothing in the house to interest me; there is Patty in the kitchen, I have just been paying her a visit. She is as busy as a bee, and as happy as a queen. I believe poor people are happier than the rich, in such weather as this, at least."

"Because they are useful, Alice; go busy yourself about some physical labour for an hour or two, then come back to me, and I predict your face will be as sunshiny as ever. I am in earnest—you need not look so incredulous!"

"What shall I do?" asked the young girl laughing. "I don't know how to do a single thing in domestic matters. Mother says I shall never work. It would spoil my fairy fingers, I presume, a terrible consequence!"

"But seriously Alice, you are not so entirely incapable of doing anything, are you?"

"I am positively, but I can learn if I choose. I believe I will sweep my room and put it in order, as a beginning. That will be something new: now I will try my best!" Alice sprang from her chair, and tripped from the apartment quite pleased with the idea. A smile broke over Miss Clinton's features, after her niece had left her alone. "How easily Alice might be trained to better things, by love and gentleness," she said half aloud. "Oh! if she would only love me, and turn to me fondly. How I would delight to breathe a genial prayer over the buds of promise in her youthful heart, and fan them to warmer life." More than an hour flew by, as Mary Clinton sat in thought, devising plans to awaken her favourite to a true sense of her duties—to a knowledge of her capabilities for happiness and usefulness. We may be useful with a heart full of sadness; but we can rarely taste of happiness, unless we are desirous to benefit some one besides ourselves. 'A quietness came over the lonely one as she mused—a spirit of beautiful repose; for she forgot all thoughts of her own enjoyment, in caring for another.

"You are quite a physician, Aunt Mary, to a mind diseased," exclaimed Alice, breaking her revery as she came in with a smiling face, after the performance of her unaccustomed labour. "I am quite in tune again now. I believe there is a little philosophy in being busy occasionally, after all."

"There is really," replied Miss Clinton, raising her deep blue eyes to Alice's face, with their pleasant expression; "and there is also philosophy in recreation—in abandoning yourself for a time to innocent gayety. An hour of enjoyment is refreshing and beneficial."

"Why, Aunt Mary!" said Alice in some surprise, "I had no idea that you thought so. You are always so industrious and quiet, I imagined you disapproved of the merriment of ordinary people. When we have a large company you almost always retire early. Why do you do so, aunt, may I ask you?"

Mary Clinton was silent a moment, then she said gently, "When I think I can add to the ease or enjoyment of any person present, I take pleasure in staying; but when I feel that I am rather a restraint than otherwise, I retire—to weep. You are yet young and beautiful, my child, for you have never known such feelings. I am too selfish, or I would not be sad so often; it is right that I should pass through such a school of discipline. I hope it has already made me better." The look of resignation that beamed from Miss Clinton's tearful eyes, caused a chord in Alice's heart to tremble with a strange blending of love, sweetness, and sorrow.

"*You* should be happy, if any one should, dear aunt," she said in a low voice, and she partly averted her head, to conceal the tears that started down her cheek. "I am happy so often," she resumed, turning around and seating herself upon an ottoman at her aunt's feet. "You deserve so much more than I—to be as good as you are, Aunt Mary, I would almost change situations, for then I should be sure of going to heaven."

"You can be just as sure in your own position, as in that of any other person. But, dear child, the more deeply we scan our hearts, the more we see there to conquer, in order that we may become fit companions for the angels."

Alice remained thoughtful for some moments, then she folded her hands over Aunt Mary's lap, and lifted her eyes to the loving face that bent over her. "Be my guardian angel," she prayed tearfully, "your love is so pure; a gentleness comes over me, when I am with you. All tumultuous feelings sink down to repose. I have not known you, Aunt Mary; you have shown me to-day how lovely goodness is. I can feel it in your presence. Oh! to possess it! I fear it will be long years before I grow so gentle in my spirit—so unselfish—so like a child of Heaven!"

"Hush, hush!" was Mary Clinton's gentle interruption. "You do not know me yet, Alice. Perhaps I appear far better than I am."

Alice smiled, and laying her arm around Aunt Mary's neck, drew down her face, and kissed her affectionately, whispering, "You will be my guide, I ask no better."

"Thank you, thank you," broke from Aunt Mary's lips; she pressed Alice's cheek with the ardent haste of love and gratitude; then yielding to the emotions that thrilled her heart, she burst into tears, and wept with a joy she had long been a stranger to. She felt that her life would no longer be useless, if she could live for Alice, and lift up to God her heart. How beautiful in its freshness, is the early day when the light of a good resolve breaks like a halo over the soul, and by its power, seeks to win it from its selfish idols! Earnest and strong is the hopefulness that bids us labour trustingly to become all we yearn to be—all we may be. How tremblingly Mary Clinton leaned upon her Saviour! experience had taught her the weakness of her fluttering heart; sorrow was familiar, yet she prayed not to shrink from it. How clear and vigorous was the mind of Alice—how shadowless was her unerring path to be—how all weakness departed before the sudden thought that rose up in her soul! How rich was the light that beamed from her steady eye—how calm and trusting the slight smile that parted her lips! How meek and confiding she was, and yet how full of strength! She was a young seeker after truth, and she realized not yet, that that same truth was the power to which she must bow every rebellious thing within her. Months rolled on, and the quiet gladness in her heart made it a delight to her to do anything and everything it seemed her duty to do. The unexplored world within opened to her gaze, and threw a glory upon creation. Infinitely priceless in her eyes, were the thousand hearts around her, in which the Lord had kindled the undying lamp of life.

One evening, at rather a late hour, Alice Clinton sought the chamber of her aunt and seated herself quietly beside her, saying in a subdued voice as she took her hand, "I am inexpressibly sad to-night, Aunt Mary. There is no very particular reason why I should feel so; no one can soothe me but you. Put your arms around me, Aunt Mary, and talk to me—give me some strength to go forward in the way I have chosen. I almost despair—I have no good influence, no moral courage. Perhaps, after all, my efforts have been in vain to become better, and I shall sink back into my former state. If all who are my friends were like you, it would be an easy thing to glide on with the stream. But I am in the midst of peril—I never knew until to-night that it was hard to speak with a cold rigour to our friends when they merit it. If I were despised, or neglected, I could more easily fix my thoughts on heaven. I dread so to hurt the feelings of any one."

"What do you refer to, dear?" inquired Aunt Mary, tenderly.

"My friend Eleanor Temple, and her brother Theodore, have been spending the evening with me. You know how gay and witty they are. In answer to a remark of mine, Theodore gravely quoted a passage of Scripture, which applied to my observation in an irresistibly ludicrous manner. I yielded to a hearty laugh which I could not restrain; it came so suddenly I had no time for thought. But in a moment after my conscience smote me, and I felt that my respect for Theodore had lessened. I had no right to rebuke him, even if I had the moral courage, for my laughter was encouragement. I turned away from him and spoke to Eleanor; I was displeased with myself, and I felt a sort of inward repugnance to him. But that was not the end; several times afterwards Theodore did the same thing.

"'There are subjects which are not fit food for merriment;' I said once in an embarrassed manner. 'If I do wrong, it is not deliberately done.' Theodore was silent a moment, and he looked at me as if he hardly knew how to understand me—then smiling, he turned the conversation, and was as gay as ever. When they had taken their leave, I entered the parlour again, and threw myself in a seat by the open window. I turned the blind, and looked out after them. Eleanor had caught the fringe of her mantilla in the railing of the area. I was about to speak with her on the little accident, when Theodore laughed, and said to his sister, 'Alice is as fond of taking characters, as an actress. She attempted to reprove me, for the very thing she had laughed at a little while before. Rather inconsistent in our favourite, Nelly, don't you think so?' Eleanor laughed, and said good-naturedly, 'Alice is impulsive, she don't measure what she says, before it comes out.'

"I rose, and left the window. I felt sad, and peculiarly discomposed and dissatisfied with myself. I knew that I had tried to do right in some degree, and it grated on my feelings that my effort should be called 'a taking of character.' Oh! if I could only live with good people altogether, who would bear with me, and trust my motives! You have my story, Aunt Mary, it amounts to nothing, but I am so sad."

"Life is made up of trifles," said Miss Clinton. "Few circumstances are so trivial that we may not draw a lesson from them. Do not feel sad, Alice, because you are misunderstood. Do not repine on account of your position; no one could fill it but yourself, or you would not be placed in it. Be resigned to meet those who call out unpleasant feelings; they teach you better your own nature than ever the angels could. They bring forth what is evil in you, that it may be conquered. Do not understand me to mean that you should ever seek those who may harm you. But a day can hardly pass over our heads, that we do not meet with persons who ruffle that harmony of soul we so labour after. It is keenly felt when one is as young in a better life as you are. You need strength, and then you will be calm and even. Time, patience, combating, prayer, good-will to man, must bring your soul to order, then you will bear upon the spirits of others with a still, purifying power which will soothe and soften like far-off music. You have it in your power to do much good; your Creator has blessed you with that inexpressible sympathy which may glide gently into another human heart and open its secret springs almost unconsciously to the possessor. I have watched you, child of my love, and perhaps I know you better than you know yourself. There are many latent germs within your being; Oh! Alice, pray God to expand them to heavenly life. Bear on—and live for something worthy a creature God has made." Mary Clinton paused in an unusual emotion; her cheek glowed deeply, and the burning softness of her eyes chained Alice's look as with a spell, to their angel expression. The heart of the young girl throbbed almost to bursting, with the world of undeveloped feeling that rushed over her. It was a moment which many have experienced—a moment which breaks over the young for the first time with such a thrill—she realized that God had gifted her with power—with a soul that might and *must* have its influence. Bowing her head upon Aunt Mary's knee, she wept; and a flood of joy, humility, and thanksgiving came over her, as she more deeply dedicated herself to the holy Lord, and laid her gifts upon His altar. Aunt Mary's words sunk peacefully into her soul, and a clear light irradiated it and filled it with a calmness that made all things right. With a look of irrepressible tenderness, and a voice full of low music, Alice said to Aunt Mary, as she rose to retire, "You have charmed away every discordant note that was touched to-night, dear aunt. How unaccountable are our sudden changes of mood! You have now thrown over me your own spirit of peaceful repose and contentment. Good-night, and think you!"

"Well, I am content, entirely content," soliloquized Mary Clinton, when the loved form of the child of her heart had disappeared. "To try to bless another, how richly does the blessing fall back upon my own soul! Yes! I have my joys. Why am I ever so ungrateful as to murmur at aught that befalls me? I am blest—a sunshine is breaking over the tender earth for me; all clouds are gone." With feelings much changed from what they were a few months previous, Mary Clinton sought the window, and with loving and devoted eyes dwelt upon the night and stillness of the heavens—so boundless and so pure. The moon was full; near it was one bright cloud of silver drapery, upon the edge of which rested a single star. "So shall it be with me," she murmured, "be the clouds that float over the heavens of my soul bright or dark, the star of holy trust shall linger near, ever bringing to my bosom—peace."

About two years after, on a winter evening, there was a large company assembled at Mr. Clinton's dwelling. It was in compliment to Alice, for that day completed her twentieth year. As she moved from one spot to another, her sweet face radiant with happiness, Aunt Mary's eyes followed her with a devoted expression, which betrayed that the lovely being was her dearest earthly treasure. The merry girl was now a glad-hearted, but thoughtful woman. An innocent mirthfulness lingered around her, which time itself would never subdue, except for a brief season, when her sweet laugh broke out with a natural, rich suddenness; there was a catching joy in it, that could not be withstood. She was the gentle hostess to perfection; with tact enough to discover congenial spirits, and bring them together, finding her own pleasure in the cheerful home thus made. She possessed the rare but happy art of making every body feel perfectly at home, one knew not why. For a moment, Alice stood alone with her little hand resting upon the centre-table. Behind her, two rather fashionable young men were talking and laughing somewhat too loud, and jesting upon sacred things. A look of pain passed over the face of the fair listener as she slowly turned round, and said in a low but earnest tone, "Don't, Theodore! Excuse me, but *such* trifling pains me." The young gentlemen both appeared mortified. "Pardon me! Alice," exclaimed Theodore Temple, "I will try to break that habit for your sake. I was not aware that it pained you so much—a lady's word is law!" and he bowed gallantly.

"No, no! Base your giving up of the habit upon principle, then it will be permanent. Much obliged for the compliment"—Alice bowed with assumed dignity, and her sweet face dimpled into a playful smile, "but I have no faith in these pretty speeches. Remember, now, I have your promise to try to break the habit; you will forfeit your word if you do not; so you see your position, don't you?" Thus saying, and without waiting for a reply, the young lady left them.

"I believe Miss Clinton is right, after all," remarked Temple's companion. "What is the use of jesting on such subjects? We never feel any better after it, and we subject ourselves to the displeasure of those who respect these things. I pass my word to give it up, if you will, Temple."

"Agreed!" was Theodore's brief answer. Without saying how mingled the motive might have been, which induced the young men to forsake the habit, they *did* forsake it permanently. Aunt Mary's lonely life was at last smiled upon by a sunbeam—and that sunbeam was the soul of Alice, which she had turned to the light. For that cherished being Mary Clinton could have offered up her life, and there would have been a joy in the sacrifice. Strongly and nobly were their hearts knit together—beautiful is the devotedness of holy, unselfish love! Blest are two frank hearts, which may be opened to each other, pouring out like lava the tide of feeling hoarded in the inward soul—such revelations are for moments when the yearning heart will not be hushed to calmness. But "there is a moonlight in human life," and there is also a blessing in that subdued hour which whispers wearily to the loving one, of weaknesses and sins, with a prayer for consoling strength to triumph yet, leaving them in the dust. Thus was it with Mary and Alice Clinton; their souls were open as the day to each other. They travelled along life's pathway with earnest purpose, fulfilling the many and changing duties that fell upon them, ever catching rich gleams of joy from above. And sorrows came too! but they purified, and taught the slumbering soul its rarest wealth—its deepest sympathies with all things good and heavenly. It seemed a slight thing that took away the desolation from the heart of Mary Clinton—she turned away from *self*, and devoted her efforts to the eternal happiness of another. Is there one human being in the wide world so desolate, that he may not do likewise? Only a mite may be cast in, but God has made none of his children so poor, as to be without an influence. The humblest effort, if it is all that *can* be made, is as full of greatness at the core, as the most ostentatious display.

THE DEAD

IT is strange what a change is wrought in one hour by death. The moment our friend is gone from us for ever, what sacredness invests him! Everything he ever said or did seems to return to us clothed in new significance. A thousand yearnings rise, of things we would fain say to him—of questions unanswered, and now unanswerable. All he wore or touched, or looked upon familiarly, becomes sacred as relics. Yesterday these were homely articles, to be tossed to and fro, handled lightly, given away thoughtlessly— to-day we touch them softly, our tears drop on them; death has laid his hand on them, and they have become holy in our eyes. Those are sad hours when one has passed from our doors never to return, and we go back to set the place in order. There the room, so familiar, the homely belongings of their daily life, each one seems to say to us in its turn, "Neither shall their place know them any more." Clear the shelf now of vials and cups, and prescriptions; open the windows; step no more carefully; there is no one now to be cared for—no one to be nursed—no one to be awakened.

Ah! why does this bring a secret pang with it when we know that they are where none shall any more say, "I am sick!" Could only one flutter of their immortal garments be visible in such moments; could their face, glorious with the light of heaven, once smile on the deserted room, it might be better. One needs to lose friends to understand one's self truly. The death of a friend teaches things within that we never knew before. We may have expected it, prepared for it, it may have been hourly expected for weeks; yet when it comes, it falls on us suddenly, and reveals in us emotions we could not dream. The opening of those heavenly gate for them startles and flutters our souls with strange mysterious thrills, unfelt before. The glimpse of glories, the sweep of voices, all startle and dazzle us, and the soul for many a day aches and longs with untold longings.

We divide among ourselves the possessions of our lost ones. Each well-known thing comes to us with an almost supernatural power. The book we once read with them, the old Bible, the familiar hymn; then perhaps little pet articles of fancy, made dear to them by some peculiar taste, the picture, the vase!—how costly are they now in our eyes.

We value them not for their beauty or worth, but for the frequency with which we have seen them touched or used by them; and our eye runs over the collection, and perhaps lights most lovingly on the homeliest thing which may have been oftenest touched or worn by them.

It is a touching ceremony to divide among a circle of friends the memorials of the lost. Each one comes inscribed—"*no more;*" and yet each one, too, is a pledge of reunion. But there are invisible relics of our lost ones more precious than the book, the pictures, or the vase. Let us treasure them in our hearts. Let us bind to our hearts the patience which they will never need again; the fortitude in suffering which belonged only to this suffering state. Let us take from their dying hand that submission under affliction which they shall need no more in a world where affliction is unknown. Let us collect in our thoughts all those cheerful and hopeful sayings which they threw out from time to time as they walked with us, and string them as a rosary to be daily counted over. Let us test our own daily life by what must be their now perfected estimate; and as they once walked with us on earth, let us walk with them in heaven.

We may learn at the grave of our lost ones how to live with the living. It is a fearful thing to live so carelessly as we often do with those dearest to us, who may at any moment be gone for ever. The life we are living, the words we are now saying, will all be lived over in memory over some future grave. One remarks that the death of a child often makes parents tender and indulgent! Ah, it is a lesson learned of bitter sorrow! If we would know how to measure our work to living friends, let us see how we feel towards the dead. If we have been neglectful, if we have spoken hasty and unkind words, on which death has put his inevitable seal, what an anguish is that! But our living friends may, ere we know, pass from us; we may be to-day talking with those whose names to-morrow are to be written among the dead; the familiar household object of to-day may become sacred relics to-morrow. Let us walk softly; let us forbear and love; none ever repented of too much love to a departed friend; none ever regretted too much tenderness and indulgence, but many a tear has been shed for too much harshness and severity. Let our friends in heaven then teach us how to treat our friends on earth. Thus by no vain fruitless sorrow, but by a deeper self-knowledge, a tenderer and more sacred estimate of life, may our heavenly friends prove to us ministering spirits.

The triumphant apostle says to the Christian, "All things are yours—Life and Death." Let us not lose either; let us make *Death* our own; in a richer, deeper, and more solemn earnestness of life. So those souls which have gone from our ark, and seemed lost over the gloomy ocean of the unknown, shall return to us, bearing the olive-leaves of Paradise.

DO YOU SUFFER MORE THAN YOUR NEIGHBOUR?

"WHOSE sorrow is like unto my sorrow?"

Such is the language of the stricken soul, such the outbreak of feeling, when affliction darkens the horizon of man's sunny hopes, and dashes the full cup of blessings suddenly from the expectant lips.

"Console me not; you have not felt this pang," cries the spirit in agony, to the kind friend who is striving to pour the balm of consolation in the wounded heart.

"But I have known worse," is the reply.

"Worse! never, never; no one could suffer more keenly than I now do, and live."

In vain the friend reasons; sorrow is always more or less selfish; it absorbs all other passions; it consecrates itself to tears and lamentations, and the bereaved one feels alone; utterly alone in the world, and of all mankind the most forsaken. Every heart knoweth its own bitterness, and there is a canker spot on every human plant in God's garden. Some are blighted and withered, ready to fall from the stalk; others are blooming while a blight is at the root.

What right have you to say, because you droop and languish, that your neighbour, with a fair exterior and upright mien, is all that his appearance indicates? What evidence have you that because you suffer from want, and your neighbour rides in his carriage, that he is, therefore, more abundantly blessed, more contentedly happy than you?

As you walk through the streets of costly and beautiful mansions, you feel vaguely, that, associated with so much of beauty, of magnificence and ease, there must be absolute content, enviable freedom, unmixed pleasure, and constant happiness. How deplorably mistaken. Here, where gold and crimson drape the windows, is mortal sickness; there, where the heavy shutters fold over the rich plate glass, lies shrouded death. Here, is blasted reputation, there, is an untold and hideous grief. Here, is blighted love, striving to look and be brave, but with a bosom corroded and full of bitterness; there the sad conduct of a wayward child. Here is the terrible neglect of an unkind and perhaps idolized husband; there the wilful and repeated faults of an unfaithful wife. Here is dread of bankruptcy, there dread of dishonour or exposure. Here is bitter hatred, lacking only the nerve to prove another Cain. There silent and hidden disease, working its skilful fangs about the heart, while it paints the cheek with the very hue of health. Here is undying remorse in the breast of one who has wronged the widow and the fatherless; there the suffering being the victim of foul slander; here is imbecility, there smothered revenge. The bride and the belle, both so seemingly blessed, have each their sacred but poignant sorrow.

Have you a worse grief than your neighbour? You think you have; you have buried your only child—he has laid seven in the tomb. Seven times has his heart been rent open; and the wounds are yet fresh; he has no hope to sustain him; he is a miserable man, and you are a Christian.

Have you more trouble than your neighbour? You have lost your all—no, no, say not so; your neighbour has lost houses and lands, but his health has gone also; and while you are robust, he lies on the uneasy pillow of sickness, and watches some faithful menial prepare his scanty meal, and then waits till a trusty hand bears the food to his parched lips.

Do you suffer more than your neighbour? True; Saturday night tests your poverty; you have but money enough for the bare necessaries of life; your children dress meagerly, and your house is scantily furnished; you do not know whether or not work will be forthcoming the following week. Your neighbour sees not, nor did he ever see, want. House, wife and children are sumptuously provided for; his barn is a palace to your kitchen. Step into his parlour and look at him for a moment; papers surround him, blazing Lehigh floods the grate, velvet carpets yield to the step; luxurious chairs invite to rest—check the sigh of envy; there is a ring at the bell—hurrying footsteps on the stairs—a jarring sound against the polished door, and in bursts the rich man's son, his brow haggard, his eyes fierce and red. He is a notorious profligate; gambling is his food and drink, debauchery his glory and his ruin. Would you be that father? Go back to your honest sons and look in their faces; throw the bright locks from their brows, and bless

God that there the angel triumphs over the brute; be even thankful that you are not burdened with corrupt gold, for their sakes; say not again that you suffer more than your neighbour.

Do you toil, young girl, from daylight to midnight, while the little sums eked out with frowns and reluctant fingers, hardly suffice to provide for you food and raiment? And the wife of your rich employer, who passes stranger-like by you, may sit at her marble toilet-table for hours, and retouch the faded brow of beauty before a gilded mirror; may lounge at her palace window till she is weary of gazing, and being gazed at; do you envy your wealthier neighbour, young sewing-girl? Go to her boudoir, where pictures and statuary, silken hangings and perfumes delight every sense, and where costly robes are flung around with a profusion that betokens lavish expenditure; ask her which she deems happiest, and she will point her jewelled finger towards you, and—if she speaks with candour—tell you that for your single soul and free spirits, she would barter all her riches. The opera, where night after night the wealth of glorious voices is flung upon the air till its every vibration is melody, and the spirit drinks it in as it would the incense of rare flowers, is to her not so exquisite a luxury as the choice songs, warbled in a concert room, to which you may listen but few times in the year; such pleasure palls in repetition, on the common mind, for nature's favourites are among the poor, and gold, with all its magical power, can never attune the ear to music, nor the taste to an appreciation of that which is truly beautiful in nature or art. Keep then your integrity, and you never need envy the wife of your employer. A round of heartless dissipation has sickened her of humanity; and if it were not for the excitement of outshining her compeers in the ranks of fashion, she would lay down her useless life to-morrow.

Mothers, worn out and enfeebled with work, labouring for those who, however good they may be, are at the best unable to pay you for you unceasing toil, unable to realize your great sacrifices, do you look upon your neighbour who has more means and a few petted children, and wish that your lot was like hers? You pause often over your task, and think it greater than you can bear.

"Tell mothers," said a lady to us a short time since, "who have their little ones around them, that they are living their happiest days; and the time will come when they will realize it. Tell them to bend in thankfulness over the midnight lamp, to smile at their ceaseless work and call it pleasure.

I can but kneel in fancy by the distant graves of my children; they are all gone. Could I but have them beside me now, I would delve like a slave for them; I would think no burden too hard, no denial beyond my strength, if I might but labour for their good and be rewarded by their smiles and their love."

Then in whatever situation we are, we should remember that even but a door from our own dwelling there may be anguish, compared with which ours is but as the whisper of a breath to the roll of the thunder. We do not say then, let us *console* ourselves by the reflection that there are always those in the world who suffer keener afflictions than ourselves, "but let us feel that though our cup of sorrow may be almost full, there might be added many a drop of bitterness;" and never, never should we breathe the expression, "there is no sorrow like unto mine."

WE ARE LED BY A WAY THAT WE KNOW NOT

WE are to consider the facts and circumstances which confirm the doctrine that the Lord's providence is at once universal and particular; and indeed that he leads us by a way unknown to ourselves.

And who that has reflected upon his own life, or upon the life of others, or upon the current events of the day, will not bear witness to the universal application of this principle?

Look to the affairs of the world, to the nations and governments of all the earth, and tell me, where is anything turning out according to the forethought and prudence of man?

Look to the movements of our own country, and say whether human prudence ever devised what we behold? What party or what individuals have ever, in the long run, brought things about as they expected? And how is it in our own city, and under our own eyes?

In the societies of the church, and in organizations for church extension, the same rule applies. And I might ask, where does it not apply? I might give examples. But this is unnecessary, when they are so numerous, and so fresh in the memory of every one.

But when we turn to the experience of individuals, we meet with the most unlimited application of our subject. The life of every one is a standing memento of its truth. For who is there, that has come to his present standpoint in life, by the route that he had marked out for himself? I will imagine that ten, fifteen, or twenty years ago each one of you fixed on your plan of life, for a longer or shorter period. It matters not what the original plan was. It matters not what prudence, sagacity, and forethought were employed in making it. It matters not how much money and power have come to the support of it. Still its parts have never been filled up as you originally sketched them.

Many particulars were altered and amended, from day to day, as you went along. Some things were abandoned as useless; some as hopeless; some as impossible; some as injurious; some things were neglected, and others forgotten. An unknown hand now and then interposed, turning the tables entirely. An unaccountable influence was found operating on certain individuals, changing their tone, and modifying their conduct. An unknown individual has come alongside of you, and has become your friend. He has mingled his emotions and his plans with yours. You have modified your plans. He has changed his. Business and commerce have taken an unexpected turn. You are the gainer or the loser, it matters not; your plans are changed by the event. An intimate friend has left you and become your open enemy; an open enemy has been reconciled and has returned to the affection and confidence of your heart. Your plans in life have to be changed to suit such events as these. Several friends and relatives, that were near to you, have been removed into the spiritual world. It may be that by such providences, your feelings, thoughts, and actions have been changed—changed utterly and for ever. Darkness of mind, gloominess of life, and anguish of spirit may have come upon you, by some such unexpected providence, and thus your plans may have been changed, or even utterly abandoned.

But beyond matters of this description, which are somewhat external, and as we say accidental, and certainly incidental, to a life in this world, and in all of which we are led in a way that we know not; there are unexpected changes of another kind, that we all have experienced. I now refer to changes in the inner man, and in the inner life.

For there is a Divinity within us that shapes our ends, and while the things of the outward life remain much the same, we experience changes of the inner life, that are at times amazing and terrible. They come like the swelling of the tide, and like the beating of the waves rolling on from a distant ocean; the deep emotions of the soul arise and swell and sweep away; the fire of thought is kindled; the imagination paints the canvas; the tongue stands ready to utter the influx of love and wisdom; and the hand to illustrate it.

As these internal states of the soul change, by conjunction with the Lord and communion with Heaven, on the one hand; or by opposition to God and alliance with Hell, on the other, we see all things of the outward world in a different light.

The changes of our internal man are, to appearance, much more directly of the Lord's Divine Providence, than the events of the outward life. Nevertheless, the two are so related by the constitution of the mind, that each individual determines, in rationality and freedom, which of the emotions and thoughts of the *inner life*, he will bring forth into *ultimate acts*; and it is here that the man may ally himself with the good and the true on one hand, or with the evil and the false on the other; and in this manner determine his destiny for heaven or hell.

The practical bearings of our subjects hinge chiefly on this; we are to confide in the Lord; lean upon his great arm; and look to Him, with the assurance that although He leads us by a way that we know not, nevertheless He is leading us aright; and if we trust to Him, and do His will, He will finally bring us to heaven.

Casting our eyes from one extreme of the Lord's vast dominions to the other, we find the same Divine Providence everywhere operating and operative. The angels of heaven, from the highest to the lowest, are continually led by the Lord in paths that they have not known; darkness is made light before them, and crooked things straight. Nevertheless they are not led into infinite good nor infinite delight. For this would be impossible. But constantly they are led into a higher degree of good than they would naturally choose; and they are defended from evil into which they would naturally subside. So also it is with us.

Hence we may rest assured, that however meagre may be the good we experience, it is vaster by far than we should inherit, if we had been permitted to carry out our own plans and to have our own way in those numerous particulars in which we have been frustrated in our plans and disappointed in our hopes.

THE IVY IN THE DUNGEON

THE ivy in a dungeon grew,
Unfed by rain, uncheered by dew;
Its pallid leaflets only drank
Cave-moistures foul, and odours dank.

But through the dungeon-grating high
There fell a sunbeam from the sky;
It slept upon the grateful floor
In silent gladness evermore.

The ivy felt a tremor shoot
Through all its fibres to the root;
It felt the light, it saw the ray,
It strove to blossom into day.

It grew, it crept, it pushed, it clomb—
Long had the darkness been its home;
But well it knew, though veiled in night,
The goodness and the joy of light.

Its clinging roots grew deep and strong;
Its stem expanded firm and long;
And in the currents of the air
Its tender branches flourished fair.

It reached the beam—it thrilled—it curled—
It blessed the warmth that cheers the world;
It rose towards the dungeon bars—
It looked upon the sun and stars.

It felt the life of bursting Spring,
It heard the happy sky-lark sing.
It caught the breath of morns and eves,
And wooed the swallow to its leaves.

By rains, and dews, and sunshine fed,
Over the outer wall it spread;

And in the day-beam waving free,
It grew into a steadfast tree.

Upon that solitary place,
Its verdure threw adorning grace.
The mating birds became its guests,
And sang its praises from their nests.

Wouldst know the moral of the rhyme?
Behold the heavenly light! and climb.
To every dungeon comes a ray
Of God's interminable day.

THE GARDEN OF EDEN

ONE day little Alice hung about her mother's neck covering her cheeks with kisses, and saying in her pretty, childish way,

"I love you, you nice, sweet mother! You are good—so good!" But her mother answered earnestly,

"Dear child, God is good; if I have any good it is from Him; He has given it to me; it is not mine."

Then the little one unclasped her caressing arms, and putting back her hair with both hands gazed with a look of surprise into her mother's face.

Presently she said—"But if He has given it to you, it is yours."

"No, darling," replied the lady, "you do not quite understand. Listen. Suppose your dear father had a great garden full of all most beautiful things that ever grew in gardens, and he should say to you—'Come and live in my garden; you shall have as much ground as you are able to cultivate, and I will give you seeds of all fruits and flowers you love best, as many as you want. Here no evil thing can ever come to harm you, but every day you will grow happier and stronger, and then I will give you more ground and more seeds, and you shall live with me for ever!' Suppose you were so glad to hear this that you lost no time, but went in, at once, and began to plant the seeds in your little plot, close by the gate—you know it would be a tiny little plot at first, because you are small and weak; and soon your flowers were to grow up and bloom, so tall, and so beautiful, and your trees hang heavy with such delightful fruit that every one passing by would exclaim,

"'Oh, what a beautiful garden! Are these flowers and fruit trees yours?'

"Would you not say—

"Oh, no! they are not mine; they are all my father's. This is his beautiful garden, but he said if I were willing I might stay here always, and I have come to live with him because he is good. Nothing at all here belongs to me, though my father likes me to give away the fruits and flowers that grow in my plot to all who ask for them. I am a great deal happier, all the time, when I think that even the wild flowers in this grass, and the small berries, and the little birds that eat them, belong to him, than I could be if they were mine, and I had no one to love for them.'

"Should you not feel, dearest, as though you were telling a wicked story, and almost as though you were stealing something, if you said, 'Yes, they are all mine,' so that the people would not even know you had a father?"

"Oh, yes! that would be very naughty indeed. I would give the people some of the fruit and flowers, and say they grew on my father's trees, and then they would love him too; but tell me more about the garden."

"I will tell you all I think you can understand, and you must be attentive, for I want you to remember it all your life. Did you ever hear of the Garden of Eden?"

"Yes; that is where Adam and Eve lived."

"Well, that's the beautiful garden I've been telling you about, and God is your good father. You can begin your journey there this very day if you like."

"Is it a very long journey?—and will you go with me? Is there really, *really* such a garden? Oh, tell me where it is!"

"I desire nothing in the world so much as to lead you there, but the path is rough and steep; I cannot carry you in my arms along that road; you must walk on your own little feet, and I am afraid they will sometimes get—very tired."

"You know, mother, I never do get tired when I am going to a pleasant place; but, oh, dear! I do believe now it is all a dream-story; you smiled and kissed me just as if it were."

"No, you need not look so disappointed, little one, for though it is something like a 'dream-story,' there is nothing in the world half so true and real. Think in that little head of yours, and tell me what seems to you most like this beautiful garden."

"I cannot think of anything at all like it, except heaven.—Oh, yes!—that is it! Heaven, is it not?"

"And what is heaven?"

"The place where good people go when they die."

"Think again. What is heaven?"

"I have thought again, and I cannot think of anything but the place where God and the angels are. I do not know how you want me to think."

"I want you to think why it is heaven, and why the angels are happy. Do you understand?"

"Yes. Being beautiful and so pleasant makes it heaven; and the angels are happy because they are in heaven."

"Then, of course, if you put even such wicked people into a beautiful and pleasant place they would be angels, and happy?"

"Oh, now I see! You mean the angels are happy because they are good."

"Why should that make them happy?"

"I don't know why, but I know the Bible says so. I suppose just the same as when you promise me, in the morning, that if I say my lessons all nicely you will tell me a beautiful fairy-tale after tea."

"No, my little Alice, not exactly in that way, though at first thought it does seem to be so. I want you very much indeed, to understand the truth about it, but I am afraid you will not find it easy. You know that God is good, and wise, and happy—ah, dearest! better, wiser, happier than the purest angels will ever know, though they go on learning it to eternity. When I say to you God is infinitely good, and wise, and happy, you cannot understand that, and neither can I; but one thing about it I can understand, and this I will tell you. Just as every joyous ray of light and heat comes to us from the sun, so all wisdom, all goodness, all beauty, all joy, flow forth from God, and are His, alone. Our very souls would go out of existence like the flames of a lamp when the oil is spent, if, for the least fraction of a second, He ceased to give us life. This truth that I am teaching you now is not mine, nor yours; it is only a tiny stream flowing from the fountains of His infinite wisdom, and would be the truth, all the same, if we had never been born, or never learned to see it. The good and joyous feelings in your heart, too, are also from God, just as the truth is, though they seem to you more as if they were your own. You must never think of them as your own, never; but thank God for them very gratefully and humbly, for they are His fruits that grow in the garden of your father, the Garden of Eden."

"Why do you call it the Garden of Eden?"

"Because, by the Garden of Eden, is signified the state of those who live in obedience to God; and by the beauty and pleasantness of the garden we are taught that, when we receive goodness and truth from God, we, at the same time, receive happiness from Him, because He is infinitely happy, as well as infinitely good, and when His spirit fills our hearts, we are happy too. Happiness comes with goodness, just as the flowers and songs of birds come with summer."

"Then are all good people happy? I thought not."

"It is true, there are many trials in this world, but do you not see that if we were good we should acknowledge that God sent them as blessings, and should be willing to accept them from him, and should, therefore, not be made very unhappy by them. You may be sure that people are really, in their heart of hearts, happy exactly in proportion as they are good. I have known persons who had suffered a great deal in many ways, and who yet said that nothing had been so bitter to them as the consciousness of their own sins. Good people see a thousand things to love and enjoy which the wicked world find no pleasure in; they are sure to make friends, and, what is far better, sure to love and do good to all about them. They take delight in everything beautiful that God has created. They think of Him, and all His goodness, and, in the midst of sorrow, their hearts are comforted, and filled with heavenly peace."

"Why did you say the road was rough and long to that beautiful garden?—is it so very, very hard to be good?—and does it take so very long?"

"You must not feel sad because it is not easy to be good; you must think of it bravely, and joyfully. Why, my Alice! did you not say you never felt tired when you were going to a pleasant place? It is not always easy to do right; sometimes we are sorely tempted, and then it seems very difficult; but what of that? It is possible, always, for God never requires of us what we cannot do. When you feel discouraged, remember that angels in heaven were little children once, and that some of them found it as hard as you do to be good and true, but they tried over and over again, and are blessed angels now. They love to acknowledge that it was not by their own strength they overcame evil, but that all the good and truth and happiness they have are from God. He does not love you less than He did them, for His love is infinite to all His children, and if you are willing He will lead you also into His Garden of Eden."

HAVE A FLOWER IN YOUR ROOM

A FIRE in winter, a flower in summer! If you can have a fine print or picture all the year round, so much the better; you will thus always have a bit of sunshine in your room, whether the sky be clear or not. But, above all, a flower in summer!

Most people have yet to learn the true enjoyment of life; it is not fine dresses, or large houses, or elegant furniture, or rich wines, or gay parties, that make homes happy. Really, wealth cannot purchase pleasures of the higher sort; these depend not on money, or money's worth; it is the heart, and taste, and intellect, which determine the happiness of men; which give the seeing eye and the sentient nature, and without which, man is little better than a kind of walking clothes-horse.

A snug and a clean home, no matter how tiny it be, so that it be wholesome; windows, into which the sun can shine cheerily; a few good books (and who need be without a few good books in these days of universal cheapness?)—no duns at the door, and the cupboard well supplied, and with a flower in your room!—and there is none so poor as not to have about him the elements of pleasure.

Hark! there is a child passing our window calling "wallflowers!" We must have a bunch forthwith: it is only a penny! A shower has just fallen, the pearly drops are still hanging upon the petals, and they sparkle in the sun which has again come out in his beauty.

How deliciously the flower smells of country and nature! It is like summer coming into our room to greet us. The wallflowers are from Kent, and only last night were looking up to the stars from their native stems; they are full of buds yet, with their promise of fresh beauty. "Betty! bring a glass of clear water to put these flowers in!" and so we set to, arranging and displaying our pennyworth to the best advantage.

But what do you say to a nosegay of roses? Here you have a specimen of the most beautiful of the smiles of Nature! Who, that looks on one of these bright full-blown beauties, will say that she is sad, or sour, or puritanical! Nature tells us to be happy, to be glad, for she decks herself with roses, and the fields, the skies, the hedgerows, the thickets, the green lanes, the dells, the mountains, the morning and evening sky, are robed in loveliness. The "laughing flowers," exclaims the poet! but there is more than gayety in the blooming flower, though it takes a wise man to see its full significance—there is the beauty, the love, and the adaptation, of which it is full. Few of us, however, see any more deeply in this respect than did Peter Bell:—

"A primrose by a river's brim,
A yellow primrose was to him,
And it was nothing more."

What would we think or say of one who had invented flowers—supposing, that before him, flowers were things unknown; would it not be the paradise of a new delight? should we not hail the inventor as a genius as a god? And yet these lovely offsprings of the earth have been speaking to man from the first dawn of his existence till now, telling him of the goodness and wisdom of the Creating Power, which bade the earth bring forth, not only that which was useful as food, but also flowers, the bright consummate flowers, to clothe it in beauty and joy!

See that graceful fuchsia, its blood-red petals, and calyx of bluish-purple, more exquisite in colour and form than any hand or eyes, no matter how well skilled and trained, can imitate! We can manufacture no colours to equal those of our flowers in their bright brilliancy—such, for instance, as the Scarlet Lychnis, the Browallia, or even the Common Poppy. Then see the exquisite blue of the humble Speedwell, and the dazzling white of the Star of Bethlehem, that shines even in the dark. Bring one of even our common field-flowers into a room, place it on your table or chimney piece, and you seem to have brought a ray of sunshine into the place. There is ever cheerfulness about flowers; what a delight are they to the drooping invalid! the very sight of them is cheering; they are like a sweet draught of fresh bliss, coming as messengers from the country without, and seeming to say:—"Come and see the place where we grow, and let thy heart be glad in our presence."

What can be more innocent than flowers! Are they not like children undimmed by sin? They are emblems of purity and truth, always a new source of delight to the pure and the innocent. The heart that does not love flowers, or the voice of a playful child, is one that we should not like to consort with. It was a beautiful conceit that invented a language of flowers, by which lovers were enabled to express the feelings that they dared not openly speak. But flowers have a voice to all,—to old and young, to rich and poor, if they would but listen, and try to interpret their meaning. "To me," says Wordsworth,

The meanest flower that blows can give Thoughts that do often lie too deep for tears."

Have a flower in your room then, by all means! It will cost you only a penny, if your ambition is moderate; and the gratification it will give you will be beyond all price. If you can have a flower for your window, so much the better. What can be more delicious than the sun's light streaming through flowers—through the midst of crimson fuchsias or scarlet geraniums? Then to look out into the light through flowers—is not that poetry? And to break the force of the sunbeams by the tender resistance of green leaves? If you can train a nasturtium round the window, or some sweet-peas, then you have the most beautiful frame you can invent for the picture without, whether it be the busy crowd, or a distant landscape, or trees with their lights and shades, or the changes of the passing clouds. Any one may thus look through flowers for the price of an old song. And what a pure taste and refinement does it not indicate on the part of the cultivator!

A flower in your window sweetens the air, makes your room look graceful, gives the sun's light a new charm, rejoices your eye, and links you to nature and beauty. You really cannot be altogether alone, if you have a sweet flower to look upon, and it is a companion which will never utter a cross thing to anybody, but always look beautiful and smiling. Do not despise it because it is cheap, and everybody may have the luxury as well as you. Common things are cheap, and common things are invariably the most valuable. Could we only have a fresh air or sunshine by purchase, what luxuries these would be; but they are free to all, and we think not of their blessings.

There is, indeed, much in nature that we do not yet half enjoy, because we shut our avenues of sensation and of feeling. We are satisfied with the matter of fact, and look not for the spirit of fact, which is above all. If we would open our minds to enjoyment, we should find tranquil pleasures spread about us on every side. We might live with the angels that visit us on every sunbeam, and sit with the fairies who wait on every flower. We want some loving knowledge to enable us truly to enjoy life, and we require to cultivate a little more than we do the art of making the most of the common means and appliances for enjoyment, which lie about us on every side. There are, we doubt not, many who may read these pages, who can enter into and appreciate the spirit of all that we have now said; and, to those who may still hesitate, we would say—begin and experiment forthwith; and first of all, when the next flower-girl comes along your street, at once hail her, and "Have a flower for your room!"

WEALTH

THE error of life into which man most readily falls, is the pursuit of wealth as the highest good of existence. While riches command respect, win position, and secure comfort, it is expected that they will be regarded by all classes only with a strong and unsatisfied desire. But the undue reverence which is everywhere manifested for wealth, the rank which is conceded it, the homage which is paid it, the perpetual worship which is offered it, all tend to magnify its desirableness, and awaken longings for its possession in the minds of those born without inheritance. In society, as at present observed, the acquisition of money would seem to be the height of human aim—the great object of living, to which all other purposes are made subordinate. Money, which exalts the lowly, and sheds honour upon the exalted—money, which makes sin appear goodness, and gives to viciousness the seeming of chastity—money, which silences evil report, and opens wide the mouth of praise—money, which constitutes its possessor an oracle, to whom men listen with deference—money, which makes deformity beautiful, and sanctifies crime—money, which lets the guilty go unpunished, and wins forgiveness for wrong—money, which makes manhood and age respectable, and is commendation, surety, and good name for the young,—how shall it be gained? by what schemes gathered in? by what sacrifice secured? These are the questions which absorb the mind, the practical answerings of which engross the life of men. The schemes are too often those of fraud, and outrage upon the sacred obligations of being; the sacrifice, loss of the highest moral sense, the destruction of the purest susceptibilities of nature, the neglect of internal life and development, the utter and sad perversion of the true purposes of existence. Money is valued beyond its worth—it has gained a power vastly above its deserving. Wealth is courted so obsequiously, is flattered so servilely, is so influential in moulding opinions and judgment, has such a weight in the estimation of character, that men regard its acquisition as the most prudent aim of their endeavours, and its possession as absolute enjoyment and honour, rather than the means of honourable, useful, and happy life. While riches are thus over-estimated, and hold such power in the community, men will forego ease and endure toil, sacrifice social pleasures and abandon principle, for the speedy and unlimited acquirement of property. Money will not be regarded as the means of living, but as the object of life. All nobler ends will be neglected in the eager haste to be rich. No higher pursuit will be recognised than the pursuit of gold—no attainment deemed so desirable as the attainment of wealth. While the great man of every circle is the rich man, in the common mind wealth becomes the synonyme of greatness. No condition is discernable superior to that which money confers; no loftier idea of manhood is entertained than that which embraces the extent of one's possessions.

There is a wealth of heart better than gold, and an interior decoration fairer than outward ornament.—

There is a splendour in upright life, beside which gems are lustreless; and a fineness of spirit whose beauty outvies the glitter of diamonds. Man's true riches are hidden in his nature, and in their development and increase will he find his surest happiness.

HOW TO BE HAPPY

OLD Mr. Cleveland sat by his comfortable fireside one cold winter's night. He was a widower, and lived alone on his plantation; that is to say, he was the only white person there; for of negroes, both field hands and house servants, he had enough and to spare. He was a queer old man, this Mr. Cleveland; a man of kind, good feelings, but of eccentric impulses, and blunt and startling manners. You must always let him do everything in his own odd way; just attempt to dictate to him, or even to suggest a certain course, and you would be sure to defeat your wisest designs. He seemed at times possessed by a spirit of opposition, and would often turn right round and oppose a course he had just been vehemently advocating, only because some one else had ventured openly and warmly to approve it.

The night, as I have said, was bitter cold, and would have done honour to a northern latitude, and in addition to this, a violent storm was coming on. The wind blew in fitful gusts, howling and sighing among the huge trees with which the house was surrounded, and then dying away with a melancholy, dirge-like moan. The old tree rubbed their leafless branches against the window panes, and the fowls which had roosted there for the night, were fain to clap their wings, and make prodigious efforts to preserve their equilibrium. Mr. Cleveland grew moody and restless, threw down the book in which he had been reading, kicked one of the andirons till he made the whole blazing fabric tumble down, and finally called, in an impatient tone, his boy Tom.

Tom soon popped his head in at the door, and said, "Yer's me, sir."

"Yer's me, indeed!" exclaimed Mr. Cleveland, "what sort of a way is this to build a fire?"

"I rispec you is bin kick um, sir," said Tom.

"Hey? What? Well! suppose I did bin kick um, if it had been properly made, it would not have tumbled down. Fix it this minute, sir!"

"I is gwine to fix um now, sir," said Tom, fumbling at the fire.

"Well! fix it, sir, without having so much to say about it; you had better do more, and say less," said Mr. Cleveland.

"Yes, sir," answered Tom.

"You *will* keep answering me when there is no occasion!" exclaimed Mr. Cleveland; "I just wish I had my stick here, I'd crack the side of your head with it."

"Yer's de stick, sir," said Tom, handing the walking cane out of the corner.

"Put it down, this instant, sir," said Mr. Cleveland; "how dare you touch my stick without my leave?"

"I bin tink you bin say you bin want um, sir," said Tom.

"You had better tink about your work, sir, and stop answering me, sir, or I'll find a way to make you," said Mr. Cleveland. "Bring in some more light wood, and make the fire, and shut in the window shutters. Do you hear me, sir?"

"Yes, sir," replied Tom.

"Well, why don't you answer, if you hear, then? How am I to know when you hear me, if you don't answer?" said Mr. Cleveland.

"I bin tink you bin tell me for no answer you, sir," said Tom.

"I said when there was no occasion, boy; that's what I said," exclaimed Mr. Cleveland, reaching for his stick.

"Yes, sir," said Tom, as he went grinning out of the room.

Mr. Cleveland was, in the main, a very kind master, though somewhat hasty and impatient. Tom and he were for ever sparring, yet neither could have done without the other; and there was something comical about Tom's disposition which well suited his master's eccentric and changeable moods. Tom evidently served as a kind of safety valve for his master's nervous system, and many an explosion of superfluous excitability he had to bear.

On the night in question, Mr. Cleveland was particularly out of sorts. The truth is, he was naturally a generous, warm-hearted man, but in consequence of early disappointment, had lived a solitary life, and was really suffering for the want of objects of affection. His feelings, unsatisfied, unemployed, yet morbidly sensitive, were becoming soured, and his untenanted heart often ached for want of sympathy.

He rose and took several diagonal turns across the room. At length he opened a window, and looked out upon the stormy night. "What confounded weather!" he muttered to himself, "it makes a man feel like blowing his brains out! There are no two ways about it, I'm tired of life. What have I to live for? If I were to die to-morrow, who would shed a tear?"

Then whispered conscience, "It is thine own fault. A man need not feel alone because there are none in the world who bear his name, or share his blood. All men are thy brethren. Thou art one of the great human family, and what hast thou done to relieve the poor and suffering around thee? Will not thy Master say to thee at the last day, 'I was an hungered, and you gave me no meat; I was thirsty, and you gave me no drink; I was a stranger, and ye took me not in; naked, and you clothed me not; sick, and in prison, and you visited me not. Inasmuch as you did it not to one of the least of these my brethren, *you did it not to me.*'"

This was a strong and direct appeal, and it was not without its effect. Then muttered Mr. Cleveland to himself again, "Well, how can I help it? It has not been for want of inclination. Heaven knows I am always ready to put my hand in my pocket whenever people call on me for charity. How can I help it if the poor and suffering do not make their wants known to me?"

Then again spake Conscience: "Thou art trying to deceive thyself, but thou canst not deceive nor silence *me*. Thou hast known of the existence of suffering, and thine indolence has prevented thee from going abroad to relieve it. Did thy Master thus? Did he not *go about* to do good? Did he not sit down to meat with publicans and sinners? Can you stand here, and look out upon such a night as this, and not think of those who are exposed to its bitterness? Can thy human heart beat only for itself when thou thinkest of the thousand miseries crying to Heaven for relief? Resolve, now, before thy head touches its comfortable pillow, that with the morning's dawn thou wilt resolutely set about thy work; or, rather, thy Master's work."

"It is very hard," still muttered Mr. Cleveland to himself, "that these thoughts will continually intrude themselves upon me. They give me no peace of my life. Stifle them as I may, they come with tenfold force. People have no business to be poor. I was poor once, and nobody gave charity to me. I had to help myself up in the world as well as I could. I hate poor people; I hate unfortunate people; in fact, confound it! I hate the world and everybody in it."

Then answered once again the still, small voice: "For shame, Mr. Cleveland, for shame! You will ruin your soul if you thus darken the light within. You know better than all this, and you are sinning against yourself. You want to be happy; well, you may be so. There is a wide field of duty open before you; enter, in God's name, and go to work like a man. What you say about having helped yourself, is perfectly true, and you deserve all credit for it. But remember that the majority of the poor are entirely destitute of your advantages. You had the foundation rightly laid. A thousand circumstances in your early life conspired to render you energetic and self-relying. You had the right sort of education, and Providence also helped to train you. Besides, once more I ask you, did your Master stop to inquire how human misery was brought about before he relieved it? Away with this unmanly, selfish policy! Follow thy generous impulses, follow out the yearnings of thy heart, without which you never can have peace; above, all, follow Christ."

Mr. Cleveland shut the window, heaved a deep sigh, and took several more turns across the room. "I believe it is all true," at length he said, "and I have been a confounded fool. I'll turn about, and lead a different life, so help me Heaven! I have wealth, and not a chick nor a child to spend it on, nor to leave it to when I die, and so I'll spend it in doing good, if I can only find out the best way; that's the trouble. But never mind, I'll be my own executor." He now rang the bell for Tom.

Tom immediately appeared, with his usual "Yer's me, sir."

"Tom," said Mr. Cleveland, "put me in mind in the morning, to send a load of wood to old Mrs. Peters."

"Yes, sir," said Tom, "an' you better sen' some bacon, 'cause I bin yerry (hear) little Mas Jack Peter say him ain't bin hab no meat for eat sence I do' know de day when. I rispec dey drudder hab de meat sted o' de wood, 'cause dey can pick up wood nuf all about."

"You mind your own business, sir," said Mr. Cleveland, "I'll send just what I please. How long is it since I came to you for advice? Confound the fellow!" he muttered aside, "I meant to send the woman some meat, and now if I do it, that impudent fellow will think I do it because he advised it. Any how, I'll not send bacon, I'll send beef or mutton."

Just at this moment, there was a knock at the door, and Tom, going to open it, admitted Dick, the coachman.

"What do you want, Dick, at this time of night?" inquired his master.

"Dere's a man down stays, sir," replied Dick, "and he seem to be in great 'fliction. He says dey is campin' out 'bout half a mile below, sir, and de trees is fallin' so bad he is 'fraid dey will all be killed. He ask you if you kin let dem stay in one of de out-houses tell to-morrow."

"Camping out such a night as this?" exclaimed Mr. Cleveland, "the Lord have pity on them! How many are there of them, Dick?"

"He, an' his wife, and six little children, sir," answered Dick.

"No negroes?" inquired his master.

"Not a nigger, sir," said Dick. "I ain't like poor buckrah, no how, sir, but I 'spect you best take dese people in, lest dey might die right in our woods."

Tom, knowing his master's dislike of advice, and fearing that Dick had taken the surest method to shut them out, now chimed in, and said, "Massa, ef I bin you, I no would tek dem in none 't all."

"What do you mean, sir?" exclaimed Mr. Cleveland; "you surely must be taking leave of your senses. Dick, you'll have to give that boy of yours a thrashing. I'll not stand his insolence much longer. Don't stand there, grinning at me, sir."

"No, sir," snickered Tom, skulking behind Dick, who was his father.

"Let the man come up here, Dick," said Mr. Cleveland.

When the traveller made his appearance, Mr. Cleveland was startled at his wan and wo-begone appearance. "Sit down, my man," said he.

"I thank you, sir," replied the stranger, "but I must be back as soon as possible to my family. Can you grant us a night's lodging, sir?"

"Certainly, sir," replied Mr. Cleveland; "have you any means of getting your family hither? I am told you have six little ones."

"They must walk, sir," replied the stranger, "for our only horse has been killed by a falling tree; but I have not a word to say. It might have been my wife or one of my little ones, and, poor as I am, I can spare none of them."

Mr. Cleveland, whose feelings were at this time in an usually softened state, got up, and walked rapidly to the book-case to conceal his emotion, dashed away a tear, and muttered to himself, as was his wont, "'Tis confoundedly affecting, that's a fact." Then turning to the stranger, who was in the act of leaving the room, he said, "If you will wait a few moments I will have my carriage got; your wife and little ones must not walk on such a night as this."

"God bless you, sir!" said the stranger, in a trembling voice; "but I am too uneasy to stay a moment longer."

"Well, go on," said Mr. Cleveland, "and the carriage shall come after you, and I will go in it myself." The stranger brushed his hand across his eyes, and left the room without speaking a word; while Dick and Tom exchanged glances of surprise at their master's uncommon fit of philanthropy; Tom feeling fully assured that the "poor buckrahs," as he termed them, owed their good fortune to his seasonable interference.

The carriage was soon in readiness, and Mr. Cleveland rode in it to the spot. He found the family all gathered around the dead horse, and lamenting over it; while the father, having just arrived, was expatiating upon his kind reception by Mr. Cleveland. It took them some little time to stow themselves away in the carriage, and Mr. Cleveland actually carried two sturdy children on his knees. Yes, there he was, riding through the dreadful storm, in danger every moment from the trees which were falling all around him, with an infant in its mother's arms squalling with all its might, and a heavy boy on each knee, and squeezed almost to death into the bargain—for there were nine in the carriage—and yet feeling so happy! ay, far happier than he had felt for many a long day. Truly, charity brings its own reward.

When they arrived at Mr. Cleveland's house, instead of being stowed away in an out-building, as the poor man had modestly requested, they were comfortably provided for beneath his own roof. That night, as he laid his head upon his pillow, he could not help feeling surprised at his sudden accession of happiness. "Well, I will go on," he soliloquized; "I will pursue the path I have this night taken, and if I always feel as I do now, I am a new man, and will never again talk about blowing my brains out." He slept that night the sleep of peace, and rose in the morning with a light heart and buoyant spirits.

His first care was to take the father of the family aside, and gather from him the story of his misfortunes. It was a long and mournful tale, and Mr. Cleveland was obliged, more than once, to pretend a sudden call out of the room, that he might hide his emotion. And the tale was by no means told in vain. True to his new resolutions, Mr. Cleveland thankfully accepted the work which Providence had given him to do, and the family of emigrants, to this day, mention the name of Cleveland with tears of gratitude and love, and, when they implore God's mercy for themselves, never forget to invoke, for their kind benefactor, Heaven's choicest blessings. Nor is that the only family whose hearts glow at the mention of Mr. Cleveland's name. Far and wide his name is known, and honoured, and beloved.

And Mr. Cleveland has found out the real secret of happiness. It is true that he and Tom still have their squabbles, for Tom is really a provoking fellow, and Mr. Cleveland is, and always will be, an eccentric, impulsive man, but his heart, which, when we first introduced him to our readers, was far from being right with God, or with his fellow-men, is now the dwelling-place of love and kindness, and the experience of every day contributes to strengthen the new principles he has imbibed, and to confirm him in the right.

Reader! art thou sad or solitary? I can offer thee a certain cure for all thy woes. Contemplate the life of Him who spake as never man spake. Follow him through all those years of toil and suffering. See him wherever called by the sorrows of his human brethren, and witness his deeds of mercy and his offices of love, and then — "go thou and do likewise."

REBECCA

HER words were few, without pretence
To tricks of courtly eloquence,
But full of pure and simple thought,
And with a guileless feeling fraught,
And said in accents which conferred
Poetic charm on household word.

She needed not to speak, to be
The best loved of the company—
She did her hands together press
With such a child-like gracefulness;
And such a sweet tranquillity
Upon her silent lips did lie,
And such unsullied purity
In the blue heaven of her eye.

She moved among us like to one
Who had not lived on earth alone;
But felt a dim, mysterious sense
Of a more stately residence,
And seemed to have a consciousness
Of an anterior happiness—
To hear, at times, the echoes sent
From some unearthly instrument
With half-remembered voices blent—
And yet to hold the friendships dear,
And prize the blessings of our sphere—
In sweet perplexity to know
Which of the two was dreamy show,
The dark green earth, the deep blue skies,
The love which shone in mortal eyes,
Or those faint recollections, telling
Of a more bright and tranquil dwelling.

We could not weep upon the day
When her pure spirit passed away;
We thought we read the mystery

Which in her life there seemed to be—
That she was not our own, but lent
To us little while, and sent
An angel child, what others preach
Of heavenly purity, to teach,
In ways more eloquent than speech—
And chiefly by that raptured eye
Which seemed to look beyond the sky,
And that abstraction, listening
To hear the choir of seraphs sing.

We thought that death did seem to her
Of long-lost joy the harbinger—
Like an old household servant, come
To take the willing scholar home;
The school-house, it was very dear,
But then the holidays were near;
And why should she be lingering here?
Softly the servant bore the child
Who at her parting turned and smiled,
And looked back to us, till the night
For ever hid her from our sight.

LIFE A TREADMILL

WHO says that life is a treadmill?

You, merchant, when, after a weary day of measuring cotton-cloth or numbering flower barrels, bowing to customers or taking account of stock, you stumble homeward, thinking to yourself that the moon is a tolerable substitute for gas light, to prevent people from running against the posts—and then, by chance, recall the time when, a school-boy, you read about "chaste Dian" in your Latin books, and discovered a striking resemblance to moonbeams in certain blue eyes that beamed upon you from the opposite side of the school-room.

Ah! those were the days when brick side-walks were as elastic as India rubber beneath your feet; shop windows were an exhibition of transparencies to amuse children and young people, and the world in prospect was one long pleasure excursion. Then you drank the bright effervescence in your glass of soda-water, and now you must swallow the cold, flat settlings, or not get your money's worth. Long ago you found out that the moon is the origin of moonshine, that blue eyes are not quite as fascinating under gray hair and behind spectacles, and that "money answereth all things."

You say so, clerk or bank-teller, when you look up from your books at the new-fallen snow glistening in the morning light, and feel something like the prancing of horses' hoofs in the soles of your boots, and hear the jingling of sleigh bells in your mind's ear, long after the sound of them has passed from your veritable auriculars.

You say so, teacher, while going through the daily drill of your A B C regiments, your multiplication table platoons, and your chirographical battalions.

You say so, factory girl, passing backward and forward from the noise and whirl of wheels in the mills, to the whirl and noise of wheels in your dreams.

You say so, milliner's apprentice, as you sit down to sew gay ribbons on gay bonnets, and stand up to try gay bonnets on gay heads.

You say so, housemaid or housekeeper, when the song of the early bird reminds you of crying children, whose faces are to be washed; when the rustling of fallen leaves in the wind makes you wonder how the new broom is going to sweep; when the aroma of roses suggests the inquiry whether the box of burnt coffee is empty; and when the rising sun, encircled by vapoury clouds, brings up the similitude of a huge fire-proof platter, and the smoke of hot potatoes.

There is a principle in human nature which rebels against repetitions. Who likes to fall asleep, thinking that to-morrow morning he must get up and do exactly the same things that he did to-day, the next day ditto, and so forth, until the chapter of earthly existence is finished!

It is very irksome for these soaring thoughts winged to "wander through eternity," to come down and work out the terms of a tedious apprenticeship to the senses. And yet, what were thoughts unlocalized and unembodied? Mere comets or vague nebulosities in the firmament, without a form, and without a home.

All things have their orbit, and are held in it by the power of two great opposing forces.

Outward circumstances form the centripetal force, which keeps us in ours. Let the eccentric will fly off at ever so wide a tangent for a time, back it must come to a regular diurnal path, or wander away into the "blackness of darkness." And if these daily duties and cares come to us robed in the shining livery of Law, should we not accept them as bearers of a sublime mission?

"What?" you say, "anything sublime in yardstick tactics or ledger columns? Anything sublime in washing dishes or trimming bonnets? The idea is simply ridiculous!"

No, not ridiculous; only a simple idea, and great in its simplicity. For the manner of performing even menial duties, gives you the gauge and dimensions of the doer's inward strength. The power of the soul asserts itself, not so much in shaping favourable circumstances to desired ends, as in resisting the pressure of crushing circumstances, and triumphing over them.

Manufactures, trades, and all the subordinate arts and occupations that keep the car of civilization in motion, may be to you machines moving with a monotonous and unmeaning buzz, or they may be like Ezekiel's vision of wheels involved in wheels, that were lifted up from the earth by the power of the living creature that was in them.

Grumbling man or woman, life *is* a treadmill to you, because you look doggedly down and see nothing but the dull steps you take. If you would cease grumbling, and look up, your life would be transformed into a Jacob's ladder, and every step onward would be a step upward too. And even if it were a treadmill, to which you and other mortals were condemned for past offences, a kindly sympathy for your fellow-prisoners could carpet the way with velvet, and you might move on smilingly together, as through the mazes of an easy dance.

It is of no use to preach the old sermon of contentment with one condition, whatever it may be, a sermon framed for lands where aristocracies are fixtures, in this generation and on this continent. Discontent is a necessity of republicanism, until the millennium comes.

Yet it is not sensible to complain of the present, until we have gleaned its harvests and drained its sap, and it has become capital for us to draw upon in the future. Most of the dissatisfied grumblers of our day are like children from whom the prospect of a Christmas pie, intended for the climax of a supper, takes away all relish for the more solid and wholesome introductory exercises of bread and butter.

What is it we would have our life? Not princely pop and equipments, nor to "marry the prince's own," which used to form the denouement of every fairy tale, will suffice us now; for every ingenious Yankee school-boy or girl has learned to dissect the puppet show of royalty, and knows that its personages move in a routine the most hampered and helpless of all.

The honour of being four years in stepping from one door of the "White House" to the other, ceases to be the meed of a dignified ambition when it results from a skilful shuffling of political cards, rather than from strength and steadiness of head and an upright gait.

If we ask for freedom from care, and leisure to enjoy life—until we have learned, through the discipline of labour and care, how to appreciate and use leisure—we might as well petition from government a grant of prairie land for Egyptian mummies to run races upon.

If one might get himself appointed to the general overseership of the solar system, still, what would his occupation be but a regular pacing to and fro from the sun to the outermost limits of Le Verrier's calculations, and perhaps a little farther? A succession of rather longish strides he would have to take, to be sure; now burning his soles in the fires of Mercury; now hitting his corns against some of the pebbly Asteroids, and now slipping upon the icy rim of Neptune. Still, if he made drudgery of his work by keeping his soul out of it, he would only have his treadmill life over again, on a large scale.

The monotony of our three-score years and ten is wearisome to us; what can we think then of the poor planets, doomed to the same diurnal spinning, the same annual path, for six thousand years, to our certain knowledge? And, if telescopes tell us the truth, the universe is an ever-widening series of similar monotonies.

Yet space is ample enough to give all systems variety of place. While each planet moves steadily along on the edge of its plane, the whole solar equipage is going forward to open a new track on the vast highway of the heavens.

We too, moving in our several spheres with honest endeavours and aspirations, are, by the stability of our motions, lifting and being lifted, with the whole compact human brotherhood, into a higher elevation, a brighter revelation of the Infinite, the Universe of Wisdom and Love.

And in this view, though our efforts be humble and our toil hard, life can never be a treadmill.

ARTHUR LELAND

ARTHUR LELAND was a young lawyer of some twenty-seven years of age. His office stood a stone's throw from the court-house, in a thriving town in the West. Arthur had taken a full course in a Northern college, both in the collegiate and law department, and with some honour. During his course he had managed to read an amazing amount of English literature, and no man was readier or had a keener taste in such things than he. He had a pleasing personal appearance, a fluent and persuasive manner, an unblemished character. Every morning he came to his office from one of the most pleasant little cottage homes in the world; and if you had opened the little front gate, and gone up through the shrubbery to the house, you would have seen a Mrs. Leland, somewhere in-doors, and she as intelligent and pleasant a lady as you ever saw. You would have seen, moreover, tumbling about the grass, or up to the eyes in some mischief, as noble-looking a little fellow of some three years old as you could well have wished for your own son.

This all looks well enough, but there is something wrong. Not in the house. No; it is as pleasant a cottage as you could wish—plenty of garden, peas and honeysuckles climbing up everywhere, green grass, white paint, Venetian blinds, comfortable furniture.

Not in Willie, the little scamp. No; rosy, healthy, good head, intelligent eyes, a fine specimen he was of an only son. Full of mischief, of course, he was. Overflowing with uproar and questions and mischief. Mustachios of egg or butter-milk or molasses after each meal, as a matter of course. Cut fingers, bumped forehead, torn clothes, all day long. Yet a more affectionate, easily-managed child never was.

The mischief was not in Lucy, the Mrs. Leland. I assure you it was not. Leland knew, to his heart's core, that a lovelier, more prudent, sensible, intelligent wife it was impossible to exist. Thrifty, loving, lady-like, right and true throughout.

Where was this mischief? Look at Leland. He is in perpetual motion. Reading, writing, walking the streets, he is always fast, in dead earnest.

Somewhat *too* fast. There is a certain slowness about your strong man. You never associate the idea of mental depth and power with your quick-stepping man. You cannot conceive of a Roman emperor or a Daniel Webster as a slight, swift man. The bearing of a man's body is the outward emblem of the bearing of his soul. Leland is rather slight, rather swift. He meets you in his rapid walk. He stops, grasps your hand, asks cordially after your health. There is an open, warm feeling in the man. No hypocrisy whatever. Yet he talks too fast. He don't give you half a chance to answer one of his rapid questions, before he is asking another totally different. He is not at ease. He keeps you from being at ease. You feel it specially in his house. He is too cordial, too full of effort to make your visit pleasant to you. You like him, yet you don't feel altogether at home with him. You are glad when he leaves you to his more composed wife. You never knew or heard of his saying or doing anything wrong or even unbecoming. You look upon him as a peculiar sort of man—well, somehow—but! He is at the bar defending that woman, who sits by him, dressed in mourning—some chancery case. Or it is a criminal case, and it is the widow's only son that Leland is defending. If you had been in his office for the last week, you would have acknowledged that he has studied the case, has prepared himself on it as thoroughly as a man can. He is an ambitious man. He intensely desires to make for himself a fortune and a position. His address to the judge, or to the jury, as the case may be, is a good one. Yet, somehow, he does not convince. He himself is carried away by his own earnestness, but he does not carry away with him his hearers. His remarks are interesting. People listen to him from first to last closely. Yet his arguing does not, somehow, convince. His pathos does not, somehow, melt. He is the sort of man that people think of for the Legislature. No man ever thinks of him in connexion with the Supreme Bench or Senate.

Wherein lies the defect? Arthur Leland is well read, a gentleman of spotless character, of earnest application, of popular manners. Why is not this man a man of more weight, power, standing? Why, you answer, the man is just what he is. He fills just the position up to which his force of mind raises him. Did he have more talent, he would be more. No, sir. Every acquaintance he has known, he himself knows, that he is capable of being much more than he is—somehow, somehow he does not attain to it! It is this singular impression Leland makes upon you. It is this singular, uneasy, unsatisfied feeling he himself is preyed upon by. "He might be, but he is not," say his neighbours. "I am not, yet I might be," worries him as an incessant and eternal truth.

It broke upon him like a revelation.

He was at work one fine morning in his garden, in a square in which young watermelon plants of a choice kind were just springing. Willie was there with him, just emerged fresh for fun from the waters of sleep. Very anxious to be as near as possible to his father, who was always his only playmate, Willie had strayed from the walk in which his father had seated him, and stood beside his father. With a quick, passionate motion, Leland seized his child, and placed him violently back in the walk, with a harsh threat. The child whimpered for a while, and soon forgetting himself, came to his father again over the tender plants. This time Leland seized him still more violently, seated him roughly in the walk, and, with harsh threats, struck him upon his plump red cheek. Willie burst into tears, and wept in passion. His father was in a miserable, uneasy frame of mind. He ceased his work, bared his brow to the delicious morning air. He leaned upon his hoe, and gazed upon his child. He felt there was something wrong. He always knew, and acknowledged, that he was of a rash, irritable disposition. He now remembered that ever since his child's birth he had been exceedingly impatient with it. He remembered how harshly he had spoken to it, how rudely he had tossed it on his knee when it awoke him with its crying at night. He remembered that the little one had been daily with him for now three years, and that not a day had passed in which he had not spoken loudly, fiercely to the child.

Yes, he remembered the heavy blows he had given it in bursts of passion, blows deeply regretted the instant after, yet repeated on the first temptation. He thought of it all; that his boy was but a little child, and that he had spoken to it, and expected from it, as if it were grown. All his passionate, cruel words and blows rushed upon his memory; his rough replies to childish questions; his unmanly anger at childish offences. He thought, too, how the little boy had still followed him, because its father was all on earth to him; how the little thing had said, he "was sorry," and had offered a kiss even after some bitter word or blow altogether undeserved. Leland remembered, too, as the morning air blew aside his hair, how often he had shown the same miserable, nervous irritability to his dog, his horse, his servants; even the branch of the tree that struck him as he walked; yea, even to his own wife. He remembered how the same black, unhappy feelings had clouded his brow, had burst from his lips at every little domestic annoyance that had happened. He could not but remember how it had only made matters worse—had made himself and his family wretched for the time. He felt how undignified, how unmanly all this was. He pictured himself before his own eyes as a peevish, uneasy, irritable, unhappy man—so weak-minded!

He glanced at the house; he knew his wife was in it, engaged in her morning duties; gentle, lady-like, loving him so dearly. He glanced at his sobbing child, and saw how healthful and intelligent he was. He glanced over his garden, and orchard, and lawn, and saw how pleasant was his home. He thought of his circle of friends, his position in business, his own education and health. He saw how much he had to make him happy; and all jarred and marred, and cursed by his miserable fits of irritation; the fever, the plague increasing daily; becoming his nature, breathing the pestilent atmosphere of hell over himself and all connected with him.

As he thus thought, his little boy again forgot himself, and strayed with heedless feet toward his father. Leland dropped his hoe, reached toward his child. The little fellow threw up his hands, and writhed his body as if expecting a blow.

"Willie," said the father, in a low, gentle voice. Willie looked up with half fright, half amazement. "Willie, boy," said the father in a new tone, which had never passed his lips before, and he felt the deep, calm power of his own words. "Willie, boy, don't walk on pa's plants. Go back, and stay there till pa is done."

The child turned as by the irresistible power of the slow-spoken, gentle words, and walked back and resumed his seat, evidently not intending to transgress again.

As Leland stood with the words dying on his lips, and his hand extended, a sudden and singular idea struck him. He felt that he had just said the most impressive and eloquent thing he had ever said in his life! He felt that there was a power in his tone and manner which he had never used before; a power which would affect a judge or a jury, as it had affected Willie. The curse cursed here too! It was that hasty, nervous disposition, which gave manner and tone to his very public speaking; which made his arguments unconvincing, his pathos unaffecting. It was just that calm, deep, serene feeling and manner, which was needed at the bar as well as with Willie. Arguing with that feeling and manner, he felt, would convince irresistibly. Pleading with that quiet, gentle spirit, he felt would melt, would affect the hearts as with the very emotion of tears.

Unless you catch the idea, there is no describing it, reader. Leland was a Christian. All that day he thought upon the whole matter. That night in the privacy of his office he knelt and repeated the whole matter before God. For his boy's sake, for his wife's sake, for his own sake, for his usefulness' sake at the bar, he implored steady aid to overcome the deadly, besetting sin. He pleaded that, indulging in that disposition, he was alienating from himself his boy and his wife; yea, that he was alienating his own better self from himself, for he was losing his own self-respect. And here his voice sank from a murmur into silence; he remembered that he was thus alienating from his bosom and his side—God!

And then he remembered that just such a daily disposition as he lacked was exactly that disposition which characterized God when God became man. The excellence of such a disposition rose serenely before him, embodied in the person of Jesus Christ; the young lawyer fell forward on his face and wept in the agony of his desire and his prayer.

From that sweet spring morning was Arthur Leland another man; a wiser, abler, more successful man in every sense. Not all at once; steadily, undoubtedly advanced the change. The wife saw and felt, and rejoiced in it. Willie felt it, and was restrained by it every drop of his merry blood; the household felt it, as a ship does an even wind; and sailed on over smooth seas constrained by it. You saw the change in the man's very gait and bearing and conversation. Judge and jury felt it. It was the ceasing of a fever in the frame of a strong man; and Leland went about easily, naturally, the strong man he was. The old, uneasy, self-harassing feeling was forgotten, and an ease and grace of tone and manner succeeded. It was a higher development of the father, the husband, the orator, the gentleman, the Christian. Surely love is the fountain of patience and peace. Surely it is the absence of passion which makes angels to be the beings they are.

Men can become very nearly angels or devils, even before they have left the world.

THE SCARLET POPPY

ONE warm morning in June, just as the sun returned from his long but rapid journey to the distant east, and sailed majestically up through the clear blue sky, the many bright flowers of one of the prettiest little parterres in the world, who had opened their eyes—those bright flowers—to smile at the sunbeams which came to kiss away the tears night had shed over them, were very much surprised, and not a little offended to find in their very midst an individual who, though most of them knew her, one might have supposed, from their appearance, was a perfect stranger to them all.

The parterre, I have said, was small, for it was in the very heart of a great city, where land would bring almost any price; but the gentleman and lady who lived in the noble mansion which fronted it, would not, for the highest price which might have been offered them, have had those sweet flowers torn up, and a brick pile reared in the place—their only child, the dear little Carie, loved the garden so dearly, and spent so much of her time there.

Oh, it was a sweet little place, though it was in the midst of a great city where the air was full of dust and coal smoke; for the fountain which played in the garden kept the atmosphere pure and cool, and every day the gardener showered all the plants so that their leaves were green and fresh as though they were blooming far away in their native woods and dells. There were sweet roses of every hue, from the pure Alba to the dark Damascus; and pinks, some of the most spicy odour, some almost scentless, but all so beautiful and so nicely trimmed. The changeless amaranth was there, the pale, sweet-scented heliotrope, always looking towards the sun; the pure lily; and the blue violet, which, though it had been taught to bloom far away from the mossy bed where it had first opened its meek eye to the light, had not yet forgotten its gentleness and modesty; and not far from them were the fickle hydrangea, the cardinal flower with its rich, showy petals, and the proud, vain, and ostentatious, but beautiful crimson and white peonias. The dahlias had yet put forth but very few blossoms, but they were elegant, and the swelling buds promised that ere long there would be a rich display of brilliant colours. Honeysuckles, the bright-hued and fragrant, the white jasmine, and many other climbing plants, were latticing the little arbour beside the clear fountain, half hiding their jewel-like pensile blossoms and bright red berries among the smooth green leaves which clustered so closely together as to shut out completely the hot sun from the little gay-plumaged and sweet-voiced songsters whose gilt cage hung within the bower. But I cannot speak of the flowers, there were so many of them, and they were all so beautiful and so sweet-scented.

Well, this June morning, as I was saying, when the flowers, as they were waked from their sleep by the sunbeams which came to kiss away the tears night had shed over them, opened their eyes and looked about them, they were surprised and offended to see a stranger in their company.

There had been, through all the season, some little rivalries and jealousies among the flowers; but from the glances which they turned on each other, this morning, it was evident that their feelings towards the stranger were exactly alike. However, as might be expected from their different dispositions, they expressed their dislike and contempt for her in different ways; but at first all hesitated to address her, for no one seemed to find language strong enough to express the scorn they felt for her; until the balsam, who never could keep silent long, inquired of the stranger, in a very impatient tone, what was her name, and how she came there.

The poor thing hesitated an instant, and her face grew very red; she must have known that her presence in that company was very much undesired, and when she spoke, it was in a low and embarrassed tone.

"My name is Papaver, and—"

But the Marygold laughed aloud. "Papaver!" she repeated in her most scornful tone; "she is nothing more nor less than a Poppy—a great offensive Poppy, whose breath fairly makes me sick. Long ago, when—"

But here the Marygold stopped short, it would not do, to confess to her genteel friends, that she had formerly been acquainted with the disreputable stranger. They did not heed her embarrassment, however, for every one, now that the silence was broken, was anxious to speak; all but the Mimosa, who could not utter a word, for she had fainted quite away—the red Rose who was very diffident, and the Dahlia who was too dignified to meddle with such trifling affairs.

"You great, red-faced thing!" said the Carnation, "how came you here in your ragged dress? Do you know what kind of company you are in? Who first saw her here?"

"I saw her," said the Morning Glory, who usually waked quite early, "I saw her before she had got her eyes open; and what do you suppose she had on her head? Why a little green cap which she has just pulled off and thrown away. There it lies on the ground now. Only look at it! no wonder she was ashamed of it. Can you think what she wore it for?"

"Why, yes!" said the Ladies' Slipper. "She is so handsome and so delicate that she was fearful the early hours might injure her health and destroy her charms!"

"No, no!" interrupted another; "she was afraid the morning breeze might steal away her sweet breath!"

"You had better gather up your sweet leaves, and put on your cap again," said the London Pride. "I see a golden-winged butterfly in Calla's cup; your spicy breath will soon bring him here to drink of your nectar!"

The most of the flowers laughed, but the Carnation still called out— "How came she here?"

The Amaranth, however, who never slept a wink through the whole night, would not answer the question, though the flowers were certain that she could, were she so inclined.

"I do not see how you who are in her immediate neighbourhood, can breathe!" said the Syringa, who was farthest removed from the poor Poppy.

"I do feel as if I should faint!" said the Verbena.

"And I feel a cold chill creeping over me!" said the Ice Plant.

"That is not strange!" remarked the Nightshade, who had sprung up in the shadow of the hedge, "she carries with her, everywhere she goes, the atmosphere of the place whence she comes. Do you know where that is?"

Some of the flowers shuddered, but the Nightshade went on:—

"The Poppy is indigenous now only on the verdureless banks of the Styx. When Proserpine, who was gathering flowers, was carried away to the dark Avernus, all the other blossoms which she had woven in her garland withered and died, but the Poppy; and that the goddess planted in the land of darkness and gloom, and called it the flower of Death. She flourishes there in great luxuriance; Nox and Somnus make her bed their couch. The aching head, which is bound with a garland of her blossoms, ceases to throb; the agonized soul which drinks in her deep breath, wakes no more to sorrow. Death follows wherever she comes!"

"We will not talk of such gloomy things!" said the Coreopsis, with difficulty preserving her cheerfulness.

But the other plants were silent and dejected; all but the Amaranth, who knew herself gifted with immortality, and the Box, who was very stoical. But another trial awaited the poor Poppy.

The Nightshade had hardly ceased speaking, when soft, gentle human voices were heard in the garden, and a child of three summers, with rosy cheeks, deep blue eyes, and flowing, golden hair, came bounding down the gravelled walks, followed by a fair lady. The child had come to bid good morning to her flowers and birds, and as she carolled to the latter, and paused now and then to inhale the breath of some fragrant blossom, and examine the elegant form and rich and varied tints of another, the little songsters sang more loudly and cheerily; and the flowers, it seemed, became more sweet and beautiful.

The Poppy, who was as ignorant as was any one else how she had found her way into the garden, now began to reason with herself.

"Some one must have planted me here," she said; "and though I am not as sweet as that proud Carnation, nor so elegant as that dignified Dahlia, I may have as much right to remain here as they!" and she raised her head erect, and spread out her broad, scarlet petals, with their deep, ragged fringe, hoping to attract the notice of the little girl.

And so indeed she did; for as the child paused before pale sweet-scented Verbena, the flaunting Poppy caught her eye, and she extended her hand toward the strange blossom.

"Carie, Carie, don't touch that vile thing!" said her mother, "it is poisonous. The smell of it will make you sick. I do not see how it came here. John must bring his spade and take it up. We will have nothing in the garden but what is beautiful or sweet, and this is neither!"

The poor Poppy! She had begun to love the little girl, the child had smiled on her so sweetly, and the other flowers had seemed so envious when that little white hand was stretched out towards her; and when she drew back, at her Mother's call, reluctantly, but with look of surprise and aversion, the Poppy did not care how soon she was banished from a place where she had been treated so unjustly.

However, she was suffered to remain; whether the lady neglected giving instructions to the gardener respecting her, or whether he forgot her commands, I am not sure; but there she remained, day after day, striving every morning to wake up early and pull off her little green cap before the other flowers had opened their eyes, but never succeeding in so doing.

It was no enviable position that she occupied, laughed at, despised, and scorned by all the other flowers in the garden, and in hourly expectation of being torn up by the roots and thrown into the street—the poor Poppy!

One day when the lady and her Carie were walking in the garden, the little girl, who had looked rather pale, put her hands suddenly to her head, and cried aloud. Her mother was very much frightened. She caught up the little girl in her arms, and tried to ascertain what was the matter; but the child only pressed her hands more tightly to her head, and cried more piteously. The lady carried her into the house, and the family were soon all in an uproar. The servants were all running hither and thither; no one seemed to know what was the matter; for the lady had fainted from terror at her child's pale face and agonized cries, and the little girl could tell nothing.

"It is that odious Poppy who is the cause of all this!" said the flowers one to another (little Carie was indeed playing in her immediate vicinity when she was seized with that dreadful distress), "she has poisoned her." And their suspicions were confirmed when one of the servants came running into the garden, and seizing hold of the Poppy, stripped off every one of her bright scarlet petals, and gathering them up, returned quickly to the house.

"You poor thing!" said the Elder, as the Poppy, so rudely handled, bent down her dishonoured head to the ground; but not one of the other flowers addressed to her a single word.

Through the long day she lay there—the Poppy—on the earth, trying to forget what had happened; for she did not know but their words were true, and she was the cause of the little girl's suffering—she would so gladly have soothed her pain. The other flowers thought she was dead, and the Poppy herself believed that she should never see the light of another morning; but just before the day was gone, the lady walked again into the garden accompanied by her husband; and—what do you suppose the other flowers thought?—without noticing one of them, the lady walked directly to the Poppy, lifted her head from the ground, and leaned it against the frame which supported the proud Carnation, and then, with her white hands, replaced the loosened earth about her half uptorn roots.

"Oh, I hope it will not die!" she said to her husband, "I should rather lose anything else in the garden, for I don't know but it saved dear little Carie's life! She had a dreadful headache, and nothing afforded her the least relief, till we bruised the leaves of the Poppy, and bound them on her temples, and then she became quiet, and fell into a gentle sleep. Oh, I hope it will live!"

Don't you think the Poppy did live, and was proud and happy enough? Do you think she was ever afterwards ashamed of her little green cap, or her ragged scarlet leaves? And do you think the other flowers ever laughed at her again, or were ashamed of her acquaintance?

When the summer had passed away, and the bright blossoms one by one withered and died before the autumn's cool breath, the Poppy cheerfully scattered her little seeds on the earth, and laid herself down to die; for she knew that when another spring should come, and her children should shoot up from the ground, they would be nurtured as tenderly, and prized as highly as those of the sweeter and far more beautiful flowers.

NUMBER TWELVE

WHEN I was a young man, working at my trade as a mason, I met with a severe injury by falling from a scaffolding placed at a height of forty feet from the ground. There I remained, stunned and bleeding, on the rubbish, until my companions, by attempting to remove me, restored me to consciousness. I felt as if the ground on which I was lying formed a part of myself; that I could not be lifted from it without being torn asunder; and, with the most piercing cries, I entreated my well-meaning assistants to leave me alone to die. They desisted for the moment, one running for the doctor, another for a litter, others surrounding me with pitying gaze; but amidst my increasing sense of suffering, the conviction began to dawn upon my mind, that the injuries were not mortal; and so, by the time the doctor and the litter arrived, I resigned myself to their aid, and allowed myself, without further objection, to be carried to the hospital.

There I remained for more than three months, gradually recovering from my bodily injuries, but devoured with an impatience at my condition, and the slowness of my cure, which effectually retarded it. I felt all the restlessness and anxiety of a labourer suddenly thrown out of employment difficult enough to procure, knowing that there were scores of others ready to step into my place; that the job was going on, and that, ten chances to one, I should never set my foot on that scaffolding again. The visiting surgeon vainly warned me against the indulgence of such passionate regrets—vainly inculcated the opposite feeling of gratitude demanded by my escape; all in vain. I tossed on my fevered bed, murmured at the slowness of his remedies, and might have thus rendered them altogether ineffectual, had not a sudden change been effected in my disposition by another, at first unwelcome, addition to our patients. He was placed in the same ward with me, and insensibly I found my impatience rebuked, my repinings hushed for very shame, in the presence of his meek resignation to far greater privations and sufferings. Fresh courage sprang from his example, and soon, thanks to my involuntary physician, I was in a fair road to recovery.

And he who had worked the charm, what was he? A poor, helpless old man, utterly deformed by suffering, his very name unnoticed, or at least never spoken in the place where he now was; he went only by the appellation of No. 12—the number of his bed, which was next to my own. This bed had already been his refuge during three long and trying illnesses, and had at last become a sort of property for the poor fellow in the eyes of doctors, students, nurse-tenders, in fact, the whole hospital staff. Never did a gentler creature walk on God's earth; walk—alas! for him the word was but an old memory. Many years before he had totally lost the use of his legs; but, to use his own expression, "this misfortune did not upset him;" he still retained the power of earning his livelihood, which he derived from copying deeds for a lawyer at so much per sheet; and if the legs were no longer a support, the hands worked at the stamped parchments as diligently as ever. But some months passed by, and then the paralysis attacked his right arm; still undaunted, he taught himself to write with the left; but hardly had the brave heart and hand conquered the difficulty, when the enemy crept on, and disabling this second ally, no more remained for him than to be conveyed once more, though this time as a last resource, to the hospital. There he had the gratification to find his former quarters vacant, and he took possession of his old familiar bed with a satisfaction that seemed to obliterate all regret at being obliged to occupy it again. His first grateful accents smote almost reproachfully on my ear: "Misfortune must have its turn, but *every day has a tomorrow!*"

It was indeed a lesson to witness the gratitude of this excellent creature. The hospital, so dreary a sojourn to most of its inmates, was a scene of enjoyment to him; everything pleased him; and the poor fellow's admiration of even the most trifling conveniences proved how severe must have been his privations. He never wearied of praising the neatness of the linen, the whiteness of the bread, the quality of the food; and my surprise gave place to the truest pity, when I learned that, for the last twenty years, this respectable old man could only afford himself, out of the profits of his persevering industry, the coarsest bread, diversified with white cheese, or vegetable porridge; and yet, instead of reverting to his privations in the language of complaint, he converted them into a fund of gratitude, and made the generosity of the nation, which had provided such a retreat for the suffering poor, his continual theme. Nor did his thankful spirit confine itself to this. To listen to him, you would have believed him an especial object of divine as well as human benevolence—all things working for his good. The doctor used to say that No. 12 had a "mania for happiness;" but it was a mania, that, in creating esteem for its victim, infused fresh courage into all that came within its range.

I think I still see him seated on the side of his bed, with his little black silk cap, his spectacles and the well-worn volume, which he never ceased perusing. Every morning, the first rays of the sun rested on his bed, always to him a fresh subject of rejoicing and thankfulness to God. To witness his gratitude, one might suppose that the sun was rising for him alone. I need hardly say, that he soon interested himself in my cure, and regularly made inquiry respecting its progress. He always found something cheering to say—something to inspire patience and hope, himself a living commentary on his words. When I looked at this poor motionless figure, those distorted limbs, and, crowning all, that smiling countenance, I had not courage to be angry, or even to complain. At each painful crisis, he would exclaim: "One minute, and it will be over. Relief will soon follow. *Every day has its to-morrow!*"

I had one good and true friend—a fellow-workman, who used sometimes to spare an hour to visit me, and he took great delight in cultivating an acquaintance with No. 12. As if attracted by a kindred spirit, he never passed his bed without pausing to offer his cordial salutation; and then he would whisper to me: "He is a saint on earth; and not content with gaining Paradise himself, must win it for others also. Such people should have monuments erected to them, known and read of all men. In observing such a character, we feel ashamed of our own happiness—we feel how comparatively little we deserve it. Is there anything I can do to prove my regard for this good, poor No. 12?"

"Just try among the bookstalls," I replied, "and find the second volume of that book you see him reading. It is now more than six years since he lost it, and ever since he has been obliged to content himself with the first."

Now, I must premise that my worthy friend had a perfect horror of literature, even in its simplest stages. He regarded the art of printing as a Satanic invention, filling men's brains with idleness and conceit; and as to writing—in his opinion a man was never thoroughly committed until he had recorded his sentiments in black and white for the inspection of his neighbours. His own success in life, which had been tolerable, thanks to his industry and integrity, he attributed altogether to his ignorance of those dangerous arts; and now a cloud swept across his lately beaming face as he exclaimed, "What! the good creature is a lover of books? Well, we must admit that even the best have their failings. No matter. Write down the name of this odd volume on a slip of paper; and it shall go hard with me, but I give him that gratification."

He did actually return the following week with a well-worn volume, which he presented in triumph to the old invalid. He looked somewhat surprised as he opened it; but our friend proceeding to explain that it was at my suggestion he had procured it in place of the lost one, the old grateful expression at once beamed up in the eyes of No. 12, and with a voice trembling with emotion, he thanked the hearty giver.

I had my misgivings, however, and the moment our visitor turned his back, I asked to see the book. My old neighbour reddened, stammered, and tried to change the conversation; but, forced behind his last entrenchments, he handed me the little volume. It was an old Royal Almanac. The bookseller, taking advantage of his customer's ignorance, had substituted it for the book he had demanded. I burst into an immoderate fit of laughter; but No. 12 checked me with the only impatient word I ever heard from his lips: "Do you wish our friend to hear you? I would rather never recover the power of this lost arm, than deprive his kind heart of the pleasure of his gift. And what of it? Yesterday I did not care a straw for an almanac; but in a little time it is perhaps the very book I should have desired. *Every day has its to-morrow*. Besides, I assure you it is a very improving study; even already I perceive the names of a crowd of princes never mentioned in history, and of whom, up to this moment, I have never heard any one speak."

And so the old almanac was carefully preserved beside the volume of poetry it had been intended to match; and the old invalid never failed to be seen turning over the leaves whenever our friend happened to enter the room. As to him, he was quite proud of its success, and would say to me at each time: "It appears I have made him a famous present." And thus the two guileless natures were content.

Towards the close of my sojourn in the hospital, the strength of poor No. 12 diminished rapidly. At first, he lost the slight powers of motion he had retained; then his speech became inarticulate; at last, no part obeyed his will, except the eyes, which continued to smile on us still. But one morning, at last, it seemed to me as if his very glance had become dim. I arose hastily, and approaching his bed, inquired if he wished for a drink; he made a slight movement of his eyelids, as if to thank me, and at that instant the first ray of the rising sun shone in on his bed. Then the eyes lighted up, like a taper that flashes into brightness before it is extinguished—he looked as if saluting this last gift of his Creator; and even as I watched him for a moment, his head fell gently on the side, his kindly heart ceased to beat. He had thrown off the burden of To-day; he had entered on his eternal To-morrow.

TO AN ABSENTEE

O'ER hill and dale, and distant sea,
   Through all the miles that stretch between,
My thought must fly to rest on thee,
   And would, though worlds should intervene.

Nay, thou art now so dear, methinks,
   The farther we are forced apart,
Affection's firm elastic links
   But bind thee closer round the heart.

For now we sever each from each,
   I learn what I have lost in thee;
Alas! that nothing less could teach
   How great, indeed, my love should be!

Farewell! I did not know thy worth;
   But thou art gone, and now 'tis prized:
So angels walked unknown on earth,
   But when they flew were recognised.

THE WHITE DOVE

THE little Lina opened her eyes upon this world in the arms of her father, the good Gotleib. He kissed the child with a holy joy: "For," said he, "now is a thought of God fixed in an eternal form;" and he felt that a Divine love flowed into this work of the great God—this also thrilled his warm, manly heart with a wondrous love. He felt the inmost of his being vibrating as with an electric touch, to the inmost of the little new-born innocent. But the rapture of the young father was altogether imperfect, until he had sealed his lips in a love-kiss upon those of the fraulein Anna, who lay there so white and beautiful in the new joy of a young mother. Like an innocent maiden, she twined her arms around Gotleib's neck, and grew strong in the influx of warm life that flowed into her responsive cares of the husband of her heart. Then Gotleib held up the newly-born Lina, and the mother's lips touched the soft cheek of the tiny little one with a living rapture, as if all of Heaven were embraced in this heart-possession.

And Gotleib knelt by the bedside, and thanked God for the beautiful gift of love with a pious awe and holy joy—large tears stood in the eyes of Anna. As he rose from his reverent posture, he kissed off the bright tears even as the sun exhales dew-drops from a pure flower, and said,

"Dost thou weep for joy, sweet one?"

And Anna said,

"Once—not long since—I had a dream—a beautiful dream—that this day has been realized. I dreamed that I was in a quite heavenly place—yet the place was as nothing—it was the *state*—for I sat with an infant in my arms—a bright innocent little one—and, thou dearest Gotleib, knelt beside me; and an angel-woman stood near us, in a soft heavenly glory, and said, in low musical, spirit-words—'Behold the fruit of the union of good and truth.' And then, methought, thou didst embrace me with a new joy of love, and whispered, 'an angel of God is born of us.' This little one is the dream-child, dear Gotleib."

Thus beautiful was the birth of the little Lina, who grew, daily, in a pure innocent loveliness. While she is expanding in the first days of her new, breathing, sensitive life, we will go back to the former life of Gotleib and Anna.

Gotleib Von Arnheim had first seen the light in this same small cottage, on the confines of the Black Forest of Germany. He was born with a large, loving heart. But the father and mother, and the dear God, were the only beings on whom his affections were fixed; for his sensitive nature shrank from the contact of the honest-hearted, but rough peasant neighbours, that made the little world of their simple life. But soon death came, and the good father left the earth for the beautiful Heaven-world. The little Gotleib missed his kind father; but his mother told him of the bright inner life, and how his father yet lived and loved him; and the heart of the boy was comforted: he felt a sense of elevation in having his father, whom he had known so familiarly here upon earth, now the companion of angels, and living in such a bright and beautiful world.

Ah, life had to him such an inner beauty; and, when still, dreamy moments of leisure intervened between his work and play, he revelled in such dreams of fancy, as lent light and life and joy to his whole being. But the death of the kind father had not only carried the boy's fancy to the other world; it was also drawing the mother's heart away to the fair spirit-land. Gotleib saw his mother's face growing thin and pale; he knew that she was weak—for oftentimes, in the long winter evenings, as he read to her from the holy word of God, her hand would drop wearily with the raised spindle, and she, who was never before idle, would fold her hands in a quiet, meek resignation. At such times a tremour would seize the boy's heart. The mother saw it; and, one night, when his fixed tender gaze rested on her, she raised her spiritual eyes to his, and said,

"Dear Gotleib! thou wilt yet have the good God to love."

"Ah, mother! mother!" cried the boy, "wilt thou, too, leave me?"

His head was bowed upon her knees in bitter grief, the desolation of earth was spread like an impenetrable pall over his whole future. Suddenly he looked up, full of a strange, bright hope, and said,

"Mother, I too may die."

Then the mother put off her weakness, and long and loving was the talk she held with her dear boy. She told him that from a little one he had ever loved God; that the first word he had ever pronounced was the name of the Holy One. She had taught him to clasp his tiny baby hands and look up and say "God," ere any other word had passed his lips. She had named him

Gotleib, because he was the love of God to her, and he was to be a lover of God. As she talked, the boy grew strong and calm, and said,

"Yet, oh, my mother! God is so great for the heart of a small child. God is so high and lifted up in the far heavens, that I feel myself but as a tiny blade of grass that looks up to the far sun—dear mother! the earth will be too lonely; ah, there is no hope but in death."

"No, my son," said the mother, "there is a beautiful hope for the earth also. I will tell you what will make you love God more truly than ever."

The boy was fixed attention.

"Thou didst not know, dear Gotleib, that when God created thee a strong, brave boy, He also created a tender, gentle little maiden, like unto thee in all things, save thou wert a boy and she a maiden. Thou wert strong and able to work, and she gentle and born to love thee."

"Where is she?" inquired the excited Gotleib.

"I know not," replied the mother. "But God knows, and He will watch over the two whom He has created, the one for the other; and, on earth, or in heaven, the two will meet. Is it not better, then, not to wish to die, but to leave all things to the will of God? For what if thy little maiden is left alone upon the earth, and there is no strong, manly heart upon which she may lean, and no vigorous arm to labour for her, how will her spirit droop with a weary, lonely sadness? No, my son, live! and the joy of a most beautiful, loving companionship, may yet be thine. The earth will not be desolate ever to thy orphan heart, with this beautiful hope before thee."

Thus, in the cold wintry night of a dark sorrow, did the good mother plant a living seed of truth, that afterwards sprang up into a vernal flowery Eden, that bloomed in the boy's heart with an eternal beauty.

When the early spring came, Gotleib looked calmly and lovingly on the beloved mother, who was leaving for the inner world. Death was beautiful to him now; it was simply the new birthtime of a mature, living soul.

The spirit of the mother's love seemed to linger over the home of his childhood, and it was a great sorrow to leave the cherished spot; but, his mother told him he was to seek a brother of hers in the distant town of Heidelberg. As Gotleib turned from the now voiceless home of his parents, a fervent desire arose in his heart that he might again be permitted to dwell beneath this sheltering roof and amidst its living associations.

The boy went forth into the unknown world, with a living trust in his heart in the great God. His was a simple, childish faith, born of his love—to him God was not a mystery. It was a Divine personality he loved. Jesus had walked the earth, and his father and mother also—all were now spirits, none the less to be loved and trusted than when upon earth; but now they were to him in transcendent states of glory. The Lord Jesus, as being infinitely great and glorious, was the alone One to whom he now looked for help—though ever as he knelt to pray to GOD, he felt that his angel-mother bowed with his spirit, and by her prompting beautiful words of humiliation and praise came to him, that he himself could never have thought of; hence the affections of his heart all grew up into the inner spirit-world.

And years passed in the good town of Heidelberg, years that brought blessings to the orphan boy as they flew. The God in whom he trusted had provided for him—had awakened a friendly kindness in many warm hearts. And Gotleib, who was at first designed by his relatives to spend his days over the shoemaker's awl and last, at length found himself, by his own ardent exertions and the helpful kindness of others, a student in the University. This was to him a most pure gratification—not because of a love of learning, not because of ambition, to attain a position before his fellow-men. Oh! it was quite otherwise with the good youth—he had one object in life. The hope that his dying mother had awakened in his heart was the guiding star of all his efforts. That little maiden created for him, and to be supported by him! The image was ever before him. Yes, he was a student for a high and noble use. Science was to be to him the instrument of a life of love and blessedness. To do good to others, and thus to provide for the maiden, was what led him to the arduous study of medicine.

It mattered not that cold and hunger and toil all bound him in an earthly coil. The warm, hopeful heart has a wonderful endurance. The delicate, attenuated form of the young student seemed barely sufficient to hold the bright and glowing spirit that looked out from his soft eyes, when he received his degrees. The desire of his life was growing into a fruition; and when he returned to his poor lodgings, a sense of freedom, of gratitude, and of delight, crowned his yet barren life. To work! to work! seemed now the one call of his being; but, whither was he to go? There was the childhood's home, to which his heart instinctively turned; but, alone and desolate, he could not dwell there. Gotleib had not forgotten his mother's lessons; he knelt and prayed to God for guidance. Even as he kneels, and feels his spirit in the sunshine of God's presence, there is a knock at the door, and the good Professor Eberhard enters. He has marked the student in his poverty and toil, and feels that he will now hold out a helping hand to the young beginner. As professor of anatomy, he needs the quick eye and delicate hand of an expert assistant.

Gotleib looked upon the Herr professor as Heaven-sent, and in a few days was installed in all the luxury of a life of active use.

Years passed away, and (sic) Gotlieb Von Arnheim sighed with a man's full heart for a woman's sympathy and responsive affection. He had seen bright eyes gleam and soft cheeks flush at his approach, and he had looked wonderingly into many a sweet face. But he had not yet seen the little maiden of whom his mother spoke—who was to be the reflex of himself. All these German maidens were altogether different from—and his heart remained unsatisfied in their presence. He felt no visions of eternity as he looked into their friendly faces.

Sometimes hope almost died out. But his trust in God seemed to forbid the death of this sweet hope. Often he said, "the good God would not have created this intense desire in one so wholly dependent upon Him, were he not intending to satisfy it." At all events, he thought—"If the maiden is not upon earth, she is in heaven." So he worked and waited patiently.

The wintry winds were howling, as it were, a wild requiem over the lordly ruins of the crime-stained castle of Heidelberg. Cold, and bitter, and clear was the starry night, when the weary Gotleib issued out of the Herr professor's warm house to answer the late call of a sick woman. Gotleib looked up into those illimitable depths where earths and suns hang suspended, to appeal to the material perceptions of man that this is not the alone world—the alone existence. The silent bright stars comforted the earth-wearied heart in which the day's toil had dimmed the spirit's perception. Gotleib stepped on bravely through the frosty darkness, and said hopefully to himself,

"There is yet another world—another life than this."

And now he stood before the house in which his services were needed. He entered a chamber, whose bare poverty reminded him of his student days. But far sadder was cold poverty here, for a lady lay on a hard couch before the scantily furnished grate, and her hollow cough, and the oozing blood that saturated her white handkerchief, rendered all words unnecessary.

A young girl, with blanched cheek and tearless eye of agony, knelt by the wan sufferer. Gotleib felt himself in the sphere of his life's use; cold and fatigue were alike gone. The sick and almost dying woman seemed to revive under his touch—it was as if strength flowed from the physician into the patient. His very presence diffused an air of hope and comfort through the desolate apartment, and the kind serving-girl, Bettina, who had guided him to the humble lodging, seconded all his active efforts to produce warmth and comfort, and soon returned with one of his prescriptions—an abundance of fuel for the almost exhausted grate. The cheerful blaze threw its strong light upon the young girl, who at first knelt in hopeless grief beside her dying mother.

What was it that thrilled the heart of Gotleib, as he looked upon this young maiden? Was it her beauty? No! he had seen others more beautiful. Was it her sorrow? No! he had seen others quite as sad. But, whatever it was, Gotleib felt he had met his destiny; the fulness of his being was developed to him; and, all unconsciously, the maiden turned to him as the Providence of God to her. She seemed to rest her troubled heart upon his strong understanding. He said her mother would not die immediately, and she grew calm.

It was very late that night when Gotleib retired; and very fervent were the prayers that arose from his heart before he slept. He felt a sense of gratitude for the uses he was permitted to perform to his fellow beings, and, in his prayers, he felt that light shone from the Divine sun upon that sorrowing maiden, and it was as if she knelt by his side, and his strong spirit-arms upheld her in the sunshine of God's love.

When the morning came, Gotleib awakened with a delicious sense of enjoyment in life—with a looking forth into the events of the day, that he had never before experienced. He hastened through his morning duties with an elasticity of spirit and hope that was altogether new to him. Though, as yet, his feeling was not defined into a thought, it was a faint perception, a dim consciousness that the elective affinities of his heart had all awakened. And while he thought he was in an excessive anxiety to see after his feeble patient, he was borne on rather by the attractions of his heart's love. He paused in a thrilling excitement of hope and doubt before the door of the poor chamber—he dreaded to have the agreeable impressions of the last evening dissipated. But, when he knocked, a light tread was heard; the door was gently opened, and the pale Anna stood before him, with such a gentle grace, and so earnest a look of gratified expectation, that, as she said in subdued tones,

"I hoped it was you," his heart bounded with exultation, to think that the young girl had him in her thoughts. But, as he approached the sick bed, his reason told him what was more natural than her wishing for the arrival of her mother's physician.

A careful glance, by daylight, around the humble apartment, revealed to Gotleib that Anna worked with her delicate, white, lady-looking hands, for the support of her dying mother. A table, placed by the window, was covered with artificial flowers of exquisite workmanship, and, while he yet lingered in the chamber, Bettina, the maid, entered from the street door, with a basket filled with the same flowers—looked at Anna, and shook her head mournfully. The young girl's lips quivered, and she pressed the tears back when she saw no purchaser had been found for her labour. Gotleib saw and felt with the most intense sympathy all that was passing. He lingered yet longer—he made encouraging remarks to the sick mother, and, at length, ventured to approach the table, and gazed with admiration on the beautiful flowers, while his brain was busy in devising how he was to make them the medium of conveying aid to the suffering mother and daughter. He turned to the faithful Bettina, who clung to those whom she served in their hard poverty—he told her that if she would follow him he would find a purchaser for the pretty flowers. Anna cast upon him a look of tearful smiling gratitude, and her simple, "I thank you," as she held out her hand to him, bound him as with a magnetic chain to her being. Bettina thought the Herr Doctor was a most generous man, for he more than doubled the paltry sum she asked for the flowers; though she did not consider it necessary to mention the fact to Anna, she merely stated to her that she had found a purchaser for as many flowers as she chose to make.

But Gotleib! what an Eden those flowers made of his chamber! with what a joy he returned to it after hours of absence; it seemed as if they brought him into contact with the sphere of a beloved existence. He examined them with delight, and could not avoid covering them with kisses. Never was patient visited or watched over more attentively than was Madame Hendrickson; and, as the mother revived, the daughter seemed to feel new life. Light beamed from her soft eyes, and oftentimes Gotleib thought that the roses that bloomed in her delicate face were far more beautiful and bright than those that grew under her light and skilful touch.

For him she seemed to feel an earnest trustful gratitude. She never concealed her glad recognition of his coming; she was too pure, and innocent, and good, to think it necessary to conceal anything. And Gotleib's visits were so pleasant, they grew longer and longer—for he and Madame Hendrickson were of the same religious faith—and he had a peculiar faculty for consoling her. Gotleib spoke of the other world with such a definite perception of its existences and modes of being, that the dying woman never wearied of listening to him. The high and true faith of the good Gotleib opened to him a world of beauty, which he poured forth in his earnest enthusiasm, more like a gifted poet than a being of mere prose. Oftentimes, as he talked, the light of his intelligence seemed to gleam back from the answering eye of Anna, until his whole being was filled with delight. While she felt that her hitherto dim and indistinct faith was growing into form and fixedness, and her intellect awakened to a sphere of ideas, to a world of perceptions, that endowed her all at once with a charmed existence, and flooded her with the light of a graceful beauty that made her appear to the admiring Gotleib like an angelic spirit.

Thus were the spirit links being woven through the cold bright days of winter. Madame Hendrickson was no longer confined to her bed; and on the Sabbath days Anna could attend the public worship of God, of whom, now, only she seemed truly to learn. It was to the Holy Supper she went on that first solemn Sabbath day, after months of confinement and sorrow. Oh! how blessed it was to listen to the Divine Word, through which God seemed to her awakened perception to shine, in a veiled beauty! and when she tasted the wine of spiritual truth, flowing from the wisdom of the Divine One, and ate of the bread of the celestial good of His love, Heaven seemed to open to her receptive heart and mind—and, as her heart's prayers went up with those of the shining angels round the throne of God, it was not for herself that she prayed, but for him that had spoken living truth to her virgin heart. Oh, the good child! In that holy moment she rejoiced to reveal her heart's love to the Divine Father; she knew that her love was born of her knowledge of God, and thus she knew that it was blessed from above.

As she passed out of the church, she encountered the earnest glance of surprised and delighted recognition from Gotleib. Very soon he was at her side. In the fullness and stillness of her beautiful thoughts and satisfied affections they walked on. Oh, how happy the dear mother looked, when she saw the two enter her lonely chamber! The heavenly light and warmth of love seemed to be within and around them; and she saw that two beings so exactly created the one for the other, could not but find an eternal happiness in each other. Gotleib was truly in one of his genial, sunny moods; he seemed to soar into worlds of light; his expanding heart was filling with the glory of Heaven. The teachings of his childhood were all brought forth; he talked of his beloved mother—now an angel of God—told of the beautiful hope she awakened in his heart concerning the little maiden created by God for him, when his heart shrunk in such pain from the isolation her death would leave him in. Then he turned to the blushing Anna, and said he thought the maiden was now found. She lifted her love-lighted eyes to his—he clasped her hand and said softly,

"Thou art mine!"

"I am thine," fell responsive from the maiden's lips; and an infinite blessedness flowed into the loving, satisfied heart of Gotleib.

The next day brought with it a new and beautiful joy,—a letter from the beloved one, conveyed into his hand as he tenderly pressed hers, at parting. For this his thirsty soul had yearned—for some expression of the maiden's heart-love that had as yet gleamed upon him but momentarily from her modest eyes. But alone in his chamber, with the dear letter before him! Ah, now indeed he was to lift the veil that hid his life's treasure. To have revealed to him the heart and mind of the beloved one. And his whole being went forth to her as he read the tender revealings. She wrote:

"Gotleib! my heart would fain speak to thine. It longs to say gratefully, 'I love thee, thou heaven-sent one.' And I would tell thee of a dream that came to me last night in my heart's beautiful happiness.

"I was reading aloud to my mother in the book you lent me. I read of how the angels ever have their faces turned to the Divine Sun. Of how their shining brows are ever attracted to this central point, in whatever position they may be—even as our feet are attracted to the central point of the earth. I was happy in this beautiful truth, and felt that through my love for thee, my thought was lifted upward, and my face, too, was turned to the Lord; and when sleep came, it seemed as if my happy spirit was conscious of a new and beautiful existence. I found myself in a large place, and a company of angelic spirits surrounded me; and we were seated at a table, adorned with an exceeding elegance, and having many varieties of food, of which we partook, but without a consciousness of taste—only there was a genial delight of mind arising from the mutual love of all those bright ones. An angel-woman spoke to me and said, 'This is the Lord's Supper; appropriate to thyself the goods and truths of His heavenly kingdom.' While she thus spoke, I saw thee, dear Gotleib, approach, with such a smiling and beautiful grace, and thou saidst to me, holding my hand—'Sweet one! how bright thou art! Hast thou learnt some new truth! for thou art ever bright, when thou dost perceive a new truth!' Then I answered, 'Ah, yes, indeed! I have learned a beautiful new truth;' and I led thee to an east window and pointed upward to the great Sun, that shone in such a Divine effulgence—then I told thee how the angels were held by the attraction of love in this centre of being—even as the children of the world are held by the attraction of gravitation to the earth—and as we talked, the light shone around thee, dear Gotleib! with so heavenly a glory, that my heart was filled with a new love for thee. For I saw, truly, that thou wert a child of God, and in loving thee

I loved Him who shone in such a radiant glory upon thee. Oh! was not this a pleasant dream? Gotleib! what worlds of beauty thou hast opened to me! Once my thought was so narrow, so bound down to the earth; but thou hast lifted me above the earth. A woman's heart is so weak—it is like a trailing vine, that cannot lift itself up until its curling tendrils are wound round the lofty tree-tops of a man's ascending thought. Gotleib, thus dost thou bear me up into the serene, bright heavens, and like some blooming flowery vine will my love ever seek to adorn thy noble thoughts."

Gotleib was charmed with the maiden's thoughts. Oh, yes—her flowers were already flying over his highest branches. She soared above him, and through her heavenly truths were growing clearer to him. How grateful he was to his Heavenly Father, that from his own bosom, as it were, was born his spirit's companion. But her life was from God—and how holy was her whole being to him! She was enthroned in his inmost heart, to be for ever treasured as the highest and best gift of God.

It was evening when he next stood beside her. The mother slept, and Anna and Gotleib stood in the moonlit window. Few, and softly whispered, were his loving words to her. But she smiled in a oneness of thought, when he said,

"In heaven, the sun shone upon us; upon earth the cold moonbeams unite us; but the sunshine will soon come again."

Anna felt that her letter had made Gotleib very happy; and she bent her head lovingly on his manly breast. Oh! to him, the desolate forlorn one, how thrilling was the first caress of the maiden! His lips touched her soft white brows with a delicious new joy. But brow, eyes, cheeks, and lips, were soon covered with rapturous kisses.

Ah! happy youth and maiden, thus bedewed with life's nectar of blessedness! What are earth's sorrows to you? Heaven is in you, and eternity only can satisfy the infinite desires of such hearts.

But as the days passed, the material body of the mother wasted away, and her spirit was growing bright in its coming glory. She wished much to see her beloved Anna in a holy marriage union before she left this world. So a few weeks after the betrothal, Gotleib led his bride to the marriage altar. It was a festive scene of the heart's happiness even beside the bed of death. Madame Hendrickson felt that she, too, was adorning for a beautiful bridal—and earthly care being thus removed from her heart, she was altogether happy.

And the good, true-hearted Anna, in white bridal garments and virgin innocence, looked to the loving mother and happy Gotleib like an angel of God. Even the Professor Eberhard thought thus, and quite certain it is, that the good minister spoke as if a heavenly inspiration flowed into him, as he bound the two into an eternal *oneness* of being. "Little children!" said he, "love one another! was the teaching of the great God, as he walked upon the earth. Hence love is the holy of the holies. And it flows from God even as heat flows from the material sun—and as the sun is in its own heat and light, so God is in love."

And taking the marriage ring, he placed it on the soft, white, rose-tipped finger of the bride, and said,

"How beautiful and expressive is this symbol of union, showing the conjunction of good and truth, which conjunction first exists in the Lord, for His love is the inmost, and His wisdom is like the golden bond of truth encasing and protecting love. And this love of the Lord flowing into man is received, protected, and guarded by woman's truth, until, in her fitness and perfect adaptation to him, she becomes the love of the wisdom of the man's love, and the twain are no longer two, but one."

The fresh spring days were now coming—Madame Hendrickson went to an eternal spring. But the heart of the loving Anna rose above the earthly sorrow of separation, as if upheld by her husband's strong faith; her imagination delighted itself in following the beloved mother into her new and beautiful state of being.

Gotleib felt that now it was good for him to return to the home of his childhood, for it was more delightful to live apart from the strife and toil of men. In the simple country life much good might be done, and yet there would be less of life's sorrow to look upon. It was weary to live in a crowded haunt, where a perception of vice and misery so mingled itself with the blessedness of his heart's love. Anna was charmed and delighted with the pure country life, and as business increased on the Herr Doctor's hands, it was so great a happiness to her to minister to his comfort. After the long winter rides, how she chafed his cold hands and warmed his frozen feet, and how lovingly she helped him to the warm suppers of the good Bettina, no homeless and desolate wanderer of earth can know. But to Gotleib, what an inexpressible blessedness was all this; and how often he left off to eat, that he might clasp Anna to his heart and cover her with kisses! Thus went the blessed married life until another spring brought with it the sweet "dream-child," as Anna called the little one, whom the angel said, was "the fruit of the union of good and truth."

The little Lina thus born into the very sphere of love, seemed ever a living joy. The father's wisdom guided the mother's tender love, and the little one was good and unselfish—and so gay in the infantile innocence and grace of her being, that oftentimes the young mother, leaning on the father's bosom, would whisper,

"Gotleib, she is indeed an angel of God."

One dark and wintry day, as the child thus sported in the inner glad light and joy of her heart, and Gotleib and Anna as usual were watching the light of her radiance, a beautiful White Dove flew fluttering against the friendly window. The child grew still in her wondrous joy. But the father quickly opened the window, and the half-frozen bird flew in, and nestled itself in Anna's bosom. It was fed and warmed and loved as bird never was before. For the little one thought it was the spirit of God come down upon the house, and Gotleib loved it because to him it was a living symbol of the peace and purity of his married life, and Anna received it as a heavenly gift for the loving child. Thus both literally and spiritually the White Dove of innocence and peace dwelt in their midst.

THISTLE-DOWN

THERE is no time like these clear September nights, after sunset, for a revery. If it is a calm evening, and an intense light fills the sky, and glorifies it, and you sit where you can see the new moon, with the magnificent evening star beneath it, you must be a stupid affair, indeed, if you cannot then dream the most *heavenly* dreams!

But Rosalie Sherwood, poor young creature, is in no dreaming mood this lovely Sabbath night. Her heart is crushed in such an utter helplessness, as leaves no room in it for hope: her brain is too acutely sensitive, just now, for visions. The thistle-down, in beautiful fairy-like procession, floats on and up before her eyes, and as she watches the frail things, they assume a new interest to her; she feels a human sympathy with them. Like the viewless winds they come, from whence she knows not; and go, whither? none can tell. They are homeless, and she is like them; but she is not as they, purposeless.

If you could look into her mind, you would see how she has nerved it to a great determination; how that, mustering visions and hopes once cherished, she had gone forward to a bleak and barren path, and stands there very resolute, yet, in the first moment of her resolve, miserable; no, she had not yet grown strong in the suffering; she cannot *this* night stand up and bear her burden with a smile of triumph.

Rosalie Sherwood was an only child, the daughter of an humble friend Mrs. Melville had known from girlhood. *She,* poor creature, had neither lived nor died innocent.

On her death-bed, Cecily Sherwood gave her unrecognised child to the care of one who promised, in the sincerity of her passion, to be a mother to the unfortunate infant. And during the eighteen years of that girl's life, from the hour of her mother's death to the day when she was left without hope in the world, Rosalie *had* found a parent in the rigid but always kind and just Mary Melville.

This widow lady had one son; he was four years old when her husband died, which was the very year that the little Rosalie was brought to Melville House. The boy's father had been considered a man of great wealth, but

HESTER

WHILE Hester lived, the day was bright
With something more than common light—
'Twas the moon's difference to the night.

As summer sun and summer shower
Revive the tree, the herb, and flower,
Hers was the gift of warmth and power.

She was not what the world calls wise;
Yet, the mute language of her eyes
Was worth a thousand homilies.

She was so crystal pure a thing,
That sin to her could no more cling
Than water to a sea-bird's wing.

Like memory-tones heard long ago,
Her gentle voice was soft and low,
But plaintive in its underflow.

Her life so slowly loosed its springs,
Long ere she passed from earthly things,
We saw the budding of her wings.

She lingered so in taking leave—
Heaven granted us a long reprieve—
That when she went we could not grieve.

The very night that Hester died,
There came and stood my couch beside,
A gentle spirit glorified.

And often in my darker mood,
When evil thoughts subdue the good,
I see her clasp the holy Rood.

But when my better hopes illume
The narrow pathway to the tomb,
My Hester's presence fills the room.

when his affairs were settled, after his decease, it was found that the debts of the estate being paid, little more than a competency remained for the widow. But the lady was fitted, by a life of self-discipline, even in her luxurious home, to calmly meet this emergency. With the remnant of an imagined fortune, she retired to an humbler residence, where, in quiet retirement, she gave her time to managing household affairs, and superintending the home education of the children.

Her son Duncan, and the young Rosalie, had grown up together, until the girl's twelfth birth-day, constant playmates and pupils in the same school. No one, not even the busiest busy-body, had ever been able to detect the slightest partiality in Mrs. Melville's treatment of her children; and, indeed, it had been quite impossible that she should ever regard a child so winningly beautiful as Rosalie, with other than the tenderest affection. Under a light and careless rein, the girl had been a difficult one to manage, for there was a light little fire in her eyes, that told of strong will and deep passions; and besides, her striking appearance had won sufficient admiration to have completely spoiled her, if a guardian the most vigilant as well as most discerning, had not been ever at hand to speak the right word to and do the right thing with her.

Mrs. Melville was a thoroughly religious woman, and seriously conscious of the responsibility she incurred in adopting the infant. She could not quiet her conscience with the reflection that she had done a wonderfully good thing in giving Rosalie a home and education; the chief pity she felt for the unfortunate orphan, led her to exercise an uncommon care, that all tendency to evil should be eradicated from the heart of the brilliant girl while she was yet young; that a sense of right, such as should prove abiding, might be impressed on her tender mind. And her labour of love met with a return which might well have made the mother proud.

There had been no officious voice to whisper to Rosalie Sherwood the story of the doubtful position which she occupied in the world. She was an orphan, the adopted child of the lady whom she devoutly loved with all a daughter's tenderness; this she knew, and it was all she knew; and Mrs. Melville was resolved that she should never know more.

The son of the widow had been educated for the ministry. He was now twenty-two years old, and was soon to be admitted to the priesthood. In this he was following out his own wish, and the most cherished hope of his mother, and it seemed to all who knew him, as though the Head of the Church had set his seal upon Duncan from his boyhood. He was so mild and forbearing, so discreet and generous, so earnest and so honest; meek, and holy of heart, was the thought of any one who looked upon his placid, youthful face. Yet, he had, besides his gentleness, that without which his character might have subsided into a mere puerile weakness; a firmness of purpose; a reverence for duty; a strict sense of right, equal to that which marked his mother among women. Duncan Melville's abilities were of a high order; perhaps not of the very highest, though, if his ambition were only equal to his powers, they would surely seem so to the world.

His voice had a sweet persuasive tone, that was fitted to *win* souls, yet it could ring like a clarion, when the grandeur of his themes fired his soul. With the warmest hopes and the deepest interest, they, who knew the difficulties and trials attending the profession he had chosen, looked on this young man.

Duncan and Rosalie had long known the nature of the tie which bound them together—members of one family—and they never called themselves brother and sister, after the youth came home a graduate from college. For, from the time when absence empowered him to look as a stranger would look on Rosalie, from that time he saw her elegant and accomplished, and bewitching, as she was, and other than fraternal affection was in his heart for her.

And Rosalie, too, loved him, just as Duncan, had he spoken his passion, would have prayed her to love him. She had long ago made him the standard of all manly excellence; and when he came back, after three years of absence, she was not inclined to revoke her early decision; therefore was she prepared to read the language of Duncan's eyes, and she consecrated her heart to him.

During the years which followed his return from college, till he was prepared for ordination, as a priest, he did not once *speak* to her of his love, which was growing all the while stronger and deeper, as the river course that, flowing to the ocean, receives every day fresh impetus and force from the many tiny springs that commingle with it. Duncan Melville never *thought* of wedding another than Rosalie Sherwood.

It was, as I said, near the time appointed for his ordination, when he felt, for the first time, as though he had a *right* to speak openly with her of all his hopes. He asked her, then, what, in soul language, he had long before asked, a question which she had as emphatically, in like language, answered—to be his partner for life, in weal or woe.

He had tried to calmly consider Rosalie's character as a Christian minister should consider the character of her whom he would make the sharer of his peculiar lot; and setting every preference aside, Duncan felt that she was fitted to assist, and to bear with him. She was truthful as the day, strong-minded and generous; humane and charitable: and though no professor of religion, a woman full of reverence and veneration.

He knew that it was only a fear that she should not *adorn* the Christian name, that kept her back from the altar of the church, and he loved her for that spirit of humility, knowing that she was "on the Lord's side," and that grace, ere long, would be given to her, to proclaim it in doing *all* His commandments.

It was certainly with a joyful and confident heart that, after he had spoken with Rosalie, Duncan sought his mother, to tell her of the whole of that bright future which opened now before him.

How then was he overcome with amazement and grief when Mrs. Melville told him it was a union to which she could never consent! Then, for the first time in his life, the astonished young man heard of that stain which was on the name poor Rosalie bore.

He heard the story to the end, and, with a decision and energy that would have settled the matter with almost any other than his mother, he declared,

"Yet for all that, I will not give her up."

"It would not be expected that you would fulfil the engagement. Rosalie herself would not allow it, if she knew the truth of the matter."

"But she need not know it. There is no existing necessity. Is it not enough that she is good and precious *to me*? She is a noble woman, whose life has been, thanks to your guidance, beautiful and lofty."

"God knows, I *have* striven to do my duty by her, but I know what I should have done if I had ever thought you would wish to change your relations with her, Duncan."

"The world has not her equal! It is cruel—it is sinful—in you, mother, to oppose our union."

"She *is* a lovely woman; but, my son, there are myriads like her."

"No *not one*! Tell me you will never breathe a word of what you have told me *to her*!"

"Never."

"Oh! thank you! thank you, mother! you could not wish another daughter."

"But for that I have told you, I could not wish another."

"Then I say you must not work this great injustice on us. Rosalie loves me. She has promised to be mine. You will break my heart."

"You are deluded and strongly excited, my son, or you would never speak so to me," said the mother, with that persisting firmness with which the physician resorts to a desperate remedy for a desperate disease. Then she spoke to him of all the relations in life he might yet be called upon to assume; of the misery which very possibly might follow this union in after days. Hours passed on, and the conference was not ended, until, with a crushed heart, and a trembling voice, Duncan arose, abruptly, while his mother yet spoke, and he said,

"If the conclusion to which you have urged me, in God's sight, is just, He will give me—He will give Rosalie, too—strength to abide by it. But I can never speak to her of this, and I must find another home than yours and hers. You must speak *for me*, mother; and let me charge you, do it gently. Do not tell her *all*. Let her think what she will, believe, as she must, that I am a wretch, past pardon; but do not blight her peace by telling *all*."

"I promise you, Duncan," was the answer, spoken through many tears, and in the deepest sorrow.

An hour after, he was on the way from the village that he might spend the coming Sabbath in another town.

And, after he was gone, the mother sought her younger, her dearly loved child. Rosalie heard that familiar step on the stairway; she had seen Duncan hurrying away from the house, and she knew the conference was over; but she had no fear for the result. So she hushed the glad tumultuous beating of her heart, and tried to veil the brightness of her eyes as she heard the gentle tapping at her door that announced the mother coming.

As for Mrs. Melville, her heart quite failed her when she went into the pleasant room, and sat down close by Rosalie. In spite of all the strengthening thoughts of duty which she had taken with her as a support in that interview, she was now at a sore loss, for it had been a bitter grief to her kind heart when, of old, for duty's sake, she made her children unhappy. How then could sh endure to take away their life's best joy, their richest hope? It was a hard thing; and many moments passed before she could nerve her strong spirit to utter the first word. Rosalie, anxious and impatient, too, but unsuspecting, at last exclaimed,

"What can it be that so much troubles you, mother?"

Then Mary Melville spoke, but with a voice so soft and sad, so faint with emotion, that it seemed not at all her voice. She said,

"I want you to consider that what I say to you, dear child, has given me more pain even to think of than I have ever felt before. Duncan has told me of your engagement to marry with him; and it has been my duty, my most sorrowful duty, oh! believe me, to tell him that such a tie must never unite you. He can never be your husband; you can never be his wife."

She paused, exhausted by her emotion; she could not utter another syllable. Rosalie, who had watched her with fixed astonishment as she listened to the words, was the first to speak again, and she tried to say, calmly,

"Of course, you have a reason for saying so. It is but just that I should know it."

"It cannot *be* known. If I had ever in my life deceived you, Rosalie, you might doubt me now, when I assure you that an impediment, which cannot be named, exists to the marriage. Have I not been a mother to you always?" she asked, appealingly, imploringly: "I love you as I love Duncan, and it cuts me to the heart to grieve you."

"Has Duncan given you an answer?"

"Yes, Rosalie."

"And it—?"

"He has trusted to his mother!" she said, almost proudly.

"Rather than me," quickly interrupted Rosalie.

"Rather than do that which is wrong; which might hereafter prove the misery of you both, my child."

"Where is he? Why does he not come himself to tell me this? If the thing is really true, *his* lips should have spoken it, and not another's."

"Oh! Rosalie, he could not do it. I believe his heart is broken. Do not look so upon me. Is it not enough that I bitterly regret, that I shall always deplore, having not foreseen the result of your companionship? Say only that you do believe I have striven to do the best for you always, as far as I knew how. I implore you, *say it*."

"Heaven knows I believe it, mother. When will Duncan come home again?"

"Monday; not before."

When Monday morning came, on the desk in Rosalie's room this letter was found:—

"I cannot leave you for ever, Duncan; I cannot go from your protecting care, mother, without saying all that is in my heart. I have no courage to look on you, my brother, again. Mother! our union, which we had thought life-lasting, is broken. I cannot any longer live in the world's sight as your daughter by adoption. I would have done so. I would have remained in any capacity, as a slave, even, for I was bound by gratitude for all that you have done for me, to be with you always—at least so long as you could wish. If you had unveiled the mystery, and suffered me to stand before you, recognising myself as *you* know me, I would have stayed. I would have been to you, Duncan, only as in childhood—a proud yet humble sister, rejoicing in your triumphs, and sharing by *sympathy* in your griefs. I would have put forth fetters on my heart; the in-dwelling spirit should henceforth have been a stranger to you. I *know* I could have borne even to see another made your wife; but in a mistaken kindness you put this utterly beyond my power. Too much has been required, and I am found—wanting! If even the most miserable fate that can befall an innocent woman; if the curse of illegitimacy were upon me, I could bear that thought even, and acknowledge the justice and wisdom that did not consider me a fit associate for one whose birth is recognized by a parent's pride and fondness.

"But, dear Mrs. Melville, I must be cognisant of the relation, whatever it is, that I bear you. I cannot, I will not, consent to appear nominally your daughter, when you scorn to receive me as such.

"*Mother*—in my dear mother's name, I thank you for the generous love you have ever shown me: for the generous care with which you have attended to the development of the talents God gave me. For I am now fitted to labour for myself. I thank you for the watchful guardianship that has made me what I am, a woman—self-reliant and strong. I thank you for it, from a heart that has learned only to love and honour you in the past eighteen years. And I call down the blessings of the infinite God upon you, as I depart. Hereafter, always, it will be my endeavour to live worthily of you—to be *all* that you have, in your more than charity, capacitated me to be. Duncan, you will not forget me?

"I do not ask it. But pray for me, and live up to the fullness of your being—of your heart and of your intellect. There is a happy future for you. I have no word of counsel, no feeble utterance of encouragement to leave you—you will not need such from *me*. God bless and strengthen you in every good word and work—it shall be the constant hope of the sister who *loves* you. Mother, farewell!"

This letter was written on the Sabbath eve on which our story opens—written in a perfect passion—yes, of grief, and of despair. The anger that

Rosalie may at first have felt, gave way to the wildest sorrow now, but her resolution was taken, and her heart was really strong to bear the resolution out.

After the sudden and most unlooked-for disappearance, the mother and son sought long, and I need not say how anxiously, for Rosalie. But their search was vain, and, at last, as time passed on, she became to the villagers as one who had never been. But never by the widow was she forgotten; and oh! there was in the world one heart that sorrowed with a constant sorrow, that hoped with a constant hope for her.

He had lost her, and Duncan sought for no other love among women. When all his searching for Rosalie proved unavailing, the minister applied himself with industry to the work of his calling, and verily he met here with his reward; for as he was a blessing to the people of his parish, in time they almost adored him. He was a spiritual physician whom God empowered to heal many a wounded and stricken heart; but there was a cross of suffering that he bore himself, which could not be removed. It was his glory that he bore it with martyr-like patience—that he never uttered a reproachful word to her through whom he bore it.

As years passed away, the gifted preacher's impassioned eloquence, and stirring words, bowed many a proud and impenitent soul with another love than that he wished to inspire, still he sought not among any of them companionship, or close friendship. They said, at last, considering his life spent in the most rigid performance of duty, that *"he was too high-church to marry,"*—that he did not believe such union consonant with the duties of the cloth! But the mother knew better than this—*she* knew a name that was never spoken now in Rosalie's old home, that was dearer than life to the heart of her son; and desolate and lonely as he oft-times was, she never *dared* ask him to give to her a daughter—to take unto himself a wife.

In a splendid old cathedral a solemn ceremonial was going forward, on the morning of a holy festival. A bishop was to be consecrated.

A mighty crowd assembled to witness the ceremony, and the mother of Duncan Melville was there, the happiest soul in all that company, for it was on *her* son that the high honour was to be laid.

How beautiful was the pale, holy countenance of the minister, who, in the early strength of his manhood, was accounted worthy to fill that great office for which he was about to be set apart! He was a man "acquainted with grief,"—you had known it by the resigned, submissive expression of his face; you had known that the passions of mortals had been all but chilled in him, by the holy light in his tranquil eyes. Duncan *had* toiled—he *had* born a burden!

A thousand felt it, looking on the noble front where religion undefiled, and peace, and holy love, and charity, had left for themselves unmistakable evidences: and, more than all, one being felt it who had not looked upon that man for years—not since the lines of grief and care had marked the face and form of Duncan Melville. There was reason for the passionate sobs of one heart, crushed anew in that solemn hour; there was pathos such as no other voice could give to the prayers which went up to God from one woman's heart, in the great congregation, for him. Poor, loving, still-beloved Rosalie! She was there, her proud, magnificent figure bent humbly from the very commencement to the close of the ceremonial; there, her beautiful eyes filled with tears of love, and grief, and despair, and pride; there, crushed as the humblest flower—the glorious beauty!

And the good man at the altar, for whom the prayers and the praise ascended, thought of her in that hour! Yes, in that very hour he remembered how *one* would have looked on him that day, could she have come, his wife, to witness how his brethren and the people loved and honoured him. He thought of her, and as he knelt at the altar, even there he prayed for her; but not as numbers thought upon the name of Rosalie Sherwood that day; for she also was soon to appear before a throng, and there was a myriad hearts that throbbed with expectancy, and waited impatiently for the hour when they should look upon her.

Bishop Melville had retired at noonday to his study, that he might be for a few moments alone. He was glancing over the sermon (sic) the was to deliver that afternoon, when his mother, his proud and happy mother, came quickly into the room, laid a sealed note on the table and instantly withdrew, for she saw how he was occupied. When he had finished his manuscript, the bishop opened the note and read—could it have been with careless eyes?

"Duncan, I have knelt in the house of the Lord, to-day, and witnessed your triumph. Ten years ago, when I went desolate and wretched from your house, I might have prophesied your destiny. Come, to-night, and behold *my* triumph—at—the opera-house!

"Your sister,
ROSALIE."

Do you think that, as he read that summons, he hesitated as to whether he should obey it? If his bishopric had been sacrificed by it, he would have gone; if disgrace and danger had attended his footsteps, he would have obeyed her bidding! The love which had been strengthening in ten long years of loneliness and bereavement, was not now to stop, to question or to fear.

"Accompany me, dear mother, this evening; I have made an engagement for you," he said, as he went, she hanging on his arm, to the cathedral for afternoon service.

"Willingly, my son," was the instant answer, and Duncan kept her to her word.

But it was with wondering, with surprise that she did not attempt to conceal, and with questions which were satisfied with no definite reply, that Mrs. Melville found herself standing with her son in an obscure corner of the opera-house that night. Soon all her expressions of astonishment were hushed, but by another cause than the mysterious inattention of her son: a queenly woman appeared upon the stage; she lifted her voice, and sobbed the mournful wail which opens the first scene in — —.

For years there had not been such a sensation created among the frequenters of that place, as now, by the appearance of this stranger. The wild, singular style of her beauty made an impression that was heightened by every movement of her graceful figure, every tone of her rich melodious voice. She seemed for the time the very embodiment of the sorrow to which she gave an expression, and the effect was a complete triumph.

Mary Melville and her son gazed on the *debutante*—they had no word, no look for each other: for they recognised in her voice the tones of a grief of which long ago they heard the prelude—and every note found its echo in the bishop's inmost heart.

"Come away! let us go home! Duncan, this is no place for us—for *you*. It is disgrace to be here," was the mother's passionate plea, when at last Rosalie disappeared, and other forms stood in her place.

"We will stay and save her," was the answer, spoken with tears and trembling, by the man for whom, in many a quiet home, prayers in that very hour ascended. "She is mine *now*, and no earthly consideration or power shall divide us."

And looking for a moment in her son's face steadfastly, the lady turned away sighing and tearful, for she knew that she must yield then, and she had fears for the future.

A half-hour passed and the star of the night reappeared, resplendent in beauty, triumphing in hope;—again her marvellous voice was raised, not with the bitter cry of despair that was hopeless, but glad and gay, angelic in its joy.

Again the mother's eyes were turned on him beside her—and a light was on that pale forehead—a smile on that calm face—a gladness in those eyes—such as she had not seen there in long, long years; but though she looked with a mother's love upon the one who stood the admiration of all eyes, crowned with the glory-crown of perfection in her art, she could not with Duncan hope. For, alas! her woman-heart knew too well the ordeal through which the daughter of her care and love must have passed before she came into *that* presence where she stood now, who could tell if still the mistress of herself and her destiny? who could tell if pure and undefiled?

That night and the following day, there were many who sought admittance to the parlours of Rosalie Sherwood; they would lay the homage of their trifling hearts at her feet. But all these sought in vain; and why was this? Because such admiring tribute was not what the noble woman sought; *and* because, ere she had risen in the morning, a letter, written in the solitude of night, was handed to her, which barred and bolted her doors against the curious world.

"Rosalie! Rosalie! look back through the ten years that are gone; I am answering your letter of long ago with words; I have a thousand times answered them with my heart, till the thoughts which have crowded there, filled it almost to breaking. We have met—met at last—you and I! But did you call that a triumph when you stood in God's house, and saw them lay their consecrating hands upon me? Heaven forgive me! I was thinking of you then—and thinking, too, that if this honor was in any way to be considered a *reward*, the needful part was wanting—you were not there! Yet you *were* there, you have written me; ah! but not *Rosalie, my wife*, the woman I loved better than *all* on earth—the *acknowledged* woman, her whose memory I have borne about with me till it was a needful part of my existence. You were by when the people came to see me consecrated—and I obeyed your call; I saw *you* when the people anointed you with the tears of their admiration and praise. If you read my heart at all, to-day, you *knew* how I had suffered—you *saw* that I had grown old in sorrow. Was I mistaken to-night in the thought that you, too, had not been unmindful of *our* past; that you were not satisfied with the popular applause; that you, also, have been lonely, that you have wept; that you have trodden in the path of duty with weariness?

"There is but one barrier now in the wide world that shall interpose between us—Rosalie, it is your own will. If I was ever anything to you, I beseech you think calmly before you answer, and do not let your triumph, to-night, blind you to the fact which you once recognised, which can make us happy *yet*. I trust you as in our younger days; nothing, nothing but your own words could convince me that you are not worthy to take the highest place among the ladies of this land. Oh, let the remembrance that I have been faithful to you through all the past, plead for me, if your pride should rise up, to condemn me. Let me come and plead *with* you, for I know not what I write."

The answer returned to this letter was as follows:—

"I learned long ago, the bar that prevented our union; it is in existence still, Duncan. Your mother only shall decide if it be insurmountable. I have never, even for a moment, doubted your faithfulness; and it has been to me an unspeakable comfort to *know* that none had supplanted me in your affections. In the temptations, and struggles, and hardships, I have known, it has kept me above and beyond the world, and if the last night's triumph proves to be but the opening of a new life for me on earth, the recollection of what you are, and that you care for me, will prove a rock of defence, and a stronghold of hope always. Severed from, or united with you, I am yours for ever."

Seven days after there was a marriage in the little church of that remote village, where Duncan Melville and Rosalie Sherwood passed their childhood. Side by side they stood now, once again, where the baptismal service had long since been read for them, and the mother of the bishop gave the bride away!

THE LITTLE CHILDREN

IT was Sabbath morning. Soft and silvery, like stray notes from the quivering chords of an archangel's harp, floated the clear, sweet voice of the church-bells through the hushed heart of the great metropolis, while old men and little children—youth in its hope, and manhood in its pride—came forth at their summons, setting a mighty human tide in the direction of the sanctuaries, beneath whose sacred droppings they should hear again the tidings which come to us over the waves of nearly two thousand years, fresh and full of exceeding melody, as when the Day-Star from on high first poured its blessed beams over the mountain heights of Judea, and the song, pealing over the hills of jasper, rolled down to the shepherds who kept their night-watches on her plains; "Peace on earth and good-will to men."

A child came forth with his ragged garments, unwashed face and uncombed hair, from one of those haunts of darkness and misery which fill the city with crime and suffering. He was a little child, and yet there was none of its peace on his brow, or its light in his eye, as he looked up with a strange, wistful earnestness at the strip of blue sky that looked down with its serene heaven-smile between the frowning and dilapidated pile of buildings which rose on either side of the alley. The sunshine flitted like the soft-caressing fingers of a spirit over his forehead, and the voice of the bells fell upon his spirit with a strange, subduing influence; and the child kept on his way until the alley terminated in a broad, pleasant street, with its crowd of church-goers, and still the boy kept on, unmindful of dainty robe and silken vesture that waved and rustled by him.

He stood at last within the broad shadow of the sanctuary, while far above him rose the tall spire, with the sunbeams coiling like a heaven-halo around it, pointing to the golden battlements of the far-off city, within whose blessed precincts nothing "which defileth shall ever enter." The massive church doors swung slowly open as one and another entered, and the child looked eagerly up the long, mysterious mid-aisle, but the silken garments rustled past—there was no hand outstretched to lead the ragged and wretched little one within its walls, and no one paused to tell him of the Great Father, within whose sight the rich and poor are alike. But while he stood there, an angel with golden hair and gleaming wings bent over him, holding precious heart-seed, gathered from the white plains of the spirit-land, and as the child drew nearer the church steps, the angel followed.

Suddenly the little dapper sexton, with his broad smile and bustling gait, came out of the church. His eyes rested a moment upon the young wistful face and on the ragged garments, and then he beckoned to the child.

"Shall I take you in here, my boy?" asked a voice kinder and pleasanter than any which the child had ever heard; and as he timidly bowed his head, the sexton took the little soiled hand in his own, and they passed in, and the angel followed them.

Seated in one corner of the church, the child's eyes wandered over the frescoed walls, with the sunshine flitting like the fringe of a spirit's robe across it, and up the dim aisle to the great marble pulpit, with a kind of bewildered awe, for he had seen nothing of the like before, unless it might be in some dim, half-forgotten dream; but when the heavy doors swung together and the Sabbath hush gathered over the church, and the hallelujahs of the organ filled the house of the Lord and thrilled the heart of the child; he bowed his head and wept sweet tears—he could not tell whence was their coming. Then the solemn prayer from the pulpit—"O, Thou who lovest all men, who art the Father of the old and the young, the rich and the poor, and in whose sight they are alike precious, grant us Thy blessing," came to the ears of the child, and a new cry awoke in his soul. *Where* was this Father? It did not seem true that He could love him, a poor little, hungry, ragged beggar; that such a one could be his child. But, oh! it was just what his heart longed for, and if all others were *precious* to this Great Father, he did not believe He would leave him out. If he could only find Him—no matter how long the road was, nor how cold and hungry he might be, he would keep straight on the way, until he reached Him, and then he would go right in and say, "Father, I am cold and hungry, and very wretched. There is no one to love me, none to care for me. May I be your child, Father?" And perhaps He would look kindly upon him, and whisper softly, as no human being had ever whispered to him, "My child!" and stronger and wilder from his heart came up that cry, "Oh, if I could only find Him!"

Again the tones of the deep-toned organ and the sweet-voiced choir floated on the Sabbath air, and crept, a strange, soft tide, into the silent places of the boy's heart, softening and subduing it; while during the long sermon, of which he heard little, and comprehended less, that spirit cry rolled continually up from the depths of his soul—"*Where* is the Father?"

The benediction had been pronounced, and the house was disgorged of most of its vast crowd of worshippers, and yet the boy lingered—he could not bear to return to his dark and dismal dwelling, to the harsh words and harsher usage of those who loved him not, without having that question, which his soul was so eagerly asking, answered. But that little timid heart lacked courage, and he knew the words would die in his throat if he attempted to speak them, and so he must go away without knowing the way to the Father—but his feet dragged unwillingly along, and his eyes searched earnestly the figures that, unwitting of his want, passed swiftly before him.

"What is it you want to know, little boy?" The voice was very musical, and the smile on the lips of the child-questioner very winning. The chestnut-brown curls floated over her silken robe, and the soft blue eyes that looked into the boy's, wore that unearthly purity of expression which is not the portion of the children of this world.

The boy looked into that fair, childish face, and his heart took courage, while very eagerly from his lips came the words, "Where is the Great Father?"

"God is in heaven!" answered the little girl in solemn tones, while a sudden gravity gathered over her features.

From lips that burned with blasphemies, amid oaths from the vile, and revilings from the scoffer, had the boy first learned that name, and never before had it possessed aught of import for him. But now he knew it was the name of the Great Father that loved him, and again he asked very earnestly, "Where is the way to God in heaven? I am going to Him now."

The child shook her head as she looked on the boy with a sort of pitying wonder at his ignorance, and again she answered, "You cannot go to Him, but He will come to you if you will call upon Him, and He will hear, though you whisper very low, for God is everywhere."

"Come, come, Miss Ellen, you must not stay here any longer," called the servant, who had been very intent at ranging the cushions in the pew, and who now hurried her little charge through the aisle, apprehensive that some evil might accrue from her contiguity with a "street-beggar."

But the words of the little girl had brought a new and precious light into the boy's heart. That "cardinal explication of the reason," the wondrous idea of the Deity, had found a voice in his soul, and the child went forth from the church, while the golden-winged angel followed him to the dark alley, and the darker home; and that night, before he laid himself on his miserable pallet in the corner, he bowed his head, and clasped his hands, and whispered so that none might hear him, "My Father, will you take care of me, and come and take me to yourself? for I love you." And the angel folded his bright wings above that scanty pallet, and bent in the silent watches of the night over the boy, and filled his heart with peace, and his dreams with brightness.

Six months had rolled their mighty burden of life-records into the pulseless ocean of the past. The pale stars of mid-winter were looking down with meek, seraph glances over the mighty metropolis along whose thousand thoroughfares lay the white carpet of the snow-king; and Boreas, loosed from his ice caverns on the frozen floor of the Arctic, was holding mad revels, and howling with demoniac glee along the streets, wrapped in the pall shadows of midnight.

Twelve o'clock pealed from the mighty tongue of the time-recorder, and then the white-robed angel of death knocked at the door of two young human hearts, in the great city.

The tide of golden hair flowed over the white pillows of crimson-draperied couch. Shaded lamps poured their dim, silvery glances upon bright flowers and circling vines, the cunning workmanship of fingers in far-off lands, which lay among the soft groundwork of the rich carpet, while small white fingers glided caressingly among the golden hair; and white faces, wild with sorrow, bent over the rigid features of the dying child, and tears, such only as flow from the heart's deepest and bitterest fountains, fell upon the cold forehead and paling lips, as the lids swept back for a moment from her blue eyes, and the light from her spirit broke for the last time into them; the lips upon which the death-seal was ready to be laid, opened; and clear and joyous through the hushed room rang the words, "I am coming! I am coming!" and the next moment the cold, beautiful clay was all which was left to the mourners.

The other, at whose heart the death-angel knocked, lay in one corner of an old and dilapidated room, on a pallet of straw. No soft hand wandered caressingly among his dark locks, or cooled with its cold touch the fever of his forehead. The dim, flickering rays of the tallow candle wandered over the features now grown stark and rigid with the death-chill. No grief-printed face bent in anguish above him; no eye watched for the latest breath; no ear for the dying word; but through the half-open door, came to the ear of the dying boy the coarse laugh of the inebriate—the jest of the vile, and the frightful blasphemies of those whose way is the way of death.

None saw the last life-light, as it broke into the dark, spiritual eyes of the boy. None saw the smile that played like the light around the lips of a seraph, about his blue and cold lips, as they spoke exceeding joyfully, "Father! Father, I have called and you have heard me; I am coming to you, coming now; for the angels beckon me;" and the pale clay on that sunken pallet was all that remained of the boy.

Together they met, those two children who had stood together in the earthly courts of the Most High, and whom the angel had simultaneously called from the earth, beneath the shining battlements of "the city of God." The white wings of the warden-angels, who stood on its watch-towers, were slowly folded together, and back rolled the massive gates from the walls of jasper; and with the great "Godlight" streaming outward, and amid the sound of archangel's harp and seraph's lyre, the ministering angels came forth. They did not ask the child-spirits there, if their earthly homes had been among the high and the honourable; they did not ask them if broad lands had been their heritage, and sparkling coffers their portion; if their paths had lain by pleasant waters, and animals followed their biddings; but alike they led them—she, the daughter of wealth and earthly splendour, whose forehead the breezes might not visit too roughly, and whose pathway had been bordered with flowers and gilded with sunshine; and he, the heir of poverty, whose portion had been want, and his inalienable heritage, suffering; whose path had known no pleasant places; whose life had had no brightness within that glorious city. They placed bright crowns, alike woven from the fragrant branches of the far-spreading "Tree of Life," around their spirit-brows; they decked them alike in white robes, whose lustre many ages shall not dim; alike they placed in their hands the harps whose music shall roll for ever over (sic) the the hills of jasper; and alike they pointed them to the gleaming battlements, to the still skies over whose surface the shadow of a cloud hath never floated; to the "many mansions" which throw the shadow of their shining portals on the rippling waters of the "River of Life," and to far more of glory "which it hath never entered into the heart of man to conceive of," and told them they should "go no more out for ever."

WHAT IS NOBLE?

WHAT is noble? to inherit
    Wealth, estate, and proud degree?
There must be some other merit,
    Higher yet than these for me.
Something greater far must enter
    Into life's majestic span;
Fitted to create and centre
    True nobility in man!

What is noble? 'tis the finer
    Portion of our mind and heart:
Linked to something still diviner
    Than mere language can impart;
Ever prompting—ever seeing
    Some improvement yet to plan;
To uplift our fellow-being—
    And like man to feel for man!

What is noble? is the sabre
    Nobler than the humble spade?
There's a dignity in labour
    Truer than e'er Pomp arrayed!
He who seeks the mind's improvement
    Aids the world—in aiding mind!
Every great, commanding movement
    Serves not one—but all mankind.

O'er the Forge's heat and ashes—
    O'er the Engine's iron head—
Where the rapid Shuttle flashes,
    And the Spindle whirls its thread;
There is Labour lowly tending
    Each requirement of the hour;
There is genius still extending
    Science—and its world of power!

THE ANEMONE HEPATICA

TWO friends were walking together beside a picturesque mill-stream. While they walked, they talked of mortal life, its meaning and its end; and, as is almost inevitable with such themes, the current of their thoughts gradually lost its cheerful flow.

"This is a miserable world," said one; "the black shroud of sorrow overhangs everything here."

"Not so," replied the other; "Sorrow is not a shroud. It is only the covering Hope wraps about her when she sleeps."

Just then they entered an oak-grove. It was early spring, and the trees were bare, but last year's leaves lay thick as snow-drifts upon the ground.

"The Liverwort grows here, one of our earliest flowers, I think," said the last speaker. "There, push away the leaves, and you will find it. How beautiful, with its delicate shades of pink, and purple, and green, lying against the bare roots of the oak-trees! But look deeper, or you will not find the flowers; they are under the dead leaves."

"Now I have learned a lesson that I shall not forget," said her friend. "This seems to me a bad world, and there is no denying that there are bad things in it. To a sweeping glance, it will sometimes seem barren and desolate; but not one buried germ of life and beauty is lost to the All-seeing Eye. I, having the weakness of human vision, must believe where I cannot see. Henceforth, when I am tempted to complainings and despair on account of the evil around me, I will say to myself, 'Look deeper, look under the dead leaves, and you will find flowers.'"

THE FAMILY OF MICHAEL AROUT

September 15th, eight o'clock.—This morning, while I was arranging my books, Mother Genevieve came in, and brought me the basket of fruit I buy of her every Sunday. For nearly twenty years that I have lived in this quarter, I have dealt in her little fruit-shop. Perhaps I should be better served elsewhere, but Mother Genevieve has but little custom; to leave her would do her harm, and cause her unnecessary pain. It seems to me that the length of our acquaintance has made me incur a sort of tacit obligation to her; my patronage has become her property.

She has put the basket upon my table, and as I wanted her husband, who is a joiner, to add some shelves to my bookcase, she has gone down stairs again immediately to send him to me.

At first I did not notice either her looks or the sound of her voice; but now, that I recall them, it seems to me that she was not as jovial as usual. Can Mother Genevieve be in trouble about anything?

Poor woman! All her best years were subject to such bitter trials, that she might think she had received her full share already. Were I to live a hundred years, I should never forget the circumstances which first made her known to me, and which obtained her my respect.

It was at the time of my first settling in the faubourg. I had noticed her empty fruit-shop, which nobody came into, and being attracted by its forsaken appearance, made my little purchases in it. I have always instinctively preferred the poor shops; there is less choice in them, but it seems to me that my purchase is a sign of sympathy with a brother in poverty. These little dealings are almost always an anchor of hope to those whose very existence is in peril—the only means by which some orphan gains a livelihood. There the aim of the tradesman is not to enrich himself, but to live! The purchase you make of him is more than exchange—it is a good action.

Mother Genevieve at that time was still young, but had already lost that fresh bloom of youth, which suffering causes to wither so soon among the poor. Her husband, a clever joiner, gradually left off working to become, according to the picturesque expression of the workshops, *a worshipper of*

Saint Monday. The wages of the week, which was always reduced to two or three working days, were completely dedicated by him to the worship of this god of the Barriers,

The cheap wine-shops are outside the Barriers, to avoid the *octroi*, or municipal excise.

and Genevieve was obliged herself to provide for all the wants of the household.

One evening, when I went to make some trifling purchases of her, I heard a sound of quarrelling in the back shop. There were the voices of several women, among which I distinguished that of Genevieve, broken by sobs. On looking further in, I perceived the fruit-woman, with a child in her arms, and kissing it, while a country nurse seemed to be claiming her wages from her. The poor woman, who without doubt had exhausted every explanation and every excuse, was crying in silence, and one of her neighbours was trying in vain to appease the countrywoman. Excited by that love of money which the evils of a hard peasant life but too well excuse, and disappointed by the refusal of her expected wages, the nurse was launching forth in recriminations, threats, and abuse. In spite of myself, I listened to the quarrel, not daring to interfere, and not thinking of going away, when Michael Arout appeared at the shop-door.

The joiner had just come from the Barrier, where he had passed part of the day at the public-house. His blouse, without a belt, and untied at the throat, showed none of the noble stains of work: in his hand he held his cap, which he had just picked out of the mud; his hair was in disorder, his eye fixed, and the pallor of drunkenness in his face. He came reeling in, looked wildly around him, and called for Genevieve.

She heard his voice, gave a start, and rushed into the shop; but at the sight of the miserable man, who was trying in vain to steady himself, she pressed the child in her arms, and bent over it with tears.

The countrywoman and the neighbour had followed her.

"Come! come! Do you intend to pay me, after all?" cried the former, in a rage.

"Ask the master for the money," ironically answered the woman from next door, pointing to the joiner, who had just fallen against the counter.

The countrywoman looked at him.

"Ah! he is the father," resumed she; "well, what idle beggars! not to have a penny to pay honest people, and get tipsy with wine in that way."

The drunkard raised his head.

"What! what!" stammered he; "who is it that talks of wine? I've had nothing but brandy. But I am going back again to get some wine. Wife, give me your money; there are some friends waiting for me at the *Pere la Tuille*."

Genevieve did not answer: he went round the counter, opened the till, and began to rummage in it.

"You see where the money of the house goes!" observed the neighbour to the countrywoman; "how can the poor unhappy woman pay you when he takes all?"

"Is that my fault, then?" replied the nurse angrily; "they owe it me, and somehow or other they must pay me."

And letting loose her tongue, as those women out of the country do, she began relating at length all the care she had taken of the child, and all the expense it had been to her. In proportion as she recalled all she had done, her words seemed to convince her more than ever of her rights, and to increase her anger. The poor mother, who no doubt feared that her violence would frighten the child, returned into the back shop, and put it into its cradle.

Whether it was that the countrywoman saw in this act a determination to escape her claims, or that she was blinded by passion, I cannot say; but she rushed into the next room, where I heard the sounds of quarrelling, with which the cries of the child were soon mingled. The joiner, who was still rummaging in the till, was startled, and raised his head.

At the same moment Genevieve appeared at the door, holding in her arms the baby that the countrywoman was trying to tear from her. She ran towards the counter, and, throwing herself behind her husband, cried,

"Michael, defend your son!"

The drunken man quickly stood up erect, like one who awakes with a start.

"My son!" stammered he; "what son?"

His looks fell upon the child; a vague ray of intelligence passed over his features.

"Robert," resumed he; "is it Robert?"

He tried to steady himself on his feet, that he might take the baby, but he tottered. The nurse approached him in a rage.

"My money, or I shall take the child away!" cried she; "it is I who have fed and brought it up; if you don't pay for what has made it live, it ought to be the same to you as if it were dead. I shall not go till I have my due or the baby."

"And what would you do with him?" murmured Genevieve, pressing Robert against her bosom.

"Take it to the Foundling!" replied the countrywoman, harshly; "the hospital is a better mother than you are, for it pays for the food of its little ones."

At the word "Foundling," Genevieve had exclaimed aloud in horror. With her arms wound round her son, whose head she hid in her bosom, and her two hands spread over him, she had retreated to the wall, and remained with her back against it, like a lioness defending her young ones.

The neighbour and I contemplated this scene, without knowing how we could interfere. As for Michael, he looked at us by turns, making a visible effort to comprehend it all. When his eye rested upon Genevieve and the child, it lit up with a gleam of pleasure; but when he turned towards us, he again became stupid and hesitating.

At last, apparently making a prodigious effort, he cried out—"Wait!"

And going to a tub full of water, he plunged his face into it several times.

Every eye was turned upon him; the countrywoman herself seemed astonished. At length he raised his dripping head. This ablution had partly dispelled his drunkenness; he looked at us for a moment, then he turned to Genevieve, and his face brightened up.

"Robert!" cried he, going up to the child, and taking him in his arms. "Ah! give him me, wife; I must look at him."

The mother seemed to give up his son to him with reluctance, and stayed before him with her arms extended, as if she feared the child would have a fall. The nurse began again in her turn to speak, and renewed her claims, this time threatening to appeal to law.

At first Michael listened to her attentively, and when he comprehended her meaning, he gave the child back to its mother.

"How much do we owe you?" asked he.

The countrywoman began to reckon up the different expenses, which amounted to nearly thirty francs. The joiner felt to the bottom of his pockets, but could find nothing. His forehead became contracted by frowns; low curses began to escape him; all of a sudden he rummaged in his breast, drew forth a large watch, and holding it up above his head—

"Here it is—here's your money!" cried he, with a joyful laugh; "a watch, number one! I always said it would keep for a drink on a dry day; but it is not I who will drink it, but the young one. Ah! ah! ah! go and sell it for me, neighbour; and if that is not enough, have my ear-rings. Eh! Genevieve, take them off for me, the ear-rings will square all. They shall not say you have been disgraced on account of the child. No, not even if I must pledge a bit of my flesh! My watch, my ear-rings, and my ring, get rid of all of them for me at the goldsmith's; pay the woman, and let the little fool go to sleep. Give him me, Genevieve, I will put him to bed."

And, taking the baby from the arms of his mother, he carried him with a firm step to his cradle.

It was easy to perceive the change which took place in Michael from this day. He cut all his old drinking acquaintances. He went early every morning to his work, and returned regularly in the evening to finish the day with Genevieve and Robert. Very soon he would not leave them at all, and he hired a place near the fruitshop, and worked in it on his own account.

They would soon have been able to live in comfort, had it not been for the expenses which the child required. Everything was given up to his education. He had gone through the regular school training, had studied mathematics, drawing, and the carpenter's trade, and had only begun to work a few months ago. Till now, they had been exhausting every resource which their laborious industry could provide to push him forward in his business; but, happily, all these exertions had not proved useless; the seed had brought forth its fruits, and the days of harvest were close by.

While I was thus recalling these remembrances to my mind, Michael had come in, and was occupied in fixing shelves where they were wanted.

During the time I was writing the notes of my journal, I was also scrutinizing the joiner.

The excesses of his youth and the labour of his manhood have deeply marked his face; his hair is thin and gray, his shoulders stooping, his legs shrunken and slightly bent. There seems a sort of weight in his whole being. His very features have an expression of sorrow and despondency. He answered my questions by monosyllables, and like a man who wishes to avoid conversation. From whence is this dejection, when one would think he had all he could wish for? I should like to know!

Ten o'clock.—Michael is just gone down stairs to look for a tool he has forgotten. I have at last succeeded in drawing from him the secret of his and Genevieve's sorrow. Their son Robert is the cause of it.

Not that he has turned out ill after all their care—not that he is idle or dissipated; but both were in hopes he would never leave them any more. The presence of the young man was to have renewed and made glad their lives once more; his mother counted the days, his father prepared everything to receive their dear associate in their toils, and at the moment when they were thus about to be repaid for all their sacrifices, Robert had suddenly informed them that he had just engaged himself to a contractor at Versailles.

Every remonstrance and every prayer were useless; he brought forward the necessity of initiating himself into all the details of an important contract, the facilities he should have, in his new position, of improving himself in his trade, and the hopes he had of turning his knowledge to advantage. At last, when his mother, having come to the end of her arguments, began to cry, he hastily kissed her, and went away, that he might avoid any further remonstrances.

He had been absent a year, and there was nothing to give them hopes of his return. His parents hardly saw him once a month, and then he only stayed a few moments with them.

"I have been punished where I had hoped to be rewarded," Michael said to me just now; "I had wished for a saving and industrious son, and God has given me an ambitious and avaricious one. I had always said to myself, that, when once he was grown up, we should have him always with us, to recall our youth and to enliven our hearts; his mother was always thinking of getting him married, and having children again to care for. You know women always will busy themselves about others. As for me, I thought of him working near my bench, and singing his new songs—for he has learnt music, and is one of the best singers at the Orpheon. A dream, sir, truly! Directly the bird was fledged, he took to flight, and remembers neither father nor mother. Yesterday, for instance, was the day we expected him; he should have come to supper with us. No Robert to-day, either! He has had some plan to finish, or some bargain to arrange, and his old parents are put down last in the accounts, after the customers and the joiner's work. Ah! if I could have guessed how it would have turned out! Fool! to have sacrificed my likings and my money, for nearly twenty years, to the education of a thankless son! Was it for this I took the trouble to cure myself of drinking, to break with my friends, to become an example to the neighbourhood? The jovial good fellow has made a goose of himself. Oh! if I had to begin again! No, no! you see women and children are our bane. They soften our hearts; they lead us a life of hope and affection; we pass a quarter of our lives in fostering the growth of a grain of corn which is to be everything to us in our old age, and when the harvest-time comes—good-night, the ear is empty!"

Whilt he was speaking, Michael's voice became hoarse, his eye fierce, and his lips quivered. I wished to answer him, but I could only think of commonplace consolations, and I remained silent. The joiner pretended he wanted a tool, and left me.

Poor father! Ah! I know those moments of temptation when virtue has failed to reward us, and we regret having obeyed her! Who has not felt this weakness in hours of trial, and who has not uttered, at least once, the mournful exclamation of "Brutus?"

But if *virtue is only a word*, what is there then in life which is true and real? No, I will not believe that goodness is in vain! It does not always give the happiness we had hoped for, but it brings some other. In the world everything is ruled by order, and has its proper and necessary consequences, and virtue cannot be the sole exception to the general law. If it had been prejudicial to those who practise it, experience would have avenged them; but experience has, on the contrary, (sic) mader it more universal and more holy. We only accuse it of being a faithless debtor, because we demand an immediate payment, and one apparent to our senses. We always consider life as a fairy tale, in which every good action must be rewarded by a visible wonder. We do not accept as payment a peaceful conscience, self-content, or a good name among men, treasures that are more precious than any other, but the value of which we do not feel till after we have lost them!

Michael is come back, and returned to his work. His son had not yet arrived.

By telling me of his hopes and his grievous disappointments, he became excited; he unceasingly went over again the same subject, always adding something to his griefs. He has just wound up his confidential discourse by speaking to me of a joiner's business, which he had hoped to buy, and work to good account with Robert's help. The present owner had made a fortune by it, and after thirty years of business, he was thinking of retiring to one of the ornamental cottages in the outskirts of the city, a usual retreat for the frugal and successful working man. Michael had not indeed the two thousand francs which must be paid down; but perhaps he could have persuaded Master Benoit to wait. Robert's presence would have been a security for him; for the young man could not fail to insure the prosperity of a workshop; besides science and skill, he had the power of invention and bringing to perfection. His father had discovered among his drawings a new plan for a staircase, which had occupied his thoughts for a long time; and he even suspected him of having engaged himself to the Versailles contractor for the very purpose of executing it. The youth was tormented by this spirit of invention, which took possession of all his thoughts, and, while devoting his mind to study, he had no time to listen to his feelings.

Michael told me all this with a mixed feeling of pride and vexation. I saw he was proud of the son he was abusing, and that his very pride made him more sensible of that son's neglect.

Six o'clock, P. M.—I have just finished a happy day. How many events have happened within a few hours, and what a change for Genevieve and Michael!

He had just finished fixing the shelves, and telling me of his son, whilst I laid the cloth for my breakfast.

Suddenly we heard hurried steps in the passage, the door opened, and Genevieve entered with Robert.

The joiner gave a start of joyful surprise, but he repressed it immediately, as if he wished to keep up the appearance of displeasure.

The young man did not appear to notice it, but threw himself into his arms in an open-hearted manner, which surprised me. Genevieve, whose face shone with happiness, seemed to wish to speak, and to restrain herself with difficulty.

I told Robert I was glad to see him, and he answered me with ease and civility.

"I expected you yesterday," said Michael Arout, rather dryly.

"Forgive me, father," replied the young workman, "but I had business at St. Germains. I was not able to come back till it was very late, and then the master kept me."

The joiner looked at his son sideways, and then took up his hammer again.

"It is right," muttered he, in a grumbling tone; "when we are with other people we must do as they wish; but there are some who would like better to eat brown bread with their own knife, than partridges with the silver fork of a master."

"And I am one of those, father," replied Robert, merrily; "but, as the proverb says, *you must shell the peas before you can eat them*. It was necessary that I should first work in a great workshop"—

"To go on with your plan of the staircase," interrupted Michael, ironically.

"You must now say M. Raymond's plan, father," replied Robert, smiling.

"Why?"

"Because I have sold it to him."

The joiner, who was planing a board, turned round quickly.

"Sold it!" cried he, with sparkling eyes.

"For the reason that I was not rich enough to give it him."

Michael threw down the board and tool.

"There he is again!" resumed he, angrily; "his good genius puts an idea into his head which would have made him known, and he goes and sells it to a rich man, who will take the honour of it himself."

"Well, what harm is there done?" asked Genevieve.

"What harm!" cried the joiner, in a passion; "you understand nothing about it—you are a woman; but he—he knows well that a true workman never gives up his own inventions for money, no more than a soldier would give up his cross. That is his glory; he is bound to keep it for the honour it does him! Ah! thunder! if I had ever made a discovery, rather than put it up at auction I would have sold one of my eyes! Don't you see, that a new invention is like a child to a workman! he takes care of it, he brings it up, he makes a way for it in the world, and it is only poor creatures who sell it."

Robert coloured a little.

"You will think differently, father," said he, "when you know why I sold my plan."

"Yes, and you will thank him for it," added Genevieve, who could no longer keep silence.

"Never!" replied Michael.

"But, wretched man!" cried she, "he only sold it for our sakes!"

The joiner looked at his wife and son with astonishment. It was necessary to come to an explanation. The latter related how he had entered into a negotiation with Master Benoit, who had positively refused to sell his business unless one-half of the two thousand francs was first paid down. It was in the hopes of obtaining this sum that he had gone to work with the contractor at Versailles; he had an opportunity of trying his invention, and of finding a purchaser. Thanks to the money he received for it, he had just concluded the bargain with Benoit, and had brought his father the key of the new work-yard.

This explanation was given by the young workman with so much modesty and simplicity, that I was quite affected by it. Genevieve cried;

Michael pressed his son to his heart, and in a long embrace he seemed to ask his pardon for having unjustly accused him.

All was now explained with honour to Robert. The conduct which his parents had ascribed to indifference, really sprang from affection; he had neither obeyed the voice of ambition nor of avarice, nor even the nobler inspiration of inventive genius; his whole motive and single aim had been the happiness of Genevieve and Michael. The day for proving his gratitude had come, and he had returned them sacrifice for sacrifice!

After the explanations and exclamations of joy, were over, all three were about to leave me; but the cloth being laid, I added three more places, and kept them to breakfast.

The meal was prolonged; the fare was only tolerable; but the overflowings of affection made it delicious.

Never had I better understood the unspeakable charm of family love. What calm enjoyment in that happiness which is always shared with others; in that community of interests which unites such various feelings; in that association of existences which forms one single being of so many! What is man without those home affections, which, like so many roots, fix him firmly in the earth, and permit him to imbibe all the juices of life? Energy, happiness, does it not all come from them? Without family life, where would man learn to love, to associate, to deny himself? A community in little, is not it which teaches us how to live in the great one? Such is the holiness of home, that to express our relation with God, we have been obliged to borrow the words invented for our family life. Men have named themselves the *sons* of a heavenly *Father*.

Ah! let us carefully preserve these chains of domestic union; do not let us unbind the human sheaf, and scatter its ears to all the caprices of chance, and of the winds; but let us rather enlarge this holy law; let us carry the principles and the habits of home beyond its bounds; and, if it may be, let us realize the prayer of the Apostle of the Gentiles when he exclaimed to the newborn children of Christ:—"Be ye like-minded, having the same love, being of one accord, of one mind."

BABY IS DEAD

"BABY is dead!" How many hearts have throbbed with anguish, and eyes overflowed with tears at the utterance of these thrilling words! A tender bud is intrusted to a rejoicing family. Very precious does it become to them. With what ecstatic joy do they note the first dawn of intelligence as it beams from the starry eyes! How merry their own hearts now, as they listen to the shouts of childish glee as they burst from the coral lips! Ay, very, very dear is this little one, and their cup of bliss seems full without alloy; when suddenly the relentless destroyer enters their happy home, and sets his seal on that snowy brow, so like a lily's leaf, in its pure beauty. Disease fastens itself upon the loved one, and, like a tender bud nipped by the untimely frost, it withers, droops, and dies. Then come the fearful words, "Baby is dead!" With what a crushing weight do they fall on the ears of that mourning family! How reluctantly do their bruised hearts acknowledge the sad truth! But stern reality avers it so, and the spectre Grief claims them for its own, as they gaze upon the pale face of the little sleeper.

Ah! the light of those bright eyes is for ever quenched, and the lids are closed tranquilly over them; the rose tint has fled from the round cheeks; the ruby lips are colourless, and the youthful heart has ceased its throbbings.

Yes, "Baby is dead," and silently they prepare it for the cheerless tomb. The golden tresses they so oft have wound lovingly over their fingers, are gently smoothed for the last time, while one fairy curl is severed and placed next the mother's heart; oft will she gaze upon it, as the months of her sorrow come and go, and weep over the memory of her departed treasure.

Sadly the little form is robed in the tiny shroud, and the dimpled hands crossed sweetly over the pulseless bosom. Gently he is placed in the coffin—it is a harder bed than he was wont to rest on, but he will feel it not. With unutterable anguish they follow him to the dark, cold grave; strange hands lower him into its gloomy depths, and the clods fall heavily upon the coffin. Each one seems to sink with laden weight into their hearts. It is filled up now, and the green turf covers the late smiling cherub, and the mourners turn sadly away. Oh! how dark the world seems now, which was so full of sunshine a little while ago! How desolate their once joyous house!

"Baby is dead—our idol is gone," is the language of their hearts. Yes, stricken ones, your sunbeam is gone; but where? You have buried the beauteous casket beneath the green sods of the valley; but the precious jewel it contained is beaming brightly in the coronal of God.

Your treasure is taken from your love-encircling arms, but it is sweetly pillowed on the bosom of that kind Saviour who said, "Suffer little children to come unto me, and forbid them not, for of such is the kingdom of heaven."

The bud is nipped from its parent stem in the springtime of its existence; but it hath been transplanted to a milder clime, where the rough blasts and chilling storms of mortality cannot harm, and where, watered by the soft dew of Divine love, its tiny leaves will expand and bloom with unfading lustre!

Had this bud of life, over whom your souls yearned with such unutterable fondness, been spared to you, you know not how your bright anticipations might have been darkened. When it came to thread life's strange, wild paths, mildew and blight might have settled on the pure spirit, and guilty, desolating passions scathed the guileless heart.

Then weep not, mourning ones, but rather rejoice that He, who doeth all things well, hath summoned it, in its pristine purity, to a haven of innocence, where contamination nor decay cannot defile or enter. And when you miss the childish prattle or silvery laugh which fell so sweetly on your ears, think of the baby that is dead to you, as a rejoicing angel among angelic hosts that throng the "land of the blest." Baby is dead to earth, but is living in Paradise!

"Then mourn not, though the loved one go
Early from this world of woe;
Upon yon bright and blissful shore
You soon shall meet to part no more,
'Mid amaranthine flowers to roam,
Where sin and death can never come."

THE TREASURED RINGLET

I AM thinking how, one April eve,
    Upon the old arm-chair
I sat, and how I fondly played
    With this brown lock of hair;
Your head was pillowed on my breast,
    Your eyes were fixed on mine,
I knew your heart was all my own,
    I know my own was thine.

The balmy breath of violets
    Came floating in the room,
And mingling with the rose's sigh,
    Spread round a rich perfume;
Yet sweeter was the warm breath which
    I felt upon my cheek,
Than fragrance from the blushing rose,
    Or from the violet meek.

Upon the oak the mocking-bird
    Was singing loud and clear,
But notes more musical to me
    Were falling on my ear;
For from your noble heart you poured
    Love's low, yet thrilling tone,
And every word your pure soul breathed
    Was answered by my own.

How like a glorious rainbow, then,
    The future all appeared?
No care or sorrow then we knew,
    No disappointment feared.
The world's rude waves had not begun
    Across our path to sweep,
We never—save from happiness—
    Had cause to sigh or weep.

But many weary years have passed
    Since that bright April eve,

And you have learned since then to weep,
    And I have learned to grieve;
And on thy brow, unfurrowed then,
    Time, and his sister, Care,
Have set their wrinkled seal, and strewed
    Their silver in thy hair.

Nor Time, nor Care, nor world's rude waves,
    Have had the power to chill
The holy love which then we vowed,
    That is unclouded still;
And until Death—the reaper—comes,
    It ne'er shall flow away—
Our tide of love which first began
    Upon that April day.

HUMAN LONGINGS FOR PEACE AND REST

THERE are few whose idea of happiness does not include peace as essential. Most men have been so tempest-tossed, and not comforted, that they long for a closing of all excitements at last in peace. Hence the images of the haven receiving the shattered bark, of the rural vale remote from the noise of towns, have always been dear to human fancy. Hence, too, the decline of life away from severe toil, rapid motion, and passionate action, has often a charm even beyond the kindling enterprise of youth. The cold grave itself repels not altogether, but somewhat allures the imagination.

"How still and peaceful is the grave!"

Especially has heaven risen to the religious mind in this complexion of tranquillity. It is generally conceived as free from all disturbance, broken by not a sound save of harmonious anthems, which, like murmuring water, give deeper peace than could be found in silence.

But man so longs for rest and peace, that he not only soothes himself with these images from afar, but hopes to foretaste their substance. And what are his views to this end? He means to retire from business to some spot where he can calmly enjoy what he has in vain panted for in the race of life. Perhaps he tries the experiment, but finds himself restless still, and learns the great lesson at last, that peace is not in the landscape, but only in the soul; and the calm sky, the horizon's circle, the steady stars, are only its language, not itself.

Perhaps he seeks peace in his home. Everything there is made soft to the feet; each chair and couch receives him softly; agreeable sounds, odours, viands, regale every sense: and illuminated chambers replace for him at night the splendour of the sun. But here again he is at fault. Peace comes not to him thus, though all the apparatus seems at hand to produce it. Still he may be outshone by a neighbour; or high estate may draw down upon him envy and ill-will; or his senses themselves may refuse the proffered bliss, and ache with disease. Peace is not in outward comforts, which the constitution sharply limits; which pass with time, or pall upon the taste. The human mind is too great a thing to be pleased with mere blandishments.

Man has a soul of vast desires; and the solemn truth will come home irresistibly at times, even to the easy epicure. Something is wanting still. There is more of pain than peace in the remnants of feasting and the exhausted rounds of pleasure.

Man has sometimes sought peace in yet another way. Abjuring all sensual delights, he has gone into the desert to scourge the body, to live on roots and water, and be absorbed in pious raptures; and often has he thus succeeded, better than do the vulgar hunters of pleasure. But unrest mingles even with the tranquillity thus obtained. His innocent, active powers resist this crucifixion. The distant world rolls to his ear the voices of suffering fellow-men; and even his devotions, all lonely, become selfish and unsatisfying.

All men are seeking, in a way better or worse, this same peace and rest. Some seek it objectively in mere outward activity. They are not unfrequently frivolous and ill-furnished within, seeking rest by travelling, by running from place to place, from company to company, changing ever their sky but never themselves. Such persons, deeply to be pitied, seek by dress to hide the nakedness of their souls, or by the gayety of their own prattle to chill the fire which burns away their hearts. The merriest faces may be sometimes seen in mourning coaches; and so, the most melancholy souls, pinched and pining, sometimes stare at you out of the midst of superficial smiles and light laughter.

Others seek rest in more adventurous action. Such are mariners, soldiers, merchants, speculators, politicians, travellers, impelled to adventurous life to relieve the aching void in their hearts. The hazards of trade, the changes of political life, cause them to forget themselves, and so they are rocked into oblivion of internal disquiet by the toss of the ocean waves. They forget the hollowness of their own hearts, and cheat themselves into the belief that they are on their way to peace.

Is peace, is rest, so longed for, then, never to be found? Yes! it has been found, though perhaps but seldom, and somewhat imperfectly. That is a state of rest for the soul when all man's powers work harmoniously together, none conflicting with another, none hindering another. This rest is complete when every special power in man's nature is active, and works towards some noble end, free to act, yet acting entirely in harmony, each with all, and all with each. That is what may be called self-command, self-possession, tranquillity, peace, rest for the soul. It is not indifference, it is not sluggishness; it is not sleep: it is activity in its perfect character and highest mode.

Some few men seem born for this. Their powers are well-balanced. But to most it comes only by labour and life-struggle. Most men, and above all, most strong men, are so born and organized, that they feel the riddle of the world, and they have to struggle with themselves. At first they are not well-balanced. One part of their nature preponderates over another, and they are not in equilibrium. Like the troubled sea, they cannot rest. The lower powers and propensities must be brought into subjection to the higher. All the powers must be brought into harmony. This requires correct views of life, knowledge of the truth, a strong will, a resolute purpose, a high idea, a mind that learns by experience to correct its wrongs. Thus he acquires the mastery over himself, and his passions become his servants, which were formerly masters. Reason prevails over feeling, and duty over impulse. If he has lost a friend, he does not mourn inconsolably, nor seek to forget that friend. He turns his thoughts more frequently to where that friend has gone, and so he goes on until it becomes to him a loss no longer, but rather a gain—a son, daughter, brother, or wife, immortal in the kingdom of God, rather than mortal and perishing on earth. Gradually he acquires a perfect command of himself, an equilibrium of all his active powers, and so is at rest.

What is more beautiful in the earthly life of Jesus, than this manly harmony, equipoise, and rest? He enjoyed peace, and promised it to His friends. And this peace of His, He did not for others postpone to a distant day, or shut up altogether in a future Heaven, but left it to His disciples on earth. What, then, was His peace?

His peace was not inactivity. They must mistake who give a material sense to the images of Heaven as a state of rest. If Christ's life represented Heaven, its peace is not slothful ease, but intense exertion. How He laboured in word and deed of virtue! He walked in coarse raiment from town to town, from city to city, from the dessert to the waves of the sea. His ministry was toil from the day of His baptism to the scene upon Calvary. And yet His life was peace. He expressed no wish to retire to an unoccupied ease. His absorption in duty was His joy. He was so peaceful because so engaged. His labours were the elements of His divine tranquillity.

And so active and earnest must we be, if we would have calmness and peace. An appeal may here be made to every one's experience. Every one will confess that when he had least to do, when mornings came and went, and suns circled, and seasons rolled, and brought no serious business, then time was a burthen; existence a weariness; and the hungry soul, which craves some outward satisfaction, was found fallen back upon itself and preying upon its own vitality. Are not the idlest of men proverbially the most miserable? And is not the young woman often to be seen passing restless from place to place, because exempt from the necessity of industry, till vanity and envy, growing rank in her vacant mind, makes her far more an object of compassion than those who work hardest for a living? The unemployed, then, are not the most peaceful. The labourer has a deeper peace than any idler ever knew. His toils make his short pauses refreshing. Were those pauses prolonged they would be invaded by a miserable ennui. Perfect peace will be found here or hereafter, not when we sink down into torpor, but only when the soul is wrought into high action for high ends.

Another element of the peace of Jesus was His sinlessness. And all human experience testifies that nothing has so much disturbed tranquillity as conscious guilt, or the memory of wrong-doing. Peace is forfeited by every transgression. Angry words, envious looks, unkind and selfish deeds, will all prevent peace from visiting our hearts.

We have noticed already another element of peace—mental and moral harmony. There is a spiritual proportion when every power does its work, every feeling fills its measure, and all make a common current to bear the soul along to ever new peace and joy. Our inward discords are the woes of life. The peaceful heart is quiet, not because inactive, but through intense harmonious working.

The cravings of the human heart for peace and rest must seek satisfaction in the ways indicated, or fail of satisfaction. There must be activity, abstinence from guilt, and moral harmony. Thus alone can we receive the peace which Jesus said He would leave to His true followers.

"BE STRONG"

IN the flush, and the rush, and the crush of Life's battle,
  When the stern blow of Right dashes loud on steeled Wrong,
Half-drowning the voice of the babe's holy prattle,
  Remember the watchword—the motto—"Be strong!"
When the clouds of the past gather brooding above thee,
  And gloam o'er thy pillow the aching night long,
Remember who never for once failed to love thee,
  And in deepest of loneliness thou wilt *be strong*!
When the rays of the morning seem slow in their beaming,
  Overpowered the firm Right—most tremendous bold Wrong,
Let not thy Thought's eye grow the dimmer for streaming,
  Pour thy tears in Faith's bosom—thou yet wilt BE STRONG.

THE NEGLECTED ONE

> "I never was a favourite;
> My mother never smiled
> On me with half the tenderness
> That blessed her fairer child."

"CHRISTINE, do be obliging for once, and sew this button on my glove, won't you?" cried Ann Lambert, impatiently, throwing a white kid glove in her sister's lap. "I am in such a flurry! I won't be ready to go to the concert in two or three hours. Mr. Darcet has been waiting in the parlour an age. I don't know what the reason is, but I never can find anything I want, when I look for it; whenever I don't want a thing, it is always in the way. Have you sewed it on yet?" she asked, looking around from the bureau, where she was turning everything topsy turvy, in the most vigorous manner. Christine was quietly looking out of the window, yawning and gazing listlessly up at the moon and stars.

"O no matter if you have no button on," was her reply; "I really don't feel like moving my fingers just now. You must wait on yourself. I always do."

"I shouldn't have expected anything but your usual idle selfishness, even when I most need your assistance," replied Ann, in a cool, bitter tone; the curve of her beautiful lip, and the calm scorn of the look she bent on Christine, betrayed her haughty, passionate character, and it also told that she was conscious of a certain power and strength of mind, which when roused, could and would bend others to her will. A slight, contemptuous smile was on her lip, as she picked up the glove which had fallen on the floor.

"I'll sew the button on, Ann," said Christine, taking it from her, and looking up seriously, but with a compressed expression about her face. Her cheeks burned; there was a reproof in her steady gaze, before which Ann's scornful smile vanished. "No, Christine, I will wait on myself," she answered in a rigid tone.

"Very well," and Christine turned to the window again. She had not quailed before her sister's look, but its bitter contempt rankled in her heart, and poisoned the current of her thoughts. Not a word was spoken, when Ann with her bonnet on, left their apartment. The front door closed; Christine listened to the sound of her sister's voice in the street a moment, then rose from her chair, and threw herself upon the bed, sobbing violently.

"Oh! why has God made me as I am?" she murmured. "No one loves me. They do not know me; they know how bad I am—but, oh! they never dream how often I weep, and pray for the affection that is denied me. How Ann is caressed by everybody, and how indifferently am I greeted! There is no one in the wide world who takes a deep interest in me. I am only secondary with father and mother; they are so proud of Ann's beauty and talent, they do not think to see whether I am possessed of talent or not. They think I am cold and heartless, because they have taught me to restrain my warmest feelings; they have turned me back upon myself, they have forced me to shut up in my own heart, its bitterness, its prayers for affection, its pride, its sorrow. They have made me selfish, disobliging, and disagreeable, because I am too proud to act as if I would beg the love they are so careless of bestowing. And yet, why am I so proud and so bitter? I was not so at school; then I was gentle and gay; then I too was a favourite; they called me amiable. I am not so now. Then I dwelt in an atmosphere of love, only the best impulses of my nature were called out. Now—oh! I did not know I could so change; I did not know that there was room in my heart for envy and jealousy. I did not know myself!"

Christine wept, until her head ached, and her forehead felt as if it was swelled almost to bursting. "After a storm, there comes a calm," is a truism well known. In about half an hour, she was sleeping profoundly, from mere exhaustion of feeling. But her face was pale, and sad to look upon, even in her sleep.

When Ann returned home, at a late hour, she glanced hastily at the bed, to see if she had retired, and was sleeping. More than once during the evening her heart had reproached her for the part she had acted. With a noiseless step she approached Christine, and bent over her. The tear-drop upon her pale cheek, revealed the unconscious girl to her in a new character. How her conscience smote her, for the grief upon that countenance, now so subdued by the spirit of sleep! Its meek sadness and tenderness stirred in her bosom feelings she had seldom experienced. She felt and understood better than ever before, her sister's proud reserve with herself, as well as every one else. She kissed away the tear, and knelt at the bedside in prayer, a thing she had not done for years. A flood of tender and self-reproachful feelings came over her; the spring was touched, and she wept aloud. Christine started up, and murmured a few broken sentences, before she was fully conscious of the meaning of the scene.

"What is the matter, Ann, are you crying?" she at length asked, as her sister lifted up her face. Ann arose from her knees; she hesitated, she felt as if she could throw herself into Christine's arms, and weep freely as she asked forgiveness for her conduct. She felt that she would be affectionately pardoned. And yet she stood silent; her heart brimming with tenderness all the while—something held her back; a something that too often chills a pure impulse, a gush of holy feeling. It was pride. She could not bring herself to speak words of penitence and humility. But she did not turn away from the anxious gaze riveted upon her; she drooped her eyes, and the tears rolled slowly down her face.

"Oh, Ann, dear Ann, this does not seem like you!" said Christine, tenderly approaching her. "I am your sister; if you have any sorrow, why may I not sympathize with you? How can *you* be sorrowful? you never meet with neglect, and—" the young girl paused hastily, with a suddenly flushed face; she had inadvertently betrayed what she had previously so carefully concealed under the mask of callous indifference—she had shown that she felt keenly her own position, and that of her sister as a favourite. Ann was proud of her intellect and fascinating beauty; she was selfishly fond of admiration. She knew that her sister was really as gifted as herself, if not more so; she had heard her converse at times, when her cheek glowed, and her eye kindled with enthusiasm. She had seen her, very rarely, but still she had seen her, when *expression* had lit up her face with a positive beauty— when the soul, the life of beauty beamed forth, and went to the heart with a thrill that acknowledged its power. She knew that she would have been brilliant and fascinating, if she had not been repressed; with all her faults, there was a more feminine yieldingness about her, than about herself. There was an affectionate pathos in her voice, a tender grace in her air, when she asked to sympathize in her sorrow. Ann felt for the first time fully, that she was one to love, and be beloved in the social circle. She felt that she had been most ungenerous to absorb all the attention of her friends, instead of bringing forward the reserved, sensitive Christine. The sisters had never been much together; they had never made confidants of each other;—Ann was the eldest, and all in all with her parents, while Christine was a sort of appendage. Ann felt the unintentional reproach conveyed in her last words; she marked how quickly she stopped, and seemed to retire within herself again; she scanned her face closely, and generous feelings triumphed.

"Dear Christine!" she said in a low voice, passing her arm around her. "We have never been to each other what sisters ought to be. I have been too thoughtless and careless; I have not remembered as I should have done, that you returned from school, a stranger to the majority of our friends and acquaintances. You are so reserved, even here at home; you never talk and laugh with father and mother as I do."

"Do you know why I appear cold, Ann? I am not so by nature. They do not seem to care when I speak, and I am not yet humble enough to have what I say treated with perfect indifference."

"Why, Christine, you are too sensitive," said Ann, half impatiently. "Be as noisy and lively as I am; entertain father, and say what will please mother; then you will be as great a pet as I."

"Even if I should value love, based upon my powers of pleasing, instead of the intrinsic worth of my character, I could not gain it, Ann. I came home, after my long absence, as merry and light-hearted, as full of hope, of love towards you all, as ever a happy schoolgirl did. Then I was seventeen; it seems as if long years had elapsed since the day I sprang into your arms so joyfully—since father and mother kissed me. Home, sweet home, how musical those words were to me! how often I had dreamed of nestling at father's side, your hand locked in mine, and mother's smile upon us both. It was not long before I was awakened from the dream I had cherished so long. I thought my heart would break when the reality that I was unloved, came upon me. Then I learned how deep were the fountains of tenderness within me. My heart overflowed with an intense desire for affection, when I saw that I did not possess it. Oh! how often I looked upon mother's face, unobserved, and felt that my love for her was but a wasted shower. At that time of bitterness, how sad was the revelation that came up from the very depths of my soul, teaching me a truth fraught with suffering—that affection is life itself! I felt that it was my destiny never to be cheered by its blessed light and warmth. Months passed away, and I closed up my heart; a coldness, a stoic apathy came over me, which was sometimes broken by a slight thing; the flood-gates of feeling gave way, and I wept with a passionate sorrow—over my own sinfulness—over my own lonely heart, without one joy to shed a glow on its rude desolation. Oh! then, when I was softened, when I could pray, and feel that the Lord listened to me, I would have been a different being, if mother's hand had been laid fondly upon my head, if her eyes had filled with tears, and I could have leaned upon her bosom and wept. But I was unloved, and my heart grew hard again."

"Don't say that you are unloved," interrupted Ann, pressing Christine to her heart, and sobbing with an abandonment of feeling. "Forgive me, dear, dear sister! my heart shall be your home—we will love each other always; I will never again be as I have been. Don't weep so, Christine, can't you believe me? I am selfish, I am heartless sometimes, but a change has come over me to-night; to *you* I can never be heartless again!"

At that moment, few would have recognised the haughty Miss Lambert in the tearful girl, whose head drooped on Christine's shoulder, while her white hand was clasped and held in meek affection to her lips. If we could read the private history of many an apparently cold, heartless being, we would be more charitable in our opinions of others. We would see that there are times when the better feelings, which God has given as a pure inheritance, are touched. We would see the inner life from Him, flowing down from its home in the hidden recesses of the soul, breaking and scattering the clouds of evil, which had impeded its descent—we would see the hard heart melted, though perhaps briefly, beneath angel influences. We would see that all alike are the beloved creations of the Almighty's hand, and we would weep over ourselves, as well as others, to feel how seldom we yield to the voice that would ever lead us aright. Ann Lambert, as her heart overflowed with pure affection, thought sincerely that no selfish action of hers should ever sadden Christine. She felt that she was unworthy, that she had been cruel and selfish, but she imagined her strong emotions of repentance had uprooted the evils, which had only been shaken.

Christine dried her tears, and looked earnestly and inquiringly in her sister's face, as if she suspected there was some hidden sorrow with which she was unacquainted. Ann answered her look by saying,

"You wonder what I was weeping for, when you awoke, Christine. I had met with no sorrow; but when I looked at you, the course of conduct I had pursued towards you came up before me vividly: I felt how unsisterly I had been—"

"Say nothing about it," interrupted Christine, with delicate generosity, "let the past be forgotten, the future shall be all brightness, dearest Ann. We will pour out our hearts to each other, and each will strengthen the other in better purposes. I am no longer alone, you love me and I am happy."

That night, the dreams of the sisters were pure and peaceful. One happy week passed away with Christine; Ann was affectionate and gentle, and only went out when accompanied by her. They were inseparable; they read, wrote, studied, and sewed together. For the time, Ann seemed to have laid aside her usual character; she yielded to her purest feelings; no incident had yet occurred to mar her tranquillity. One evening, when she was reading aloud to Christine in their own apartment, a servant girl threw open the door and exclaimed,

"Miss Ann, there are two gentlemen waiting in the parlour to see you; Mr. Darcet and Mr. Burns!"

"Very well," replied Ann, rising, and giving the book to Christine; but she took it away in the instant, and said,

"Come, Crissy, go down with me!"

"Oh, no matter," replied her sister, "I am not acquainted with them, and I would rather stay up here, and read. Mother will be in the parlour."

"Suit yourself," returned Ann, half carelessly, as she smoothed her hair. "When you get tired of reading, come down."

"I'll see about it," said Christine, as the door closed.

Ann looked beautiful indeed, as she entered the parlour, her features lit up with a smile of graceful welcome. After a little easy trifling, the conversation turned upon subjects which she knew Christine would be interested in. Under a kind impulse, she left the room, and hastened to her.

"Come down into the parlour, Christine," she exclaimed, laying her hand affectionately upon her shoulder, as she approached. "Mr. Darcet is telling about his travels in Europe, and I am sure you will be interested. There (sic) isn o need of your being so unsociable. Come, dear!"

Christine raised her face with an eloquent smile; she went with Ann without speaking, but her heart was filled with a sweet happiness, from this proof of thoughtful affection. When she was introduced to Ann's friends, there was a most lovely expression on her face, breathing forth from a pure joyfulness within.

"I was not aware that you had a sister, Miss Lambert," said Mr. Darcet, turning to Ann, when they were quietly seated after a brief admiring gaze at Christine.

"Perhaps I have been too much of a recluse," replied Christine quickly, in order to relieve the embarrassment of Ann, which was manifested by a deep blush. "I have yielded to sister Ann's persuasions this time to be a little sociable, and I think I shall make this a beginning of sociabilities."

"I hope so," returned Darcet; "do you think being much secluded, has a beneficial effect upon the mind and feelings?"

"I do not," was the young girl's brief answer. The colour came to her cheek, and a painful expression crossed her brow, an instant. "But sometimes—" the sentence was left unfinished. Darcet's curiosity was awakened by the sudden quiver of Christine's lip, and forgetful of what he was about, he perused her countenance longer, and more eagerly, than was perfectly polite or delicate. She felt his scrutiny, and was vexed with her tell-tale face. There was a silence which Mrs. Lambert interrupted by saying, with a smile,

"We should like to hear more of your adventures, Mr. Darcet, if it is agreeable to you."

"Oh! certainly!" he replied. And he whiled an hour quickly away. Ann was then urged to play and sing, which she did, but there was a little haughtiness mingled with her usual grace.

"Don't you sing, Miss Christine?" asked Darcet, leaving the piano, and approaching the window where she sat, listening attentively to Ann.

"I do sometimes," answered Christine, smiling, "but Ann sings far better."

"Let others judge of that. Isn't that fair?"

"We often err in thinking we do better than other people, but I think we generally hit the truth, when we discover that in some things, at least, we are not quite as perfect as others."

"Certainly, but it is the custom to speak of ourselves, as if we were inferior to those whom we really regard as beneath us in many respects. There is no true humility in that; we depart from the truth."

"Custom sanctions many falsehoods; to speak the truth always, would make us many enemies. But we might better have them, than to contradict the truth; what do you think?" Christine looked up with an earnest seriousness.

"Truth, and truth alone, should govern us in every situation, let the consequences be what they may," said Darcet, in a tone that sounded almost stern; then more gently he added, "Before all things I prize a frank spirit; for heaven may be reflected there. With all, this upright candour must in a measure be acquired. Yet, I think frankness to our own souls is acquired with far more labour. We shrink from a severe scrutiny into our tangled motives."

"And when these motives are forced upon our notice, we endeavour to palliate and excuse them. I am sure it is so," exclaimed Christine earnestly, for her own young heart's history came up before her, and she remembered that she had excused herself for acting and feeling wrong, on the plea that others had not done right, by her. "But"—she continued after a pause, "you cannot think it is well always to express the sentiments which circumstances may give rise to. Such a course might prevent us from doing a great deal of good."

"Certainly it might. The end in view should be regarded. Good sense, and a pure heart, will show us the best way in most cases."

There is a power deep and silent, exerted by good persons; the folded blossoms of the heart slowly open in their presence, and are refreshed. A new impulse, a pure aspiration for a higher life, a yearning after the perfecting of our nature, may be sown as a seed in hearts that are young in the work of self-conquest. Thus it was with Christine. The influence of Darcet strengthened all that was good within her; and as they remained long engaged in deep and earnest conversation, the elevation and purity of his sentiments gave clearness and strength to ideas that had been obscure to her before, because unexpressed. Her peculiar situation had made her far more thoughtful than many of her years. She thought she had lost the gay buoyancy of her childhood, but she was mistaken. She was one to profit by lessons that pressed down the bounding lightness of her spirit; she was yet to learn that she could grow young in glad feelings, as years rolled over her head. There was a subdued joy in her heart, that was new to her, and gave a sweetness to her manner, as she poured forth the guileless thoughts that first rose to her lips. It seemed strange to meet with the ardent sympathy which Darcet manifested by every look of his intelligent face; she could scarcely realize that it was herself, that anybody really felt interested in the thoughts and imaginings that had clustered around her solitary hours. At parting, he said with warm interest, as he slightly pressed her hand, "I hope, Miss Christine, we may have many conversations on the subjects we have touched upon to-night."

"Oh! I hope so," replied Christine, with a frank, bright smile. After the gentlemen had gone, Christine threw her arm around her sister, and said gayly, "Hav'n't we had a pleasant evening, Ann, my dear?"

"Pleasant enough," said Ann, trying to yawn, "but I felt rather stupid, as I often do."

"Stupid! Is it possible?" exclaimed the astonished girl. "You were talking with Mr. Burns; well, he didn't look as if he would ever set the North River afire with his energies, it is true."

Ann smiled very slightly, then rather pettishly disengaged herself from the detaining hand of Christine, and taking a light, retired without saying anything, but a brief good-night to her mother. Christine soon followed, wondering what made Ann so mute and sharp in her actions. "Why, Ann, are you angry with me?" she asked, going up to her, as soon as she entered the apartment.

"I don't know what I should be angry for," was the impatient reply. "Can't a person be a little short when sleepy, without being tormented with questions about it?"

"Oh, yes, I won't trouble you any more." And making due allowance for Ann's quick temper, Christine occupied herself good-humouredly with her own thoughts. The secret of Ann's shortness and sleepiness lay here. Her vanity was wounded to think, that Christine was more interesting than her own beautiful self.

"Well, he is a sort of a puritan, and now I begin to understand Christine, better, I think she is too," thought Ann, after she had mused her irritation away a little. "He is very polite and agreeable, and it was very pleasant to have him always ready to take me out when I wanted to go, but I never felt perfectly easy in his company; I was always afraid I might say something dreadful; something that would shock his wonderful goodness. But Christine seemed perfectly at home. How bright and lovely she looked! I will not allow evil thoughts to triumph over me. I will not be vexed simply because she eclipsed me, where no one ever did before. She is a dear, affectionate girl, and I made a vow before God to love her always, never to be to her as I was once."

A fervent prayer brought back to Ann all her former tranquillity, and she pressed a kiss upon Christine's forehead, full of repentant affection. Just before she went to sleep, she thought to herself,

"Well, if I may trust my woman's perception, Darcet will be exclaiming, after he has seen Christine a few times more,

"Oh! love, young love, bound in thy rosy bands."

Ann's perception proved correct. About a year after these cogitations, Christine became Mrs. Darcet. The sisters were much changed, but Christine the most so. There was a child-like simplicity and sweetness beaming from her young face, which Ann needed. Yet had much haughtiness faded from the brow of that beautiful girl; she had grown better; but as yet her heart had not been schooled in suffering as Christine's had. There was deep affection in the warm tears that fell upon the bride's cheek, as poor Ann felt that she had indeed gone to bless another with her tender goodness. Christine's warm heart grew yet more sunny in her own happy little home, and her feelings more open and expansive, beneath the genial influence of friendly eyes.

THE HOURS OF LIFE

TWILIGHT.—The dewy morning of childhood has passed, and the noon of youth has gone, and the gloom of twilight is gathering over my spirit. Alas! alas! how my heart sinks in a wan despair! One by one my hopes have died out, have faded like the gleams of sunshine that have just vanished beneath the grove of trees. Hopes! Ah, such warm, bright, beautiful, loving hopes! But, methinks, than lived upon the earth, unlike the gleaming rays of sunshine that are fed from heaven. The earth's darkness dims not their glory; pure and radiant they shine behind the black shadow. But human hopes are earth-born; they spring from the earth, like the flitting light of night, and lead us into bogs and quagmires.

Yet it is beautiful to realize that we have had hopes; they are the past light of the soul, and their glow yet lingers in this gloomy twilight, reminding one that there has been a sunny day, and memories of things pleasant and joyous mingle with the present loneliness and cheerless desolation.

Words, that excited hopes, that awoke thrilling emotions, linger on the listening ear. But, ah! the heart grows very sad, when the ear listens in vain, and the yearning, unsatisfied spirit realizes that the words, so loved, so fondly dwelt upon, were but words, empty, vain words. But, to have believed them, was a fleeting blindness. They served for food to the yearning heart, when they were given, and shall the traveller through the desolate wilderness look back with scorn upon the bread and water that once satisfied his hunger and thirst, even though it is now withheld? No—let him be thankful for the past; otherwise, the keen biting hunger, the thirsty anguish of the soul, will have a bitterness and a gall in it, that will corrode his whole being. Ah! what is this being? if one could but understand one's own existence, what a relief it would be; but to understand nothing—alas!

Life is a weary burden. I feel weighed down with it, and I do not know what is in the pack that bows me so wearily to the earth. I do know that in it are agonized feelings, bitter disappointments, and a desolation of the heart. But there is a something else in it; for, now and then, come vague, vast perceptions of a dim future; but I shut my eyes. I cannot look beyond the earth. I could have been satisfied here with a very little; a little of human love would have made me so happy. Yes, I would never have dreamed of an unknown heaven. Heaven! What is heaven? I remember when I was a little child, lying on my bed in the early morning twilight (ah! that was a twilight, unlike this, which is sinking into a black night, for that was ushering in the beautiful golden day), but it was twilight when I looked through the uncurtained window; and through the intertwining branches of a noble tree I saw the far, dim, misty sky—and I wondered, in my childish way, "if heaven is like that;" and all at once it seemed to me that the dim, distant sky opened, and my dead mother's face looked out upon me so beautifully, I did not know her, for she died when I was an unconscious infant, and yet I did know her. Yes, that beautiful face was my mother's, and my heart was full of delight. That my mother could see me, and love me, from the far heavens, was like a revelation to me. And often, on other mornings, I awakened and looked through the very same branches of the tree, out into the far sky, and thought to see my mother's face shining through the window and watching over her lonely, sleeping child. But my fancy never again conjured up the vision. Fancy! What is fancy? If one could but understand, could grasp the phantom and mystery of life! And above all, if one could but understand what heaven is!

When I was a child, heaven was to me a peopled place, a wonderful reality; and I remember a dream that I had—what a strange dream it was! For I went to heaven, and I saw a shining One, sitting on a throne, and many beautiful ones were standing and seated around the throne, and my father and mother were there; and they had crowns on their heads, and held each other by the hand, and looked down upon me so lovingly. I knew that it was my father, because my mother held him by the hand, though my father died the day I was born, and I stood before them in the great light of a Heavenly Presence, as such a poor little earth-child, but I was happy, inexpressibly happy, only they did not touch me; but I was not fit to be touched by such soft, shining hands. And what was yet a greater joy than ever to see my unknown father and mother on the other side of the throne, I saw my brother, my dear, gentle, beautiful little brother, who, seven years older than I, had loved and played with me on the earth. He was clothed in white garments, and was grown from a child to a youth, and was so full of a noble and beautiful grace. He smiled upon me; he did not speak; none spoke. All was so still, and serene, and bright, and beautiful. Next morning I awoke as if yet in my dream, so vivid was the whole scene before me. I could have danced and sung all day, "I have seen my father and mother and brother in the heavenly courts." But what are dreams?

Yet, it is wonderful to go back to the dreams and thoughts of childhood; they are so distinct; such living realities. I often remember a speech I made in those far childish days. I was lying in bed with a friend in the early gray morning. All at once I started up and said—"Oh, how I wish I had lived in the days when Jesus lived upon the earth!"

I was asked why? And I replied, "Because I could have loved Him; I would have followed as those women followed Him; I would have kissed the hem of His garment."

A laugh checked the further flow of my talk; but I lay down again, and then my thoughts wandered off to the mountains of Judea, and I saw a Divine Man walking over the hills and valleys, and women following Him. In those days I knew two passages in the Bible, and that was all that I knew of it, for I never read it. But I learned at Sunday school, Christ's Sermon on the Mount, and the first five verses of the first chapter of John. And I remember how confused I always was over the WORD, for some told me it meant "*Logos.*"

What was "*Logos?*" I could never fathom it. Now I know what "*Logos*" means. And yet the mystery is not fathomed. Well, let that go. I could never understand the Bible. However, in those days it was something holy and sacred to me; because the Bible that I owned belonged to my dear father, and I often kissed it, and loved the Book dearly, but I could not read it by myself. But I did read occasionally in the Bible, to an old woman; she lived on the way to the village school, in a dilapidated, deserted country store; she occupied the little back room, in which was a fire-place, and I was permitted to take a flask of milk to her every day, as I passed to school; and with what a glad heart I always hurried off in the morning, that I might gather broken brush-wood and dried sticks, for her to kindle her fire with. Charitable people sent her wood, but it was wet and hard to kindle, and the poor old woman, with her bent back, would go out and painfully gather the dried sticks that lay around her desolate home; but when I came, she would take my book and dinner-basket into her house, and leave me the delight of gathering the sticks. Ah! I was happy then—when I knelt on the rude hearth and blew with my mouth instead of a bellows, the smoking, smouldering wood into a blaze, and heard the loving words that the good old woman lavished upon me. She loved me—but not as much as I loved her. She was my peculiar treasure—something for me to live for, and think of. I always left my dinner with her, and at noon returned to eat it with her; though I would feel almost ashamed to spread out the cold meat and bread before her, she looked so much like a lady.

But she always asked a blessing; that was what I never did, and it gave me an awe-stricken feeling, and my meal would have something of a solemn and tender interest—what with the blessing, and the old woman's love for me, and mine for her—and we ate it in a solemn and gloomy room, for there was no table in the little back room, so we used the counter of the old store; and the empty shelves and the closed doors and shutters, with only the light from the back-door, made me often look around shudderingly into the gloom and obscurity of dark corners—for I abounded in superstitious terrors, and I pitied the poor, lonely old woman for living in such a home more than I ever pitied the cold and hunger she endured.

Often when our dinner was over, I read aloud to her in the Bible. She could read it herself. But perhaps she liked to hear the sound of a childish voice, and perhaps she thought that she was doing me good. Did she do me good? heigho!—at all events, she left a beautiful memory to gild this dark twilight that grows upon my soul.

But the loving, trusting childhood is gone, and why do I dwell upon it? Why does its sensitive life yet move and stir in my memory? Has it aught to do with the cold, dark present? The Present! Alas! what a contrast it is to that childish faith! I almost wish that I could now believe as I did then. But no. *Reason* has dissipated the visions and dreams and superstitions of childhood. It has made unreal to me that which was most real. In its cold, chilling light, I have looked into the world of tangible facts and possible realities.

Ah! this cold, cold light, how much of beauty and love it has congealed! It has fallen like a mantle of snow over the warm, living life of the earth; and blooming flowers, that sent up odours on the soft air, have crumbled to dust, and bright summer waters that reflected the heavens in their blue depths, and glittered in the light of stars and moon and sun, have now been congealed into solid, dull opaque masses, which yield not to the tread of man. Alas! no bird of beauty dips its wing in these dead waters, and plumes itself for an aerial flight of love and joy. But the cold contraction chains down all the freer, beautiful life, into a hopeless, chilling inanity.

MIDNIGHT.—The gloom has gathered into a darkness that may be felt; and seeing nothing, I would stretch forth my hands to feel if there is anything within my mind to stay my soul upon. But, alas! in a deep sorrow, how little do mental acquisitions avail! All the beautiful systems and theories that delighted my intelligence, and filled my thought in my noon of hope and life, have sunk into darkness. How is this? Sometimes I think that all light comes through the heart into the mind; and when love is quenched, behold, there is only darkness; the beauty and life and joy are gone. Ah, woe is me! Have I nothing left?—no internal resources—no wealth of knowledge, with which to minister to this poverty of hope and life? It cannot be that all past efforts, all struggles and self-sacrifices, to attain this coveted and natural knowledge, were useless, vain mockeries. I thought I should live by this knowledge; that when the outer life palled upon me, I could then retire within my own being to boundless stores of riches and beauty. Well—this time has come, and what do I find? Truly it is no Aladdin-palace, glittering with gold and gems. It is more like a cavernous depth, stored with rubbish, and from its dark deeps comes up an earthy odour, that almost suffocates my spirit. But this is my all, and I must descend from the life of the heart to the life of the mind, and scan my unsatisfactory possessions.

Well, here is a world of childish, school-day lumber. Once it was a great delight to me to learn that the world was round, and not square; but I cannot see that a knowledge of that fact affords me any great satisfaction now, for it has shaped itself to me as an acute angle. And the earth's surface! how I used to glow with the excitement of the bare thought of Rome! and Athens! and Constantinople! and their thrilling histories and wonders of art, and beauties of nature, seemed to me an indefinite world of unattainable delight and ecstasy. But now, I have lived in all these places, and the light and glory have gone. They have fallen within the freezing light of reason. They are no longer like beautiful dreams to me. They are squared down into fixed, unalterable facts. I cannot gild them with any light of fancy; and I cannot extract from them anything like the delight of my childhood. So I will turn from these fixed facts and look out for those philosophical theories, that gave me a later delight, as more interior mental pleasure.

Well, when I first broke through the shackles of the old childish faith, Percy Bysshe Shelley was my high-priest. Through him I thought I had come into a beautiful light of nature, vague, shadowy, and grand, filling vast conceptions of the indefinite. He discarded the God of the Hebrews, who was fashioned after their own narrow, revengeful passions; a Being of wrath and war. And a brooding spirit, an indefinite indwelling life of nature, was a new revelation to me. I grew mystical and sublime and sentimental, in this new mental perception. But I wearied of that. I could not walk on stilts always, and I descended to the earth and read Voltaire, and laughed and sneered at all the old forms and superstitions of man. But this does not afford me any enjoyment now—the unhappy do not feel like laughing at a ribald wit; but, alas! this rubbish is stored here, and here I must live with it. It blackened and blurred the pictures of the angels, that adorned my childish memories. It wiped out all heavenly visions, and left only the earthly life.

But the human heart cannot live without a God; and I tried hard to make one, for myself, through German pantheism. But I turn this rubbish over disconsolately, for it is a material God, and does not respond to one spiritual nature. It seems rather to react against it. Alas! alas! I sink down into a Cimmerian darkness here; it seems as if the Stygian pools of blackness had closed over me, and a cry of anguish goes forth from my inmost soul, piercing the dark depths to learn what is spirit? and what is God? What manner of existence or unity of Being is He? Who is He? Where is He? And how can I attain to a knowledge of Him? But through the echoing halls of my dark mind, there is only a wailing sound of woe, of misery, of disappointment, of a yearning anguish of spirit for a something higher and better than I have ever yet conceived of or known.

But there is yet more of this mental rubbish. Ah! here is a whole chapter of stuff—and I once thought it was so wise. I called it the "progressive chain of being," and wove it out of the Pythagorean philosophy. I said man's nature begins from the lowest, and ascends to the highest. *Nature* gives the impulse to life; and the flower that blooms in South America may die, and its inner spirit may clothe itself in a donkey born in Greece! and so it goes on transfusing itself from clime to clime, in ever new and higher forms, until man is developed. Well, was there ever such stuff concocted before? I almost hear the bray of that donkey, who originated in a flower. And pray, most sapient self! what is nature? It seems *now*, to me, a *form*, a mere dead incubus of matter. And could this inert tangible matter, sublimate in its hard, dead bosom, an essence so subtle, as to be freer of the bonds of time and space? At such a preposterous suggestion even a donkey might bow his ears with shame. So I will hand this "progressive chain of being" over to a deeper darkness, and pass on.

Lo! here lie the statues of broken gods, headless divinities. I tried to believe in Greek mythology; to fancy that the world had gone backwards, and that there were spirits of the earth and air, that took part in the life of man. But these were poetic visions that shifted and waved with every fleeting fancy. But *now* this would be a pleasant faith. What if I *could* appeal to an invisible, higher spiritual being, who sympathized with my nature, to lead me out of this darkness of ignorance into a true world of light, of truth, of definite knowledge, concerning life and its origin; concerning God and His nature? If I were only an old Greek, how I would pray to Minerva for help, and call upon Hercules to remove this Augean dirt, that pollutes and lumbers all the chambers of my mind! But when the old Greeks called, were they answered? Ah, there is nothing to hope for!

Yet Socrates believed in these spiritual existences; he ordered a cock to be sacrificed to Esculapius as he was drinking the hemlock. To him, they were not mere poetic creations; he believed to the last that he was guided and guarded by his demon. What if we all are? What if even now, in this midnight darkness, stands a beautiful being, veiled by my ignorance, who loves me, from a world of light; sees the tangled web of my thoughts, and would draw it out into form, and order, and beauty? If such there be, oh, bright and beautiful one! pity me, love me, and enlighten me. Alas, no!—all is yet dark. What would a being revelling in light and beauty, have to do with this poor, faded life of mine? Alas! that was a fleeting hope, that, like a pale, flickering ray, gilded the darkness for a moment.

But, here is a something which gives somewhat of joy and life to the mind. It is a beautiful thought of Plato, that there is a great central sun in the universe, around which all other suns revolve. What if this be an inner sun, which is the fountain of spiritual life? That is something to believe. Yet the thought sinks appalled from it. The heart desires a God that it may love, and trust in, that it may speak to and be heard; and if the fountain of life be only a sun, what is there to love in it? True, we rejoice in the light and beauty of the sun that upholds *this* world in its place; but what is this enjoyment compared to the bliss of human love? A man—a living, breathing, loving man—is the perfection of existence; and one could be happy with a perfect man, if all the suns in the universe were blotted out. A MAN! what is he, in his essential attributes? What is it that gives a delight in him? Ah! I am full of ideal visions—for in all history I find not one man that altogether fills my vision of what a man should be. From the Alexanders and Caesars I turn with loathing—their fierce, rude, outre life, their selfish, grasping ambition, suggest to me the vision of snarling wild beasts, battling over the torn and palpitating limbs of nations. These men could never have touched my soul; they could never have dispelled the darkness of my mind; they could not be friends. But was there ever a man that could have answered the questions for the solution of which my spirit yearns? Plato was beautiful; around him was a pure, intellectual light. But, after all, he *knew* very little; his writings are mostly suggestive. But suppose here was a man who could reveal all the hidden things of life? How sudden would be the delight of learning of him, of communing with his spirit? And what if he knew, not only everything relating to this world, and my own intellectual being, but could tell me of all the universe, of all the after life? Oh! what a joy such a man would be to me! How would this midnight darkness melt into the clearest and most beautiful day!

But did such an one ever exist? Why is it that now comes over me the vision of my childhood, of the Divine Man walking over the hills of Judea? Oh, Christ! who wert Thou? My thought goes forth to Thee; beautiful was Thy life upon the earth. It had in it a heavenly sanctity, a purity, a grace and mercy, a gentleness and forbearance, that seems to me God-like and Divine. Yes—what if God descended and walked on the earth? I could love Him, that He had lowered Himself to my comprehension. But God! the Infinite and Eternal! in the finite human form, undergoing death! I cannot comprehend this. But what is infinity? When I look within myself and realize my ever-changing and fleeting feelings, now glancing in expansive ranges of thought from star to star, I realize an infinity in mind, that is not of the body. What if it were thus with the Holy Man, Christ? What if He were God as to the spirit, and man as to the flesh? If this were so, well may I have wished "to live when Jesus walked the earth," for He alone could have revealed all things to me. How wonderful must have been His wisdom! And if His indwelling spirit were God, then Christ yet lives—lives in some inner world of love and beauty. Ah, beautiful hope! for, if immortality is my portion, I may yet see Him, and learn of Him in another existence. Methinks the night of my soul is passing away; upon the rayless darkness a star has risen; a fixed star of love and hope; what if like other fixed stars it prove a sun?

Oh, Christ! holy and beautiful Man! if Thou yet livest in far-away realms of light and blessedness—grant that I may see Thee, and learn of Thy wondrous wisdom. Enlighten my darkness, and suffer me to love Thee as the Divinest type of man that my thought has yet imagined.

THE DAWN OF THE MORNING.—I have gone back to my Bible with the old childish love and reverence. I read it with an object now. I know that in it, the beautiful Christ-nature was portrayed; and I read with infinite longings to find Him the "unknown God;" and bright revealings come to me through this Book. I feel that it is Divine, and the light grows upon me; and sometimes like the Apostles, who awakened in the night, and saw Christ transfigured before them, I also saw a transfiguration. I lose sight of the mere material man, and I perceive an inner glory of being, a radiance of wisdom, and purity, and love, that clothe Him in a Divine light, and make His countenance brilliant with a spiritual glory.

This transfiguration, what was it? My thought dwells upon it so—it was a wonderful thing. I know that the scoffing philosophers ridicule the idea of there being any reality in it; they regard it either as a fiction on the part of the writers, or as a dream or a delusion of the senses. But I believe that it all happened just as it was narrated. For it is beautiful to believe it. If it did not happen, I am none the worse for believing it, even if the whole life was a fiction, which all history proves to have been true; and had no Christ lived upon the earth, yet, as a work of art, this fiction would have been the highest and most beautiful dream of the human thought. But if it is all literally true; if Christ was "God manifest in the flesh," how much do I gain by believing in him! I have attained the highest and best of all knowledge—I know GOD!

And this transfiguration becomes a wonderful revelation! It was the Spirit of God shining through the Man. And this spirit was a substance and a form. And what was its form?—that of a man, with a face radiant as the sun.

Now know I how to think of God. He is no longer a vague, incomprehensible existence; an ether floating in space. But He is a living, breathing human form, a Man! in whose image and likeness we were created. Oh, how I thank God that He has revealed this to me! Now, I know what manner of Being I pray to; and like as the apostles saw Him, in His Divine spiritual human form, will I now always think of Him. I will look through His veil of flesh, I will love Him as the only God-man that ever existed.

When I think thus of the inner Divine nature, clothed in a material body, how wonderfully do the scenes of this drama of the life of Christ strike me! Imagine Him, the God of the universe, standing before the Jewish sanhedrim, condemned, buffeted, and spit upon. How at that moment in His inmost Divine soul, He must have glanced over the vast creation, that He had called into being; and felt that an Infinite power dwelt in Him. One blazing look of wrathful indignation would have annihilated that rude rabble. But He had clothed himself in flesh, to subdue all of its evil and vile passions; to show to an ignorant and sensual race, the grace and beauty of a self-abnegation—a Divine pity and forgiveness. And thus did the outer material Man die with that beautiful and touching appeal to the Infinite-loving soul, from which the body was born: "Father! forgive them, they know not what they do." Oh, Thou! Divine Jesus! make me like unto Thee in this heavenly and loving spirit.

How clear many things grow to me now! I smile when I think of the old childish trouble over the word *"Logos,"* for this *Logos,* i. e. truth, has been revealed to me. In the knowledge that Christ was the Infinite God—the Creator of the universe, I see Him as the central *truth.* Thus Christ was the *Logos,*—the *Word*; the Divine Truth, and now I read, that "In the beginning was Christ, and Christ was with God, and Christ was God." And I am happy in this knowledge—my thought has something to rest upon out of myself; and my affections grow up from the earth to that wonderful Divine Man, who, after the death of the body, was seen as a man, a living man! Immortality is no longer the dream of a Plato. It is a demonstrated fact.

In my mind is the stirring of a new life, as in the light of an early morning-glory; the voice of singing birds is in my heart, and an odour of blooming flowers expands itself in the delight of my new day. I see the morning sun in a fixed form, yet flooding worlds with the radiations of its light and heat, and shining in its glory on the dew-bespangled blade of grass. Oh Christ!—thou art my Sun—and I, the tiny blade of grass, rejoice in Thy Divine wisdom and love. Look down upon me, oh, Thou holy One! from the "throne of Thy glory, and the habitation of Thy Holiness," and exhale from me, through the dew of my sorrow, the incense of my love.

Draw me up from the earth, even as the sun draws up the bowed plants, and let me drink in the beautiful life of free heavenly airs.

NOON-DAY.—How the light grows! In the warm love of my soul a summer's day glows—so serene and bright, so full of ceaseless activities, that the fruits ripen in a smiling, rosy beauty.

The living Christ hath heard my soul's prayer; and books, which I never before heard of, have revealed to me all those wonderful truths after which my spirit yearned.

First of all, the mystery of the Bible has been made clear to me. I see it now as a beautiful whole. The Infinite knew from the beginning that He was going to descend upon the earth, and take upon Himself a human nature, weak and ignorant and vicious; and that He was to purify and enlighten, and make Divine this fallen nature, that man might know God in a material form, and love Him. All this is written out in the Bible.

I stand on the threshold of a wonderful science. There are innumerable things that I do not comprehend in the Bible; but what I see and understand awakens in me a thrilling delight, and I can never exhaust this book; for it is full of the nerves of life; and I can no more number them than I can count the sensitive fibres that spread themselves from my brain, to the innumerable cellular tissues of my skin. But as the body is full of a sentient life, so is every word of the Bible full of an indwelling life.

And now do I recognise the good that my patient, suffering old friend did me in my childhood; would that I had read the Holy Bible to her many other days. Doubtless she is now a beautiful angel in Heaven.

The angels! and Heaven! now too do I understand the inner existence; and the dreams and visions of my childhood were, after all, blessed realities; and the dead father and the dead mother, after whom my childish heart yearned so lovingly, were revealed to me as a living father and a living mother, in a wondrously beautiful life. Thus was a warm inner love kept alive in my soul; and now I know that death is but a new birth. As a glove is drawn from the hand, so is the body drawn from the spirit; and, I too, will thus be born again. Life is again crowned with a beautiful hope.

Life!—and this mystery too is solved. God is the alone life, and finite human spirits are forms receptive of life from God. God is the soul and creation is His body—and from this infinite Divine soul, life flows forth into every atom of the body. Beautiful thought! The Lord sits throned in the inmost, and is cognisant of every nerve that thrills through His boundless universe of being. Every thought and feeling that passes through my heart and mind is as clearly perceived by Him, as are the sensations of my body perceived by my soul. Thus are we in God, and God in us.

And how vast is the thought that suns, and their peopled worlds, are to the body of God but as the drops of blood to the finite human body; and who can count these drops? for as they flow forth, and back to the heart, they ever grow and change, and increase—and who can measure the Infinite! and this Being, sentient of all things in the universe, providing for all things; seeing all things; maintaining order, down to the minutest particle, in a system which the finite thought of man can never grasp—and loving his creatures in myriads of worlds, of which man never dreamed. How inconceivable must be His boundless wisdom, His infinite love! Can we wonder that a Soul so glowing with love, so radiant in intelligence, should shine as the sun? Yes—this is the Central Sun, whose spiritual beams, pouring forth their Divine influences, creating as they go angelic and spiritual intelligences, finally ultimate themselves in material suns, and material human bodies. Thus the garment of dull, opaque matter is woven by the Divine Soul, through the condensations of His emanations. Thus, were "all things made by Him; and without Him was not anything made that was made;" and "in Him was life, and the life was the light of men."

The thought sinks after this far flight—we worship and adore the Infinite. But the Lord must for ever remain apart from our weak natures, as far as the sun is above the earth. He lives, in His incomprehensible self-existence, at an immeasurable distance from us. This the Divine Man sees, and in His tender compassion and loving mercy for every human soul He creates, a twin-soul is made, that the finite may find the fullness of delight in another finite existence.

Oh, blessed and beautiful providence of God! that two human hearts and minds may intertwine in mutual support, and look up to the Infinite. And in the glorious sunshine of life, grow ever young and beautiful, in an immortal youth.

Oh, ye suffering, sorrowing children of earth! turn your affections and hopes from the fleeting things of time; from the outside-world, to the beautiful inner spirit-life, where eternity develops ever new and varying joys. Then only can the day dawn upon the human soul, and the midnight darkness be dissipated by boundless effulgence of light.

MINISTERING ANGELS

TIME and Patience! These are Angels
    By our Heavenly Father sent;
Whispering to our restless spirits,
    "Cease to murmur—be content;
God, who is thy truest friend,
Doth our aid in trials send.

When thy weary spirit faileth,
    'Neath the weary cross it bears,
God is not unmindful of thee—
    He is listening to thy prayers;
From His children's tearful pleading
He will *never* turn unheeding!"

Heart of mine! Trust thou these Angels;
    Lean on Patience, and be calm;
Trust in Time, who is preparing
    For thy grief a spirit-balm;
God is merciful, and He
Gave them charge concerning thee.

OURS, LOVED, AND "GONE BEFORE"

> The light of her young life went out,
> As sinks behind the hill
> The glory of a setting star;
> Clear, suddenly, and still.
>
> —WHITTIER.

YOU ask me to tell you of her, the sweet friend we have loved and lost. You impose on me a difficult task; I find it so harrowing to my feelings, and I also find that my pen is inadequate to the tribute my heart would pay.

I would that the privilege of knowing and loving her had been yours, for to know her was to love her.

In former letters I told you something of her; how she came to us a lovely bride of just nineteen summers; how anxiously we looked for her first appearance in church, for they arrived late Saturday evening, and no one had seen her. I told you how my heart went out to her as I looked on her sweet, bright, yet somewhat timid face; there was a perfect witchery in her eyes. I felt that I could gaze into them for ever; there was about them a spell, a fascination that I have never seen in others; they laughed as they looked at you, and yet they were not merely laughing eyes; perhaps the long, drooping lashes somewhat modified the expression, and helped to give the peculiarity so strikingly their own.

Her dress and whole appearance were captivating; the simple light straw hat, with the little illusion veil, and the pure white dress fitting so prettily the slender form. I could hardly wait for the next day, so anxious was I to see and speak with her, for I loved her already.

I had been prepared to love her, for our young pastor had told us much of his future bride. You know our house was one of his homes, and to us he had spoken often and enthusiastically of his Mary. It seemed to me that first Sabbath, that his prayers were particularly impressive, and his thanks to the Author and Giver of every perfect gift unusually appropriate; he seemed overpowered by a weight of gratitude and love.

How I admired the two as I glanced from one to the other! And I know that many prayers went up from that assembled congregation for long life and blessings on them.

It was a beautiful home that had been prepared for her. Her furniture had been sent on previous to their marriage, and our little band had vied with each other in arranging with a view both to taste and comfort. How we did wish for a peep into her own home, to get a hint with regard to arranging her things, so as to be *home-like*!

You know there is often so much in association, and we would have loved the new strange place to have a familiar look to her at first sight. Oh! what visions we conjured up as we arranged the room which was to serve both as parlour and dining-room; for the house was small, and Mr. B.'s study must be on the first floor. *There* was the best place for the piano between the windows, which looked into the garden; we heard in anticipation the sweet voice which was to fill the little room with melody, as the roses and flowers of June now filled the garden with fragrance. The pretty fire-screen must stand in a conspicuous corner, for that spoke particularly of home, and of the hours delightfully passed in the dear family circle while tracing it stitch by stitch; and I fancied that into each bright flower which stood out so life-like from the canvas some emotion of her heart had been indelibly wrought. How many lovely home associations will the pretty fire-screen bring up!

How we arranged, and disarranged, and re-arranged, before all was to our minds; and how we hoped, when all was finished, that it would look as charming to her as it did to us! And we were not disappointed; for, on the following Monday, when we called to see her, nothing could exceed the enthusiasm of her expression and gratitude; everything was lovely, perfect; she saw all *en couleur de rose*.

She had left indulgent parents, and a home of refinement and luxury, and we feared for her the untried duties of her new position; but an intimate acquaintance proved her eminently qualified for the responsibility she had assumed. She adapted herself with charming grace and readiness to her present circumstances. She was a most delightful acquisition to our limited circle; a favourite with all; and she blended so beautifully the graces of religion with those of her natural temperament that she became our idol.

The "parsonage" seemed to me a paradise, surrounded by none but bright and holy influences. There the poor always found a welcome, a willing heart, a ready hand, and listening ear; however sad and desponding on entering, they invariably came out cheerful and hopeful. There seemed a magic spell cast around every one who sought the presence of our dearly loved pastor and his wife.

With what pleasure I used to watch for their steps as they took their morning walks together that bright first year of their married life! They seemed to have the life and vivacity of children. She always accompanied him in his walks, in his visits to the poor, in relief to the sick, by the bedside of the dying; she was like his shadow, and always haunted him for good. It might be said most emphatically of both, "When the ear heard them it blessed them, and when the eye saw them it gave witness to them, because they delivered the poor that cried, and the fatherless, and him that had none to help him; the blessing of him that was ready to perish came upon them, and they caused the widow's heart to sing for joy."

Thus several years passed away; new cares and new duties devolved on them; but all were cheerfully met and delightfully performed; and they basked in the sunshine of God's love. Beautiful children sprang up around them, and we felt that "earth never owned a happier nest" than that which was placed in our midst.

How proud Mr. B. was of his family, and with what reason, too, for we all felt it with him; his wife so beautiful, so good, so in all respects fitted to make home happy, with her never-failing sunshine and light-heartedness; his two little girls, our impersonation of cherubs; and the youngest a noble boy, so dear to his mother's heart. Oh! how many attractions within that charmed circle!

I shall never forget an evening I passed in the nursery with that dear one surrounded by her happy little band. Willie, "the baby," as she called him, although more than two years old, was sitting in her lap, twirling one of her long, beautiful ringlets round his tiny fingers.

"Sing, mamma!" he said.

"Oh, do!" joined in Effie and Minnie, putting their bright innocent faces and soft brown curls close to hers; "sing The Dove, mamma, please."

She laughingly asked me to excuse her, saying, she always devoted the twilight hour to amusing and instructing the little ones. I begged her to allow my presence to be no restraint upon her usual custom. She then commenced, and I thought no seraph's voice could be sweeter, as she sang one of Mary Howitt's beautiful translations:—

"There sitteth a dove so white and fair
   All on the lily spray,
And she listeneth how to Jesus Christ
   The little children pray;
Lightly she spreads her friendly wings,
   And to Heaven's gate hath fled,

And to the Father in Heaven she bears
    The prayers which the children have said.

And back she comes from Heaven's gate,
    And brings, that dove so mild,
From the Father in Heaven, who hears her speak,
    A blessing for every child.
The children lift up a pious prayer—
    It hears whatever you say,
That heavenly dove, so white and fair,
    All on the lily spray."

I joined heartily in the thanks and admiration the children expressed when she had finished.

As she laid them in their little beds, and kissed their rosy lips and dimpled cheeks, she said, "I can never thank God enough for these sweet children." She then added, "Oh! what an affliction it must be to lose a child; I think if one of mine should die, I should die too; but," she added, "I should not say so; could I not trust them with Him who doeth all things well?" She little realized how soon she was to be put to the test. I called there a few days after. She was in the garden raising and tying up some drooping carnations which the rain of the preceding day had injured.

"Willie is not well," said she. "I have just sung him to sleep, and Mr. B. said I must take a little fresh air, for I was fatigued with holding him, and I thought I would confine myself to the garden, to be near, if he should wake."

Soon a cry from the nursery was heard; she sprang up the steps in nervous haste, while I quite chided her anxiety. I followed her into the room, and was surprised and shocked to find the dear boy in a high fever; his little arms tossing restlessly, and his lips dry and parched. Mr. B. sent immediately for the physician; we waited anxiously his arrival, hoping secretly that we were unnecessarily alarmed; but his coming did not reassure us; he saw dangerous symptoms; but still, he said, he hoped for the best. I went home, as Mr. and Mrs. B. both declined my services for the night, saying they would rather attend him alone. The next day I was pained to hear that his symptoms were more unfavourable; that the medicine had had no effect, and the physician was becoming discouraged. I flew over to the "parsonage;" the wildly anxious look of the mother distressed me. I begged her to lie down a little while, and allow me to take her place by the baby.

"Oh, no," she said, "I cannot leave him; who but his mother should be by his side?"

It seemed to me that I had never seen greater distress on any countenance. Mr. B. endeavoured to soothe her, though his anguish was apparently as keen as her own.

"If our Saviour would remove this little flower to his own garden, shall we refuse to give it up? Shall we not rather bless and thank him for allowing us to keep it so long?"

"Oh, yes!" she said, "He doeth all things well; I know that he does not willingly afflict nor grieve the children of men. I know that whom He loveth he chasteneth, and I can say, 'Thy will be done.' Nature is powerful, but my Saviour feels for me, and will forgive the inward struggle."

All that night they watched his little life fast ebbing away. Towards morning his sufferings seemed to cease; he smiled upon his parents. Hope for a moment revived in their hearts, but soon to be displaced by bitter anguish. Daylight showed the marked change in his features and complexion that told too plainly the messenger was very near.

"Speak to me, Willie," she exclaimed, bending over him in an agony of grief.

"Mamma," he said, and, with the effort, his little spirit took its flight.

Much has been said and written upon the death of infants, but when we see so much of wickedness in the world, so much of sin to blight, so much sorrow to fade, can we wonder that the Lord of Paradise loves to transplant to a fairer clime these frail buds of earth, there to have a beautiful and unfading development!

We saw no more of our precious friends till the day of the funeral. This was their first affliction, and none liked to intrude on the sanctity of their grief, though many tears were shed, and hearts went out to them; but we felt that they knew whom they had trusted, and that under the shadow of His wings they could rest securely till the storm was past.

A neighbouring clergyman was to perform the last sad office for the dead. Most lovely did little Willie look in his coffin. The child-like, beautiful expression still lingered. Rare flowers, the smallest and whitest, had been placed in the tiny hand, and shed their fragrance throughout the room.

Oh! how sad and sick appeared the mother, as she bent to take the last look at the little form she had loved and cherished so tenderly! Her nights of anxiety and watching had left their traces upon her face; her usually light and elastic step was feeble and slow, and she rested heavily upon the arm of her husband. His form also was bowed, and his countenance bore traces of the deepest grief.

One of those sudden changes which we so often experience in this our most changeful climate, took place that day. At noon it was very warm and bright, but before we returned from the funeral it was cloudy and cold.

The next day Mrs. B. was quite sick with severe cold, and the effects of the past excitement and grief. We flattered ourselves that rest and quiet, with good nursing, would soon restore her; and you may judge of our dismay upon learning, the day after, that she was dangerously ill.

"Oh no," we thought and said a hundred times, "it cannot be so; she will surely be better to-morrow."

We could not have it otherwise. We could not for an instant admit the idea that she would not recover. The bare supposition was agony. Oh! how harrowing to me is the remembrance of those long summer days, and those wakeful moonlight nights, in which, prostrated by disease, lay that young and lovely being so idolized by us all, but whom, indeed, we were destined to see no more on earth.

The Divine fiat had gone forth, and hearts were agonized, and looks grew sadder and sadder, as day after day sounded like a knell in our ears the fearful words, "Not materially better." But we could not give her up; hope would linger. No one was permitted to see her but the family and nurses, for the doctor said all excitement must be carefully avoided. We said, "She will not die; God will raise her up." In our weakness and blindness, we could see no mercy nor wisdom in this terrible bereavement, this scorching desolation of the already heavily-stricken servant of the Most High. He was naturally of a most hopeful disposition, and this, notwithstanding the discouraging words of the physician, buoyed up his soul, and he with us hoped against hope. They could not persuade him to leave her for a moment. Whole nights he watched by the side of her he loved best on earth, anticipating every word and look, and administering to her comfort.

How you would have felt for us, dear Anna, had you been here! We would walk by the house, and look up at the windows or door, not daring to knock for fear of disturbing her, but hoping to see one of the physicians or some one of the family, of whom to make inquiries. Oh, the nervousness of those days! the restless, weary nights we passed, till our fears and apprehensions became a racking torment, and we felt almost that we must die (sic) ourselves ourselves or be out of suspense; but when, on the evening of the tenth day after her illness, a messenger came with pallid face and almost wild look to say that she was *dead*, we were stunned. I really think we were almost as much shocked as though we had not heard of her illness; for we felt that, at the eleventh hour, some favourable turn *must* take place. I think we expected a miracle to be performed, so certain were we, or wished and tried to be, that she would recover.

But God's ways are not as our ways; truly, they are past finding out. We felt like putting our hands on our mouths, for fear of rebelling against *His* most righteous decrees. "Be still, and know that I am God," was all that we could say. It was hard to realize that the sun was still shining behind the cloud, for this was a darkness that might be felt. There seemed a pall over the earth and sky. Oh, how unsatisfactory seemed all on earth! how dark and strange! how mysterious and unreal! We could not weep, we were stunned, and it seemed at the time that we could never come back to earth without her. But when the touching relation of her last hours was made to us, the fountains of grief were unsealed, and we wept, as it were, rivers of tears.

I can give you no idea on paper of the beauty and sublimity of that death-scene as it was painted to me. We imagined that the heart must shrink, or at least draw back before the entrance into the dark valley. But all was peace; it flowed in upon her like a river, and she felt that underneath were the everlasting arms. Her husband and two remaining children stood by the bed. Oh, the bitterness of the cup he was called upon to drink! He shrank from it. As he bent over her, she said,

"Do not weep, love. How good God has been to give us so many bright, happy years together! Surely the lines have fallen to us in pleasant places, and I"—raising her beautiful eyes to heaven—"have a goodly heritage. I go to my Saviour. How should I feel at this moment had I not a hope in him? Oh, I am going home! I see Willie beckoning me to hasten. I will bear him in my arms to the Saviour's feet, and together we shall sing the 'new song.' I do not love you nor these sweet darlings less; but I love the Saviour more. I wish you could look in my heart and see the love I bear you. Thank you for all your indulgence, for all your kindness in bearing with my many infirmities. If I am permitted, I will be ever your guardian angel. Remember me with much and undying love to all the dear friends who have been so kind to me."

She appeared buoyed up with unnatural strength, though her end was so near. She broke into a sweet hymn; and it was, they said, as though the angel's voice had anticipated the few short moments before she should sing the "new song." She lay quiet for a little time, holding the hand of her husband in her own; then, opening her eyes and seeing the last rays of the departing sun, "I shall never look upon that bright orb again; but there is no need of the sun there. I draw near to heavenly habitations, and I would not retreat for what the world can give. Dearest, be faithful to your trust." And, imprinting a kiss upon his lips, her pure spirit went peacefully home.

We draw a veil upon the feelings of that bereaved one; too sacred are they to be looked upon; his house was left unto him desolate. That form, which had been to his eye like the well in the desert or the bow in the sky, was now cold in death.

Oh! thought we, why needed this affliction to be sent upon one so near *perfection*? Surely, *he*, of all others, needed not this discipline; and then came to our minds, soft, sweet, and soothing, the words, "Every branch in me that beareth fruit, he purgeth it that it may bring forth more fruit."

We felt that it was hard to lay in the grave the form of our dear friend; it was hard to part with the casket which had enshrined the precious jewel. Beautiful in life, she was so in death. The departing spirit had left a ray of brightness on its earthly house, and, in looking at the calm brow and peaceful smile, death seemed divested of its terror. We had twined the pure white flowers she loved around and amongst the rich dark masses of wavy hair, and she looked like a beautiful bride more than a tenant for the grave. The memory of that day will live ever in our minds. It was the last day of summer, and there seemed a beautiful appropriateness in the season; it seemed to us that the summer of our hearts had gone with her.

A sad and mournful procession, we followed her remains to the church so dear to her in life. It was but a few days since she entered it in her loveliness and bloom, and for the last time on earth commemorated a Saviour's dying love. She will partake with us here no more. May we be counted worthy to sit down with her at our Father's board in heaven! Mournful was the sight of the black pall which covered the coffin; mournful the drapery which shrouded her accustomed seat and enveloped the chancel; mournful the badges which all, as by consent, had adopted as expressive of their feelings on the occasion; but, oh! most mournful and heart-rending was the sight of that husband and father leading by the hand on either side all that remained to him of his beautiful family. It was difficult to recognise in him the man of two short weeks before; twenty years seemed added to his life; the eyes, usually beaming with light, now cast down and swollen with weeping—the countenance, index of a heart full of peace and joy, now so sorrow-stricken. Truly, he seemed "smitten of God and afflicted." We turned our eyes away as he stood by the grave which contained almost his earthly all.

It was a beautiful spot where they laid her to rest by the side of her baby. The sun was just going down in a golden flood of light, betokening a glorious morrow (beautiful emblem of the resurrection, when this perishing body should be raised in glory), and the shadows of the trees were lengthening on the grass. Every sound was in sweet accordance with the scene; the soft twittering of the birds as they sought their resting-places for the night, the quiet hum of the insects, and the sweet murmuring of the brook which flowed at a little distance.

A holy calm pervaded our minds as we wended our way between the trees and down the slope which bounded this lovely spot; and, as we left the gate, we involuntarily paused and looked back long and earnestly on the sweet view. Every object was bathed in that golden haze so peculiar to the last days of summer and the beginning of autumn; but at this time it seemed to us that the flood of soft light had escaped from the gate of heaven which we imagined had opened to receive the form lost to our sight.

Oh, we miss her more and more, everywhere! in our walks and visits; in the missionary circle, of which she was so ready and active a member; in the Sunday school; in her accustomed seat in church; and we miss the soft tones of her voice in prayer, and the rich outpourings of her melody in praise.

The poor of the parish have, indeed, lost a friend, as their tears and remembrance amply testify when they recount her kindnesses, her gentle words, her deeds of charity and love. "Flowers grew under the feet of her," said one wretchedly poor, yet, I thought, quite poetical old woman, whose declining days she had lightened of much of their weariness. A track of glory seems that which she has left behind; and there was so much that was beautiful and consoling in her last hours that it were selfishness to wish her back. She is with the Saviour she loved; she folds again to her heart the little one whose loss she had not time to realize on earth; together they have entered on their "long age of bliss in heaven."

Does not that death-scene speak volumes in attestation of the religion she professed, of the Saviour she adored? That young fair being, surrounded by all that makes life happy; friends who loved, a husband who idolized, children who clung to her; with a heart full of love and sympathy for all, rejoicing with those who rejoiced, and weeping with those who wept; of rare beauty and rarer accomplishments, a sunbeam on the face of the earth; yet she willingly left all when her Father called her. Is not her faith worth striving after?

We have reason (blessed be God!) to see already some good effects from the contemplation of her life and death. The young have received a warning, thoughtlessness a check. We have realized that neither youth nor beauty is a security against the ravages of the spoiler.

God grant that our dear pastor may experience the truth of the words of the Psalmist: "Those who sow in tears shall reap in joy." He feels that his treasure is laid up in heaven, and we know that his heart is there. To see his dear one happy had ever been his chief desire, and he would not call her back, for he knows that she is now in the enjoyment of a bliss that the world cannot give.

Though cast down, he is not destroyed; he has come unscathed from this furnace of affliction because one like the Son of God was with him. With eyes turned heavenward, he waits his appointed time. The religion of the cross glistens like a gem on his dark-robed fortunes, and points him to fairer worlds, where the love that grew here amidst clouds will be made perfect in a light that knows no shadow, where he and his departed ones will again have one home, one altar, and one resting place.

Like his Divine Master, he goes about doing good. Oftener than ever is he found amongst the sons and daughters of affliction; more than ever are they objects of his special care; his precept is blessed by his example, and thus many a prodigal son has he recalled from his wanderings, many an outcast gathered into the fold, many a wayworn pilgrim pointed to his true rest, many a mourner comforted. They saw that the resignation he preached to others he practised himself; they saw that the hand of the Lord was heavy upon him, but that yet he turned not backward; they saw that he went his way as a pilgrim pressing forward to a better country. Most brilliant will be the diadem which the Lord, the righteous Judge, shall give him in the last day, for are not these words of Holy Writ, "They who turn many to righteousness shall shine like the stars for ever and ever?"

OUTWARD MINISTERINGS

EACH owns some secret law;—the flowers that flourish
   Bloom in their season, in their season die;
Dews flow beneath, their feeble strength to nourish,
   The wind, Earth's angels, life's sweet breath supply.

As in the wondrous world of faultless Nature,
   So in the moral universe of man,
Given for the spirit's every form and feature,
   Are powers fulfilling its immortal plan.

Whether its aim be fixed on seeking Pleasure,
   Whilst draining deep her falsely-sparkling bowl,
Or in the light of Love be sought the treasure
   Whose worth may satisfy the craving soul;

Whether it court the applause of listening nations,
   And toil, with earnest energy, for fame,
Or seek with nobler hopes those elevations,
   Whence from its God with spotless robes it came:

All help to lead it on, to Truth or Error,
   Darkness or Light, as its own pathway lies;
Here, seeming seraphs, hidden shapes of terror,
   There, darksome shadows, angels in disguise.

Behold yon miser bend, with palsied fingers,
   O'er the rich gold around him glittering piled,
How, with a father's care, he tireless lingers
   By life's all-precious hope, his darling—child.

Fond wretch! his aim to narrow life is bounded,
   Yet, true to Nature, all for him hath proved;
The glorious gifts that once his path surrounded,
   Have served to strengthen feelings basely loved!

By glittering lights, behold yon splendid palace,
   See squalid youth and beauty enter there,
Eager to drown within the brimming chalice,
   All pangs of grief—all thoughts of woe or care.

Alas! for them, that such a sad fruition
  Should burst from seeds bright with the hues of Time;
These specious splendours fail not in their mission,
  But spur their spirits on the road to crime!

In yonder room, behold a beauteous maiden,
  Who bright the standard of her hope unrolls;
But, oh! that smiling bark, with evil laden,
  Leads on to fatal depths, or treacherous shoals!

Gaze on the gambler, pale with care and sorrow,
  And mark the dismal shades he long hath trod,
Who lives to witness each returning morrow,
  Sin-burdened, roll before an outraged God!

Seest thou the light from yonder casement streaming?
  Seest thou the shadow on the window cast?
There, lost in thought and poesy's wild dreaming,
  Waits one to hear Fame's loud but fickle blast.

This is his life's great aim; but what beyond it?
  Of Truth's bright treasure though he love to tell,
In barren mines of lore he hath not found it,
  Bowing beneath his idol's deadly spell.

But gaze on One, who seeks in all around him,
  Lessons of good to cheer him on his way,
As every golden year through life hath found him
  Nearer the realms of Heaven's eternal day.

With him events of earth are sweet evangels,
  All meaner things but step-stones hurled beneath;
Whilst nobler lead to Eden-realms of angels,
  With shining robes, and crown, and amaranth wreath.

Oh! fellow-pilgrims through this desert dreary,
  In all the scenes of life God's mercy trace,
Then though with grief cast down, with watching weary,
  Strong shall ye stand in His sufficient grace!

Thus sweet, melodious tones and forms of beauty,
  All glorious sights and sounds may ever prove
Angels to lure us on the path of duty,
  Echoes of symphonies that float above!

BODILY DEFORMITY, SPIRITUAL BEAUTY

WHO has not observed in passing through the crowded streets of our city, how great, comparatively, is the number of those, who are more or less deformed? My heart aches for these poor unfortunates, who are deprived of some of the legitimate avenues of enjoyment which God has so bounteously vouchsafed to me.

Here is one (and it would seem to me the most unmitigated of all the catalogue) who is groping his way along in darkness, holding fast by the hand of a little girl. There is another who has lost a limb, and makes his way along with the utmost difficulty. Yonder is one so extremely deformed, that his sensitiveness forbids him often to appear in the crowded streets. And there is another still, who is quite helpless, sitting in a little wagon drawn about by a faithful dog.

In the minds of different individuals, these various aspects of deformity produce pity, disgust, and horror; but I have often thought, could we but look, as God looks—down into the audience chamber of the spirit—the heart—how differently our minds would be affected at the sight of these bodily deformities. Perhaps yon poor blind man, grinding away upon his hand-organ, whose natural eyes for long, weary years, have been closed against the profusion of beauty around him, has had the eyes of his understanding opened, and the pure light from the eternal throne illumes the depth of his soul. Perhaps he, who hobbles slowly and sadly along upon his crutches, treads with care and unknown joy, the *narrow way*,—and when, life's journey's over, he walks through the valley of the shadow of death, he will fear no evil; for a rod and a staff unknown to his earthly pilgrimage, *they will comfort him*. Who shall say but he, whose deformity drives him from the public way, walks continually before God and Angels—a perfect man? It may be, that yon helpless one—*so* helpless that his mother feeds him—has power to move the arm that moves the world; for God hears prayer.

It is a most solemn truth that He who is the judge of quick and dead, looks not upon the *outer* man; but upon his inner, spiritual nature. With His judgment, it matters not, that a man be deformed; that his eyes be blind or his tongue be tied: is the heart all right?—has it become a sanctuary, meet for the spirit's residence and lighted by the Sun of Righteousness, where every word, thought, and deed, becomes an acceptable sacrifice to God? is it not disturbed by sin or blinded by passion? These are the things which have to do in the estimate which God puts upon every intelligent creature. Take good care then, my brother pilgrim, that the heart is all right—though the body which covers it for a little season is distorted and maimed.

THE DEAD CHILD

"Though our tears fell fast and faster,
  Yet we would not call her back;
We are glad her feet no longer
  Tread life's rough and thorny track.
We are glad our Heavenly Father
  Took her while her heart was pure;
We are glad He did not leave her,
  All life's troubles to endure.
We are glad—and yet the tear-drop
  Falleth, for, alas! we know
That our fireside will be lonely,
  We shall miss our darling so!"

HOW beautiful a young child in its shroud! Calm and heavenly looks the white face on which the blighting breath of sin never rested.

The silken curls parted from the marble brow—the once bright eyes closed—once red lips pale—little hands that have ofttimes been clasped as the lips repeated "Our Father," now meekly folded over the throbless heart, tell us that Death, cruel, relentless Death, has been there.

Surely, the *soul* that once beamed from those closed eyes is happy! Hath not the Saviour said, "Of such is the kingdom of heaven?" Robed like an angel is she now, a lamb in the Saviour's bosom. Could parental love ask more? Surely not. Cleansed from all earthly taint; secure from all trouble, care, or sin, those eyes will no more weep; but the tiny hands will sweep a golden harp, and the childish voice will be heard making music in heaven.

Often, O, how often had our hearts said, "God bless her!" And has not our prayer been answered? The yearnings of love cannot be stifled; for we miss the loving clasp of white arms—the soft pressure of fresh lips—the prattle and smile that were music and light to our world-weary hearts; our hand moves in vain for a resting-place on the golden head; yet we feel, we know that "it is well with the child," for we see how much of woe she has escaped; how much of bliss she has gained; a home with the sinless; the companionship of angels for ETERNITY. Blessed one!

Alone, yet fearlessly, didst thou pass through the "dark valley" and enter into the home prepared for thee. As fearlessly, trustingly may *we* meet the conqueror, Death, and when the conflict is ended, meet thee in thy new home to dwell for evermore!

WATER

GOD is the author of all our blessings. There is no truth, perhaps, to which we are more ready to give our assent than this; and yet, a great many people seem to act as if they did not believe it, or, at least, as if they were prone to forget it.

A traveller stopped at a fountain, and, letting the rein he held in his hand fall upon the neck of his horse, permitted the thirsty animal to drink of the cooling water that came pouring down from a rocky hill, and spread itself out in a basin below. While the weary beast refreshed himself, the traveller looked at the bright stream that sparkled in the sunlight, and said thus to himself:—

"What a blessing is water! How it refreshes, strengthens, and purifies! And how bountifully it is given! Everywhere flows this good gift of our Heavenly Father, and it is as free as the air to man and beast."

While he thus mused, a child came to the fountain. She had a vessel in her hand, and she stooped to fill it with water.

"Give me a drink, my good little girl," said the traveller.

And, with a smiling face, the child reached her pitcher to the man who still sat on his horse.

"Who made this water?" said the traveller, as he handed the vessel back to the child.

"God made it," was her quick reply.

"And do you know anything that water is like?" asked the traveller.

"Oh, yes! Father says that water is like truth."

"Does he?"

"Yes, sir. He says that water is like truth, because truth purifies the mind as water does the body."

"That is wisely said," returned the traveller. "And truth quenches our thirst for knowledge, as water quenches the thirst of our lips."

The little girl smiled as this was said, and, taking up her pitcher, went back to her home.

"Yes, water represents truth," said the traveller, as he rode thoughtfully away. "The child was right. It purifies and refreshes us, and is spread out, like truth, on every hand, free for those who will take it. Whenever I look upon water again, I will think of it as representing truth; and then I will remember that it is as important to the mind's health and purity to have truth as it is for the body to have water."

Thus, from a simple fountain, as it leaped out from the side of a hill, the traveller gained a lesson of wisdom. And so, as we pass through the world, we may find in almost every natural object that exists something that will turn our minds to higher and better thoughts. Every tree and flower, every green thing that grows, and every beast of the field and bird of the air, have in them a signification, if we could but learn it. They speak to us in a spiritual language, and figure forth to our natural senses the higher, more beautiful, and more enduring things of the mind.

BEAUTIFUL, HAPPY, AND BELOVED

WOULDST thou be beautiful?
Ah, then, be pure! be pure! An angel's face
  Is the transparent mirror of her soul.
If ghastly guilt on fairest brows you trace,
  Then do you hear the knell of beauty toll.
Let Purity her seal on thee impress,
  And thine shall be angelic loveliness.
    The pure are beautiful.

Wouldst thou be dearly loved?
Then love, love truly all that God has made;
  For by His name of love is He best known.
No damp distrust be on thy spirit laid;
  And let affection's words and deeds be one.
Thy soul's warm fountain shall not gush in vain;
  From Love's deep source it shall be filled again;
    For they who love, are loved.

And wouldst thou happy be?
Then make the truth thy talisman, thy guide.
  Be truth the stone in all thy jewels set.
Into thy heart its opal-light shall glide,
  And guide thee where are happier spirits yet.
For these three rays are in the shining crown:
  The seraph by the Throne of Light lays down,
    Truth, Love, and Purity.

"EVERY CLOUD HAS A SILVER LINING"

WHAT! can this be true in this dark world of ours, where the thick clouds of sorrow, disappointed hopes, and bereavements are continually hanging over us, obscuring even the bright star of hope; where upon every passing breeze is borne deep wailings of woe, bitter sighs ascending from bruised and broken hearts mourning over lost hopes, crushed affections, wasted love; struggling vainly for victory in the fierce battle of life; groping about in darkness to catch, if possible, one gleam of sunlight from the heavy clouds—but in vain?

"Ashes to ashes, dust to dust." Another shrine robbed of its idol; another hearth left desolate. See, how the black clouds settle down and press more closely around that lonely widowed one. Grim Death mocks at his grief from the open grave, so soon to receive his heart's idol. Ay, remove the coffin lid; gaze with all the agonizing bitterness of a *last* look upon that cold marble face; was aught on earth so lovely? Kiss for the last time the pure forehead. Ah! those pale white lips give back no answering pressure of love; sealed for ever by that last chilling blast from the cold river.

And now the damp earth presses heavily over that cherished form; far down in the darkness and silence of the grave must the loved one remain, never more to cheer by her gentle words of love and kindness, the heart of him who so needed her sympathy and love. Gone, gone for ever.

What on earth is now beautiful or bright since the dearest, best treasure is removed? Oh, no! there can be no bright spot in affliction like this; there can be no bright ray to gild this night of sorrow.

Ah! thou erring mortal, repine not. The all-wise Father knew thy frail heart, saw thy whole life and soul bound up in that one creature, weak and sinful like thyself; forgetful of the Creator; and wilt thou dare raise thy feeble voice against the Almighty when He removed the idol that He alone may reign? Wilt thou not bow meekly, kiss the rod, and accept the bitter cup of bereavement, offered as it is in mercy?

And is this all? Is there no life beyond the grave? Is the spirit which held such communion with thine for ever quenched?

Can the grave contain for ever the immortal part? Look up, oh! mourning one; thy loved one is not there.

Hark! hearest thou not soft, heavenly voices, whispering sweetly of a life beyond the dark river, where Death can never come; of glorious mansions where is peace and joy for ever more, and of another freed spirit welcomed to the blissful home? Dost thou not feel upon thy tear-moistened cheek, gentle wavings of angel wings perfumed with the breath of heavenly flowers?

Even now, may the happy glorified spirit of thy loved one be hovering around; think you it would return again to that perishing body of clay?

The sweet star of faith is already rising over thy grief; the clouds, all bright and shining with hues caught from heavenly skies, are no longer dark and rayless; and now, even with thy lonely bleeding heart, canst thou humbly receive the chastisement from Him who doeth all things well.

Henceforth will earth seem less dear, heaven nearer, and more to be desired; thy own cherished companion is there, and who can know but that her pure spirit may sometimes look down upon thee, still to encourage thy endeavours to battle manfully with life and its trials, still to cheer and console in thy hours of distress; but now, with heart and affections all purified from the dross of earth, will not the influence be more blessed than when she walked with bodily presence at thy side?

Yes, thanks to our merciful Father, every cloud *has* a silver lining, however dark the side presented to our view, ladened heavy though it be with sorrows and woes, which almost crush the life from our hearts as it presses upon us; yet there away, hidden from our short mortal vision, gleams the soft silvery lining, ever gently shining, perhaps never to be revealed in this world, reserved for us to discover after we too have been called from this to our heavenly home, and look back upon our earthly pilgrimage with rejoicings that we have been so safely borne through every trial and temptation.

Ah! then will our sky be without a cloud. All joyous and happy will we tune our harps anew to the praise of Him who loved us and hath given us the victory!

AN ANGEL OF PATIENCE

BESIDE the toilsome way,
Lowly and sad, by fruits and flowers unblest,
Which my lone feet tread sadly, day by day,
Longing in vain for rest,

An angel softly walks,
With pale, sweet face, and eyes cast meekly down,
The while from withered leaves and flowerless stalks
She weaves my fitting crown.

A sweet and patient grace,
A look of firm endurance true and tried,
Of suffering meekly borne, rests on her face,
So pure—so glorified.

And when my fainting heart
Desponds and murmurs at its adverse fate,
Then quietly the angel's bright lips part,
Murmuring softly, "Wait!"

"Patience!" she meekly saith—
"Thy Father's mercies never come too late;
Gird thee with patient strength and trusting faith,
And firm endurance wait!"

THE GRANDFATHER'S ADVICE

IT was a golden sunset, which was fondly gazed upon by an old man on whose broad brow the history of seventy winters had been written. He sat in the wide porch of a large old-fashioned house: his look was calm and clear, though years had quelled the fire of his eagle glance; his silver hair was borne mildly back, by the south wind of August, and a smile of sweetness played over his features, breathing the music of contentment. His heart was still fresh, and his mind open to receive an impress of the loveliness of earth. The dew of love for his fellow-creatures fell upon his aged soul, and pure adoration went up to the Giver of every good from its altar. He lifted his gaze to the cerulean blue above him, and dwelt upon his future, with a glow of hope upon his heart—then he turned to the past, and his beaming expression gradually mellowed into pensiveness: in thought, he travelled through the long vista of years which he had left behind him, and his mental exclamation was,

"There has not been a year of my life since manhood, that I might not have lived to a better purpose. I might have been more useful and devoted to my race. I might more fully have sacrificed the idol self, which so often I have knelt to, in worship more heartfelt than I offered the Divinity. Yet have I laboured to become pure in thy sight, oh, my God! build thy kingdom in my breast!"

A tear trembled in the aged suppliant's eye, and the calm of holy humility stole over him; the gentle look was again upon his countenance, when a young man of about twenty years, swung open the gate leading to the house, and, approaching, saluted the old man with a cordial grasp of the hand; flinging his cap carelessly down, he took a seat in a rustic chair, and exclaimed with a smile of mingled affection and reverence, which broke over his thoughtful features, making him extremely handsome,

"Well, grandfather, I believe you complete seventy years to-day!"

"Yes, my son, and I have been looking back upon them. I do not usually dwell upon the past with repining, yet I see much that might have been better. My years have not always been improved."

The young man listened respectfully; presently he asked, with sudden interest, "Pray tell me, if there ever was a whole year of your life, so perfectly happy that you would wish to live it all over again?"

"I have been perfectly happy at brief intervals," was the reply, "yet there is not a year of my long life, that I would choose to have return. I have been surrounded by many warm friends now gone to their homes in the spirit-world,—I have loved, and have been loved, and the recollection yet thrills me; still I thank God that I am not to live over those years upon earth. I have struggled much for truth and goodness, and there has not been one struggle which I would renew, though each has been followed by a deep satisfaction."

"To me, your life appears to have been dreary, grandfather," replied his companion. "I ask for happiness!" After a pause, he added with impetuosity, "If I am not to meet with the ardent happiness I dream of, and desire, I do not care to live. What is the life which thousands lead, worth? Nothing! I cannot sail monotonously down the stream—the more I *think*, and thought devours me, the more discontented do I become with everything I see. Why is an overpowering desire for happiness planted within the human breast, if it is so very rarely to be gratified? My childhood was sometimes gay, but as often, it was clouded by disappointments which are great to children. I have never seen even the moment, since I have been old enough to reflect, when I could say that I was as happy as I was capable of being. I have even felt the consciousness that my soul's depths were not filled to the brim with joy. I could always ask for more. In my happiest hours, the eager question rushes upon me, involuntarily, 'Am I entirely content?' And the response that rises up, is ever 'No.' I am young, and this soft air steals over a brow of health—I can appreciate the beautiful and exquisite. I can drink in the deep poetry of noble minds—I can idly revel in voluptuous music, and dream away my soul, but with that bewitching dream, there is still a yearning for its realization. I cannot abate the restlessness that presses upon me—I look around, and young faces are bright and smiling with cheerful gayety. I endeavour to catch the buoyant spirit, but I succeed rarely,—if I do, it floats on the surface, leaving the under-current unbroken in its flow. Yet after I have endeavoured to lighten the oppressive cares of some unfortunate creature, a sort of peace has for a time descended upon me, which has been infinitely soothing. It soon departs, and my usual bitterness again sways me. I sought for friendship, and for awhile I was relieved, but I cannot forbear glancing down into the motives of my fellow men, and that involuntarily-searching spirit has proved unfortunate to me. I met with selfishness in the form of attachment, and then I turned to look upon the hollow heart of society, and it was there."

"Alfred, you make me sad," said the old man, in a solemn and deeply pained voice. "This is the first time I knew that your heart was such a temple of bitterness."

"If I have saddened you, I wish I had not spoken: but the thoughts rushed over me, your kind heart is always open, and I gave them expression. You have lived long, and there is more sympathy in your experience, than in the laughing jest of those near my own age. Pardon me, grandfather, I will not pain you again!" Alfred turned his eyes upon his aged friend; he caught the look of kindness upon that honoured face, and it fell warmly, upon his soul.

"It is right to think deeply," said the revered adviser, "but one must think rightly, also. You must not look out upon the world, from the darkened corners of your soul, or the hue is transferred to all things which your glance falls upon. Take the torch of truth and heavenly charity to chase away the dimness within you, then powerful changes will be wrought in your vision. You will begin to regard your fellow man with new feelings of interest. I am a plain and blunt old man, Alfred, but you know that my only desire is for your good; so bear with my remarks if they be unpalatable."

"Certainly, sir, I value frankness before flattery."

"You may say that you have never been *perfectly* happy," continued the old gentleman; "that is neither strange nor uncommon, for I have met with few thoughtful persons of your years, who, upon close reflection, could say that their souls could desire no more than had been granted to them. You must seek for resignation, not entire bliss upon earth, although it is possible that you may enjoy it for a season."

"Why is joy so transitory and unquiet so lasting?" demanded the young man impatiently.

"The fault is not in the transitoriness of the joy, but in the very soul itself,—it is in a state of disorder; its nature must be changed before it can receive for ever only the image of gladness. In a chaos of the elements, can a smiling sky be always seen? Lay asleep all unruly elements in the spirit, and a pure heaven of brightness will then greet the uplifted glance."

"But how can all this be done, grandfather? hath unruly elements do you speak of? What can I do; for instance? I certainly am willing and glad to see my kind happy—if my soul be in disorder, I do not know in what it consists, or how to bring it to order. I am weary of its unsatisfied desires; it is, continually in search of something which it has never caught sight of,—and the fear, that that unknown, yet powerfully desired something may never come to quench my thirst, falls with the coldness of death upon my bosom."

"That something may be found by every human being, if sought for in the right way. Those yearnings are not given us, that they may fall back and wither the fountain from which they spring. But the question is, do we seek for happiness in the right way? Do we not rather ask for an impossibility, when we ask for permanent bliss, before we have laid a foundation in our souls for it? You wish to take this life too easy by far, my son; rouse up all your strength, look around you with the keenness of a resolved spirit, and seek to regenerate your whole being,—let that be your object, and let the desire for happiness be subservient to it. You will clasp joy to your breast, as an everlasting gift, at the end of the race. What are your aims and objects? You hardly know; you are in pursuit of that which flees, before you as a shadow, and your restless spirit sinks and murmurs,—you have no grand object in view, to buoy you up steadily and trustfully through every ill which life has power to bestow. Those very ills are seized upon, and become instruments of glory to the devoted and heaven-strengthened spirit,—they prepare for a deeper draught of all things dear and desired, and though the soul droop beneath the weight of human suffering, yet the rod that smites is kissed with a prayer. Turn away from your individual self, as far as you can, and regard the broad world with a philanthropic eye—"

"Impossible—impossible!" interrupted Alfred, hastily, "I defy any person to turn from himself, and look upon the world with a more interested gaze than he casts upon his own heart. One may be philanthropic in his feelings and devoted to alleviating the distresses of less fortunate beings, but I hold it to be impossible that our individual selves will not always be first in interest. A sudden and powerful impulse may carry us away for a time, but after that rushing influence leaves us, we see yourselves again, and, find that we had only lost our equilibrium briefly. I say only what I sincerely think, and what thousands secretly know to be the case, even while advocating views quite opposite. There is no candour in the world!"

"Softly, my good friend," said the grandfather, mildly smiling. "I also hold it to be impossible that we can lose either our individuality or our interest in ourselves, but I believe it possible that we may love others just as well, if not better than ourselves. I do not refer to one or two particular persons whom we may admire, but I speak of the mass of our fellow-creatures."

"I cannot even conceive of such a love!" returned the young man, shaking his head. "I cannot see how I could love a person who possesses no attractive qualities whatever;—I always feel indifference, if not dislike. I think I could sacrifice my life to one I loved, if thrown into sudden and imminent danger; still, I think I might give pain to that same person many times, by gratifying myself. For instance, grandfather,—suppose you were to be led to the stake, to be burned to-morrow,—I would take your place to save you; yet I do not now do all I possible can, to add to your happiness. I gratify whims of my own; I idle away hours in the woods, or by some stream, when I fully know that it would be more pleasing to you, to see me bending patiently over my Greek and Latin."

"Very true!" sighed the old man. "You prove your own position, which is that your ruling love is self-love."

Alfred lifted up his eyebrows, as if he had heard an unwelcome fact. We are often willing to confess things, which we do not like to have old us. He fell into deep thought. Finally he said, "It is universally allowed that virtue is lovely; those who practise it, appear calm and resigned, and often happy—but, to tell the truth, such enjoyment seems rather tame and flat. I wish to be in freedom, to let my burning impulses rush on as they will, without a yoke. I love, and I hate, as my heart bids me, and I scorn control of any kind."

"Yet you submit to a yoke, my son; one which is not of your own imposing either."

"What kind of a yoke?"

"The yoke of society,—you bow to public opinion in a measure. You avoid a glaring act, often, more because it will not be *approved*, than because you have a real disinclination for it. Is not that the case sometimes?"

Alfred did not exceedingly relish this probing, but he was too candid to cover up his motives from himself. He answered a decided "yes!" but it was spoken, because he could not elbow himself out of the self-evident conviction forced upon him.

"Do you think it degrading for a man to conquer and govern the strongest, as well as the weakest impulses of his soul?" pursued his grandfather.

"Certainly not degrading,—it is in the highest degree worthy of praise. It is truly noble! I acknowledge it."

"And yet you deem such enjoyment as would result from this government, tame and flat."

"I beg pardon; when I spoke of virtue, I referred to that smooth kind which is current, and seems more passive than active,—that soft amiability which appears to deaden enthusiasm, and to shut up the soul in a set of opinions, instead of expanding it widely to everything noble and generous, wherever it may be found."

"It was not genuine virtue, you referred to, then,—it was only its resemblance."

"It was what passes for virtue. But to come at the main point, grandfather;—where is happiness to be found, if we are to be warring with ourselves during a lifetime, checking every natural spring in the soul?"

"Stop there, Alfred! We only quench the streams, which prevent the spirit's purest wells of noble and happy feelings from gushing forth in freedom. We must wage a warfare, it is true; why conceal it? But it does not last for ever, and intervals of gladness come to refresh us, which the worn and blunted spirit of the man of pleasure in vain pants for. An exquisite joy, innocent as that of childhood, pervades the bosom of truth's soldier in his hours of peace and rest, and he lifts an eye of rapture to heaven—to God."

Alfred dwelt earnestly upon the noble countenance of the speaker, and his bosom filled with unwonted emotion, as the heavenly sweetness of the old man's smile penetrated into his inward soul. Goodness stood before him in its wonderful power, and he bowed down his soul in worship. How insignificant then seemed his individual yearnings after present enjoyment, instead of that celestial love which can fill a human soul with so strong a power from on high. He reflected upon that venerable being's life—so strong and upright; he dwelt upon his large and noble heart, which could clasp the world in its embrace. He remembered months of acute suffering, both physical and mental, which had been endured with the stillness of a martyr's inward strength; and then, too, he recalled times when that aged heart was more truly and deeply joyful than his own young spirit had even been. Both relapsed into the eloquent silence of absorbing thought. It was evident from the softened and meditative cast of Alfred's features, that his bitterness had given way to the true tenderness of feeling it so often quelled; he revolved in his mind all that had been advanced by his grandfather, and he dwelt upon every point with candour and serious reflection. A strong impression was made upon him, but he was entirely silent in regard to it,—he waited to try his strength, before he spoke of the better resolutions that were formed, not without effort, in his mind. He felt a conviction that a change from selfishness to angelic charity might be accomplished, if he were but willing to co-operate with his Maker,—the conception of universal love slowly dawned upon his soul, now turned heavenward for light,— his duties as a responsible being came before him, and a sigh of reproach was given to the past. Then golden visions of delight thronged up to his gaze, and it was with a severe pang he thought of losing his, hold upon the dear domains of idle fancy,—he had so revelled for hours and hours, in intoxicating dreams, which shut out the world and stern duty. He felt his weakness, but he resolutely turned from dwelling upon it. The evening air was refreshing after the warm sunset, but old Mr. Monmouth would not trust himself to bear it. Alfred went into the house with him, and made a brief call, then left, and wended his way a short distance to his own home, which was a very elegant mansion, surrounded by every mark of luxury and taste. He immediately sought his chamber, and took up a neglected Bible which his mother had given him when a child,—he turned over its leaves, and his eyes fell upon the one hundred and nineteenth psalm, "Thy word is a lamp unto my feet, and a light upon my path. I have sworn, and I will perform it, that I will keep thy righteous judgments." He read on, and the exceeding beauty and touching power of the Holy Word had never so deeply affected him,—he wept, and all that was harsh in his nature melted,— he prayed, and the angels of God approached, filling his uplifted soul with heavenly strength. Sweet was the thrill of thanksgiving, that arose from that hitherto restless spirit—quiet and blest the peace that hushed him to deep, invigorating slumber. Persons of an enthusiastic temperament are apt to fall into extremes; such was the case with Alfred Monmouth. He so feared that he would fall back into his former states of feeling, that he guarded himself like an anchorite. For three months he abstained from going into company, and even reasonable enjoyment he deprived himself of. He threw aside all books but scientific and religious ones; even poetry he shut his ears against, lest it might beguile him again to his dreamy, but selfish musings. No doubt this severe discipline was very useful to him at the time, in strengthening him against the besetting faults of his character; but it could not last long, without originating other errors. During this time he had been, perhaps, as happy as ever in his life; his mind had been fixed upon an object, and a wealth of new thoughts had crowded upon him—he rejoiced with a kind of proud humility in his capability for self-government. He thought he was rapidly verging towards perfection. But "a change came o'er the spirit of his dream" at last, and an unwonted melancholy grew upon him, until it settled like a pall over his heart. An apathy in regard to what had so lately interested him, stole over him, and indeed a cold glance fell upon almost every pursuit he had once prized. Plunged in deep gloom, he one evening sought his grandfather's dwelling, hoping, by a conversation with the cheerful old man, to regain a more healthy state of mind; to his great satisfaction, Alfred found him alone reading.

"Well, my boy, I am glad you have come in!" was the salutation, with a most cordial smile, for Mr. Monmouth had silently remarked the late alteration in his somewhat reckless grandson. He also detected the present gloom upon his fine countenance, and the earnest hope of dispelling it, added an affectionate heartiness to his manner. Alfred made several common-place remarks, then, with his usual impatience, he flung aside all preamble, and said,

"I am gloomy, grandfather, even more so than I have ever been, and I cannot explain it. The last serious conversation I had with you, produced a strong effect upon me, and for a long time after I was unusually cheerful and vigorous in mind. I seemed to have imbibed something of your spirit—I delighted in the hope of regenerating myself, through the aid of Heaven; it seemed as if angels hushed my restless spirit to repose, and I tried in humility to draw near my God. Yet I feared for myself, and I withdrew from temptation, from all society which was uncongenial to my state of mind. I was *content* for a long time, but now the sadness of apathy overwhelms me."

"Endeavour, without murmuring, to bear this state of mind, and it will soon pass off," remarked Mr. Monmouth. "We must not always fly from temptation in every form, my boy, but we must arm ourselves against its attacks, otherwise our usefulness will be greatly lessened. If those who are endeavouring to make themselves better, do so by shunning society, they are rather examples of selfishness than benevolent goodness,—the selfishness is unconscious, and such a course may be followed from a sense of duty. But the glance which discovered this to be duty was not wide enough; it took in only the claims of self, yet I would not convey the idea, that we have any one's evils to take care of but our own. We need society, and, however humble we may be, society needs us. We need to be refreshed by the strength of good beings, and we must also contribute our slight share to those whom Providence wills that we may benefit. The life of heaven may thus circulate freely, and increase in power among many hearts. Go forward, Alfred, unmindful of your feelings, and pray only to trust in Providence, and to gain a deep desire for usefulness."

"Ah! yes," returned the young man, earnestly. Light broke in upon his darkness. "I am glad that I have spoken with you, grandfather, for your words give me strength to persevere. I never knew that I was weak until lately."

"Such knowledge is precious, my dear son. We are indeed strongest when the hand of humility removes the veil that hides us from ourselves."

"Probably such is, the case, but I cannot realize it. It is with effort that I drag through the day; I am continually looking towards the future, and beholding a thousand perplexing situations where my besetting sins will be called into action. I see myself incapable of always following out the noble principles I have lately adopted."

"As thy day is, so shall thy strength be!" said Mr. Monmouth. "Be careful only to guard yourself against each little stumbling-block as it presents itself, and your mountains will be changed to mole-hills. Never fear for the future, do as well as you can in the present."

"But it is so singular that I should feel thus, when I have been trying as hard as a mortal could to change my erroneous views, and to regard all the dispensations of Providence with a resigned heart. I have cast the selfish thought of my own earthly happiness from my mind as much as possible."

"And yet there is a repining in your gloominess. You are not satisfied to bear it."

"Well, perhaps not. I am wrong,—I think that I could submit with true fortitude to an outward trial, but there seems so little reason in my low spirits. Have you ever felt so, grandfather?"

"Often; and at such times, I devote myself more earnestly than ever to anything which will take my thoughts from myself."

"I will do so!" replied Alfred, firmly. "If my purposes are right in the sight of Heaven, I will be supported."

"True, my son."

Alfred left the home of his grandsire, more at rest with himself and all the world. Fresh peaceful hopes again sprang up within him, and he began to see his way clear. He reasoned himself into resignation, and, as day after day went on, he grew grateful for the privilege and opportunity offered to school his rebellious spirit to order.

Four years passed; Alfred was engaged in the busy world, and he shrunk not from it, but rather sought to do his duty in it. One summer evening, he was called to enter the large, old-fashioned house of his grandfather. His brow was thoughtful, but calm and resigned—he sought a quiet room; it was the chamber of death,—yet was its stillness beautiful and peaceful; he knelt by a dying couch, and clasped the hand of his aged grandsire—then he wept, but the unbidden tears were those of gratitude. The serenity of heaven was upon the countenance of the noble old man.

"My hour has come, Alfred," he said, placing one hand upon the beloved head bowed before him, "and I go hence with thankfulness. Ah! even now, there is a heavenly content in my bosom. The angels are bending over me, and wait to take my spirit to its home: there is no mist before my sight, all is clear. The Father of love lifts up my soul in this hour—our parting will be short, my son—" the old man's voice trembled, an infinite tenderness dwelt in his eyes, and Alfred felt that there was a reality in the peace of the dying one. All the good that he had done him rushed before him, and he exclaimed with humility,

"How can I ever repay you, dear grandfather! for all your noble lessons to me?"

"I am repaid," was (sic) the the low reply; "they have brought forth fruit, and I have lived to see it. I trust that you will leave the world with all the peace that I do, and with deeper goodness in your spirit. My blessing be upon you, my son!"

"Amen!" came low from Alfred's fervent lips.

The eyes of the aged one closed in death, and his young disciple went forth again into the world, made better by the scene he had witnessed.

A HYMN OF PRAISE

I BLESS Thee for the sunshine on the hills,
    For Heaven's own dewdrops in the vales below,
For rain, the parent cloud alike distils,
    On the fond bridegroom's joy—the mourner's woe!
And for the viewless wind, that gently blows
    Where'er it listeth, over field and flood,
Whence coming, whither going, no man knows,
    Yet moved in secret at Thy will, Oh, God!
E'en now it lifts a ring of shining hair
    From off the brow close to my bosom pressed—
The loving angels scarce have brows more fair
    Than this, that looks so peaceful in its rest:—
We bless Thee, Father, for our darling child,
Oh, like Thine angels make her, innocent and mild!

I rise and bless Thee, for the morning hours;
    Refreshed and gladdened by a timely rest,
When thoughts like bees, rove out among the flowers,
    Still gathering honey where they find the best:
And for the gentle influence of the night,
    Oh, Heavenly Father! do we bend the knee,
That shuts the curtains of our mortal sight,
    Yet leaves the mind, with range and vision free,
For dreams! the solemn, weird, and strange that come
    And bear the soul to an elysian clime,—
Unveiling splendours of that better home,
    Where angels minister to sons of time!
For all Thy blessings that with sleep descend,
Our hearts shall praise Thee, God, our Father and our Friend!

AN ANGEL IN EVERY HOUSE

IT is a trite saying, and an unique one, that there is "a skeleton in every house." That every form however erect, that every face however smiling, covers some secret malady of mind that no physician can cure. This may be true, and undoubtedly is; but we contend that, as everything has its opposite, there is also an *angel* in every house. No matter how fallen the inmates, how depressing their circumstances, there is an angel there to pity or to cheer. It may be in the presence of a wrinkled body, treading the downward path to the grave. Or, perhaps, in a cheerful spirit looking upon the ills of life as so many steps toward heaven, if only bravely overcome, and mounted with sinless feet.

We knew such an angel once, and it was a drunkard's child. On every side wherever she moved she saw only misery and degradation, and yet she did not fall. Her father was brutal, and her mother discouraged, and her home thoroughly comfortless. But she struggled along with angel endurance, bearing with an almost saintly patience the infirmities of him who gave her existence, and then hourly embittered it. Night after night, at the hours of ten, twelve, and even one, barefoot, ragged, shawlless, and bonnetless, has she been to the den of the drunkard, and gone staggering home with her arm around her father. Many a time has her flesh been blue with the mark of his hand when she has stepped in between her helpless mother and violence. Many a time has she sat upon the cold curbstone with his head in her lap; many a time known how bitter it was to cry for hunger, when the money that should have bought bread was spent for rum.

And the patience that the angel wrought with made her young face shine, so that, though never acknowledged in the courts of this world, in the kingdom of heaven she was waited for by assembled hosts of spirits, and the crown of martyrdom ready, lay waiting for her young brow.

And she was a martyr. Her gentle spirit went up from at couch of anguish—anguish brought on by ill-usage and neglect. And never till then did the father recognise the angel in the child; never till then did his manhood arise from the dust of its dishonour. From her humble grave, he went away to steep his resolves for the better in bitter tears; and he will tell you to-day, how the memory of her much-enduring life keeps him from the bowl: how he goes sometimes and stands where her patient hands have held him, while her cheek crimsoned at the sneers of those who scoffed at the drunkard's child.

Search for the angels in your households, and cherish them while they are among you. It may be that all unconsciously you frown upon them, when a smile would lead you to a knowledge of their exceeding worth. They may be among the least cared for, most despised; but when they are gone with their silent influence, then will you mourn for them as for a jewel of great worth.

ANNIE

THE grave is Heaven's gate, they say;
And when dear Annie passed away,
   One calm June morning,
I saw upon the heavenly stairs,
A band of angels, unawares,
   Her path adorning.

The grave is Heaven's gate, they say;
And when dear Annie passed away,
   A music flowing
Filled my sad soul with love and light,
That made me seem, by day and night,
   To Heaven going.

The grave is Heaven's gate, they say;
And when dear Annie passed away,
   A saintly whiteness
O'erspread the beauty of her face,
And filled it with the tender grace
   Of angel brightness.

The grave is Heaven's gate, they say;
And when dear Annie passed away,
   An angel splendid
Cast his large glories to the ground,
While waves of throbbing music-sound
   In sweetness blended.

The grave is Heaven's gate, they say;
And when dear Annie passed away,
   In holy sweetness—
When life's sad dream with her was o'er,
Her white soul stood at Heaven's door,
   In its completeness.

MOTHER

WHEN she changed worlds, and before the time, what was she to others? A small old, delicate woman. *What was she to us?* A radiant, smiling angel, upon whose brow the sunshine of the eternal world had fallen. We looked into her large, tender eyes, and saw not as others did, that her mortal garment had waxed old and feeble; or if we saw, this, it was no symbol of decay, for beyond and within, we recognised *her* in all her beauty. Oh! how heavy and bitter would have been her long and slow decline, if we had seen her grow old instead of young! The days that hastened to give her birth into eternity, grow brighter and brighter, until when memory wandered back, it had no experiences so sweet as those through which she was passing. The long life, with its youthful romance, its prosaic cares, its quiet sunshine, and deep tragedies, was culminating to its earthly close; and, like some blessed story that appeals to the heart in its great pathos, the end was drawing, near, all clouds were rolling away, and she was stepping forth into the brilliance of prosperity. Selfishness ceased to weep under the light of her cheerful glance, and grew to be congratulation. Beside her couch we sat, and traced with loving fancy the new life soon to open before her; with tears and smiles we traced it. Doubts never mingled, for from earliest childhood we had no memories of her inconsistent with the expectations of a Christian. Deep in our souls there lay gratitude that her morning drew near; beautiful and amazing it seemed that she would never more bow to the stroke of the chastener; fresh courage descended from on high, as we realized that there was an end to suffering; it was difficult to credit that her discipline was nearly over; how brief it had been, compared with the glorious existence it had won her. How passing sweet were her assurances that she should leave us awhile longer on earth with childlike trust, knowing that our own souls needed to stay, and that the destiny of others needed it! But the future seemed very near to her, and she saw us gathered around her in her everlasting home. She grew weaker, and said her last words to us. Throughout the last day she said but little, but often her tender eyes were riveted upon us; they said "Farewell! farewell!" In the hush of the chamber, a faint, eolian-like strain came from her dying lips; it sounded as if it came from afar; *then* the angels were taking her to their companionship. She softly fell asleep, resigning her worn-out body to us, and *she* entered heaven. Ah! do we apprehend what a glorious event it is for the "pure in heart" to die? We look upon the bride's beauty, and see in the vista before her, anguish and tears, and but transient sunshine. The beauty fades, the splendour of life declines to the worldly eyes that gaze upon her. Deaf and blind are such gazers, for the bride may daily be winning imperishable beauty, yet it is not for this world. A most sad and melancholy thing it seems when children of a larger growth judge their parents by their frail and decaying bodies, rather than by their spirits. And more deeply sad still is it, when the aged learn through the young to feel that the freshness of existence has gone by with them. Gone by? when they are waiting to be born into a new and vast existence that shall roll on in increasing majesty, and never reach an end! Gone by? when they have just entered life, as it were! The glory and sweetness of living is *going by* only with those who are turning away their faces from the Prince of Peace. Sweet mother! she is breathing vernal airs now, and with every breath a spring-like life and joy are wafted through her being. Mother beautiful and beloved! some sweet, embryo joy fills the chambers of my heart as I contemplate the scenes with which she is becoming familiar. Dead and dreary winter robes the earth, and autumn leaves lie under the snow like past hopes; but what of them? I see only the smile of God's sunshine. I see in the advancing future, love and peace—only infinite peace!

GREAT PRINCIPLES AND SMALL DUTIES

IT is observable that the trivial services of social life are best performed, and the lesser particles of domestic happiness are most skilfully organized, by the deepest and the fairest heart. It is an error to suppose that homely minds are the best administrators of small duties. Who does not know how wretched a contradiction such a rule receives in the moral economy of many a home? how often the daily troubles, the swarm of blessed cares, the innumerable minutiae of arrangement in a family, prove quite too much for the generalship of feeble minds, and even the clever selfishness of strong ones; how a petty and scrupulous anxiety in defending with infinite perseverance some small and almost invisible point of frugality, and comfort, surrenders the greater unobserved, and while saving money, ruins minds; how, on the other hand, a rough and unmellowed sagacity *rules* indeed, and without defeat, but while maintaining in action the mechanism of government, creates a constant and intolerable friction, a gathering together of reluctant wills, a groaning under the consciousness of force, that make the movements of life fret and chafe incessantly? But where, in the presiding genius of a home, taste and sympathy unite (and in their genuine forms they cannot be separated)—the intelligent feeling for moral beauty, and the deep heart of domestic love,—with, what ease, what mastery, what graceful disposition, do the seeming trivialities of life fall into order, and drop a blessing as they take their place! how do the hours steal away, unnoticed but by the precious fruits they leave! and by the self-renunciation of affection, there comes a spontaneous adjustment of various wills; and not an innocent pleasure is lost, not a pure taste offended, nor a peculiar temper unconsidered; and every day has its silent achievements of wisdom, and every night its retrospect of piety and love; and the tranquil thoughts, that in the evening meditation come down with the starlight, seem like the serenade of angels, bringing in melody the peace of God! Wherever this picture is realized, it is not by microscopic solicitude of spirit, but by comprehension of mind, and enlargement of heart; by that breadth and nicety of moral view which discerns everything in due proportion, and in avoiding an intense elaboration of trifles, has energy to spare for what is great; in short, by a perception akin to that of God, whose providing frugality is on an infinite scale, vigilant alike in heaven and on, earth; whose art colours a universe with beauty and touches with its pencil the petals of a flower. A soul thus pure and large disowns the paltry rules of dignity, the silly notions of great and mean, by which fashion distorts God's real proportions; is utterly delivered from the spirit of contempt; and, in consulting for the benign administration of life, will learn many a truth, and discharge many ant office, from which lesser beings, esteeming themselves greater, would shrink from as ignoble. But in truth, nothing is degrading which a high and graceful purpose ennobles; and offices the most menial cease to be menial, the moment they are wrought in love. What thousand services are rendered, ay, and by delicate hands, around the bed of sickness, which, else considered mean, become at once holy and quite inalienable rights! To smooth the pillow, to proffer the draught, to soothe or obey the fancies of the delirious will, to sit for hours as the mere sentinel of the feverish sleep; these things are suddenly erected, by their relation to hope and life, into sacred privileges. And experience is perpetually bringing occasions, similar in kind, though of less persuasive poignancy, when a true eye and a lovely heart will quickly see the relations of things thrown into a new position, and calling for a sacrifice of conventional order to the higher laws of the affections; and alike without condescension and without ostentation, will noiselessly take the post of service and do the kindly deed. Thus it is that the lesser graces display themselves most richly, like the leaves and flowers of life, where there is the deepest and the widest root of love; not like the staring and artificial blossoms of dry custom that, winter or summer, cannot change; but living petals woven in Nature's workshop and folded by her tender skill, opening and shutting morning and night, glancing and trembling in the sunshine and in the breeze. This easy capacity of great affections for small duties is the peculiar triumph of the highest spirit of love.

"OF SUCH IS THE KINGDOM OF HEAVEN"

How quietly she lies!
Closed are the lustrous eyes,
Whose fringed lids, so meek,
Rest on the placid cheek;
While, round the forehead fair,
Twines the light golden hair,
Clinging with wondrous grace
Unto the cherub face.
Tread softly near her, dear ones! Let her sleep,—
I would not have my darling wake to weep.

Mark how her head doth rest
Upon her snowy breast,
While, 'neath the shadow of a drooping curl,
One little shoulder nestles like a pearl,
And the small waxen fingers, careless, clasp
White odorous flowers in their tiny grasp;
Blossoms most sweet
Crown her pure brow, and cluster o'er her feet,
Sure earth hath never known a thing more fair
Than she who gently, calmly, slumbers there.

Alas! 'tis Death, not sleep,
That girds her in its frozen slumbers deep.
No balmy breath comes forth
From the slight-parted mouth;
Nor heaves the little breast,
In its unyielding rest;
Dead fingers clasp
Flowers in unconscious grasp;—
Woe, woe is me, oh! lone, bereaved mother!
'Tis Death that hath my treasure, and none other.

No more I hear the voice,
Those loving accents made my heart rejoice;
No more within my arms
Fold I her rosy charms.

And, gazing down into the liquid splendour
Of the brown eyes serenely, softly tender,
Print rapturous kisses on the gentle brow,
So cold and pallid now.
No more, no more! repining heart, be still,
And trust in Him who doeth all things well.
Oh, happy little one!
How soon her race was run—
Her pain and suffering o'er,
Herself from sin secure.
Not hers to wander through the waste of years,
Sowing in hope, to gather nought but tears;
Nor care, nor strife,
Dimmed her brief day of life.
All true souls cherished her, and fondly strove
To guard from every ill my meek white dove.

Love, in its essence,
Pervaded her sweet presence.
How winning were her ways;
Her little child-like grace,
And the mute pleadings of her innocent eyes,
Seizing the heart with sudden, soft surprise,
As if an angel, unaware,
Had strayed from Heaven, here;
And, saddened at the dark and downward road,
Averted her meek gaze, and sought her Father, God.

In her new spiritual birth,
No garments soiled with earth
Cling round the little form, that happy strays,
Up through the gates of pearl and golden ways,
Where sister spirits meet her,
And angels joyful greet her.
Arrayed in robes of white,
She walks the paths of light;
Adorning the bright city of our God,
The glorious realms by saints and martyr trod!

THE OLD VILLAGE CHURCH

TWENTY years! Yes, twenty years had intervened since I left the pleasant village of Brookdale, and not once during all this period had I visited the dear old spot that was held more and more sacred by memory. Hundred times had I purposed to do so, yet not until the lapse of twenty years was this purpose fulfilled. Then, sobered by disappointments, I went back on a pilgrimage, to the home of early days.

I was just twenty years old when I left Brookdale. My father's family removed at the same time, and this was the reason why I had not returned. The heart's strongest attractions were in another place. But the desire to go back revived, after a season of affliction and some painful defeats in the great battle of life. The memory of dear childhood grew so palpable, and produced such an earnest longing to revisit old scenes, that I was constrained to turn my face towards my early home.

It was late in the evening of a calm autumnal day, at the close of the week, when I arrived at Brookdale. The village inn where I stopped, and at which I engaged lodgings for a few days, was not the old village inn. That had passed away, and a newer and larger building stood in its place. Nor was the old landlord there. Why had I expected to see him? Twenty years before, he was bent with age. His eyes were dim and his step faltered when last I saw him. It was but natural that he should pass away. Still, I felt a shade of disappointment when the truth came. He who filled his place was unknown to me; and, in all his household, not a familiar countenance was presented.

But I solaced myself for this with thoughts of the morrow, when my eyes would look upon long-remembered scenes and faces. The old homestead, with its garden and clambering vines—a picture which had grown more vivid in my thoughts every year—how earnest was my desire to look upon it again! There was the deep, pure spring, in which, as I bent to drink, I had so often looked upon my mirrored face; and the broad flat stone near by, where I had sat so many times. I would sit there again, after tasting the sweet water, and think of the olden time! The dear old mill, too, with its murmuring wheel glistening in the bright sunshine, and the race, on whose bank I had gathered wild flowers and raspberries?

I could sleep but little for thinking of these things, and when morning broke, and the sun shone out, I went I forth impatient to see the real objects which had been so long pictured in my memory.

"Am I in Brookdale? No—it cannot be. There is some strange error. Yes—yes—it is Brookdale, for here is the old church. I cannot mistake that. Hark! Yes—yes—it is the early bell! I would know its sound amid a thousand!"

On I moved, passing the ancient building whose architect had long since been called to sleep with his fathers, and over whose walls and spire time had cast a duller hue. I was eager to reach the old homestead. The mill lay between—or, once it did. Only a shapeless ruin now remained. The broken wheel, the crumbling walls, and empty forebay were all that my eyes rested upon, and I paused sadly to mark the wreck which time had made. The race was dry, and overgrown with elder and rank weeds. A quarter of a mile distant stood out sharply, against the clear sky, a large factory, newly built and thither the stream in which I had once sailed my tiny boat, or dropped my line, had been turned, and the old mill left to silence and decay. Ah me! I cannot make words obedient to my thoughts in giving utterance to the disappointment I then felt. A brief space I stood, mourning over the ruins, and then moved on again, a painful presentiment fast arising in my heart that all would not be, as I had left, it in the white cottage I was seeking. The two great elms that stood bending together, as if instinct with a sense of protection, above that dear home—where were they? My eyes searched for them in vain.

"Where is the spring? Surely it welled up here, and this is the way the clear stream flowed!"

Alas! the spring was dried, and scarcely a trace of its former existence remained. The broad flat stone was broken. The shady alcove beneath which the waters came up so cool and clear, had been removed. All was naked and barren. Near by stood an old deserted house. The door was half open, the windows were broken out, the chimney had fallen, and great patches of the roof had been torn away. Around, all was in keeping with this. The little garden was covered with weeds, the fence that once enclosed it was broken down, the old apple-tree that I had loved almost as tenderly as if it had been a human creature, was no more to be seen, and in the place where the grape-vine grew was a deep pool of green and stagnant water.

My first impulse was to turn and flee from the place, under a painful revulsion of feeling. But I could not leave the spot thus. For some minutes I stood mournfully leaning on the broken garden gate, and then forced myself to enter beneath the roof where I was born, and where I grew up with loving and happy children, under the sunlight of a mother's smile. If there was ruin without, there was desolation added to ruin within, but neither ruin nor desolation could entirely obliterate the forms so well remembered. I passed from room to room, now pausing to recall an incident, and now hurrying on under a sense of pain at seeing a place, hallowed in my thoughts by the tenderest associations of my life, thus abandoned to the gnawing tooth of decay, and destined to certain and speedy destruction. When I came to my mother's room, emotion grew too powerful, and a gush of tears relieved the oppressive weight that lay upon my bosom. There I lingered long, with a kind of mournful pleasure in this scene of my days of innocence, and lived over years of the bygone times.

At last I turned with sad feelings from a spot which memory had held sacred for twenty years; but which, in its change, could be sacred no longer. Material things are called substantial; but it is not so. Change and decay are ever at work upon them; they are unsubstantial. A real substance is the mind, with its thoughts and affections. Forms built there do not decay. How perfectly had I retained in memory the home of my childhood! Not a leaf had withered, not a flower had faded; nothing had fallen under the scythe of time. The greenness and perfection of all were as the mind had received them twenty years before. But the material things themselves had, in that brief space, passed almost wholly away. Yes; it is in the mind that we must seek for real substance.

Slowly and sadly I turned from the hallowed place, and went back towards the village inn. No interest for anything in Brookdale remained, and no surprise was created at the almost total obliteration of the old landmarks apparent on every hand. My purpose was to leave the place by the early stage that morning, and seek to forget that I had ever returned to the home of my childhood.

My way was past the old village church where, Sabbath after Sabbath, for nearly fifteen years, I had met with the worshippers; and as I drew nearer and nearer the sacred place, I was more and more impressed with the fact that, if change had been working busily all around, his hand had spared the holy edifice. That change had been there was plainly to be seen, but he had lingered only a moment, laying his hand gently, as he paused, on the ancient pile. New and tenderer feelings came over me. I could not pass the village church, and so I entered it once more, although it was yet too early for the worshippers to assemble. How familiar all! A year seemed not to have intervened since I had stood beneath that roof. The deep, arched windows, the antique pulpit and chancel, the old gallery and organ, the lofty roof, but most of all the broad tablet above the pulpit, and the words "Reverence my Sanctuary: I am the Lord," were as familiar as the face of a dear friend. There was change all around, but no change here in the house of God.

Seating myself in the old family pew, I gave my mind up to a flood of crowding associations; and there I sat, scarcely conscious of the passing time, until the bell sounded clear above me its weekly summons to the worshippers. And soon they began to assemble, one after another coming in, and silently taking their places. Conscious that I was intruding, I yet remained in the old family pew. It seemed as if I could not leave it—as if I must sit there and hearken once more to the words of life. And I was there when the rightful owners came. I arose to retire, but was beckoned to remain. So I resumed my seat, thankful for the privilege. Group after group entered, but faces of strangers were all around me. Presently a white-haired old man came slowly along the aisle, and, entering the chancel, ascended to the pulpit. I had not expected this. Our minister was far advanced in years when we left the village, yet here he was! How breathlessly did I lean forward to catch the sound of his voice when he arose to read the service! It was the same impressive voice, yet lower and somewhat broken. My heart trembled, and tears dimmed my eyes as the sound went echoing through the room. For a time I was a child again. I closed my eyes, and felt that my mother, my sister, and my brothers were with me.

I can never forget that morning. When the service closed, and the people moved away, I looked from countenance to countenance, but all were strange, except those of a few old men and women. Still lingering, I met the minister as he came slowly down the aisle towards the door. He did not know me, for his eyes were dim with age, and I had changed in twenty years. But, when I extended my hand and gave my name, he seized it with a quick energy, while a vivid light irradiated his countenance.

I will not weary the reader with a detail of the long interview held that day with the old minister in his own house. It was good for me that I met him ere leaving Brookdale under the pressure of a first disappointment. His words of wisdom were yet in my ears.

"As you have found the old church the same," said he, while holding my hand in parting, "amid ruin and change everywhere around, so will you find the truths which are given for our salvation ever immutable, though mere human inventions of thought are set aside by every coming generation for new philosophies, and the finer fancies of more brilliant intellects. Religion is built upon a rock, and the storms and floods of time cannot move it from its firm foundation."

"THE WORD IS NIGH THEE"

DWELL'ST thou with thine own people? are the joys,
    The hopes, the blessings of "sweet home" thine own?
"The Word is nigh thee;" hear the sacred voice!
At morn, bow with thy loved ones round the throne;
At noon-tide read and pray; and in the hour
    When evening's shades close round thee, let the truth
Subdue thy heart by its transforming power;
    That thou, whom God has blessed, may'st serve him
from thy youth.

Affection's ties oft sunder; and the home
    Of peace and love, sorrow and death can enter.
Art thou, indeed, a mourner? dost thou roam
    Alone and sad, where late thy joys did centre?
"The Word is nigh thee!" and though bitter grief
    Makes all the future seem one day of sorrow,—
Its words of peace shall grant thee sweet relief;
    The night of pain and fear shall find a joyous morrow

"The Word of God is nigh thee!" let it be
    The lamp that o'er thy pathway sheds its light,
Then, through the mists of error, thou shalt see
    The way of truth, all radiant and bright,
In which of old the sons of God did go,
    Leaning on Him who was their friend and guide;
Nor shall thy heart be faint, thy step be slow,
    Till thou in Heaven, thy home, shalt triumph by their side

The Word of God shall bless thee, in the hour
    When human hopes and human friends shall fail:
It was in health thy portion, and its power
    Is mightiest even in the gloomy vale.
No evil shalt thou fear while He is with thee;
    The sting of death his hand shall take away,
His rod and staff shall comfort thee and cheer thee,
    And thou with Him shalt dwell through heaven's eternal day.

AUNT RACHEL

WE remember as it were yesterday the first time we saw her, though it was a brief glance, and she was so quickly forgotten that most of us had passed into the supper-room and the rest had reached the door, heedless of the stranger, when one of our party, perhaps more thoughtful than the others, cast her eyes on the quiet little figure that stood, near the fire as if irresolute, whether to follow or remain. With lady-like politeness she received the excuses which one of the gentlemen offered for having preceded her, and entered the room.

She was very slight, and thin, and pale, her, eyes were of a light gray and her hair inclined to redness, but her forehead, was broad and smooth and, about her thin lips there hovered an expression of sweetness and repose.

We have forgotten now what first led us to feel that beneath that unprepossessing exterior were concealed the pulses of a warm, generous heart, and the powers of a strong and cultivated mind, but we remember well the morning that she set her seal upon our heart.

It was a clear, cold, brilliant morning in March. The whole broad country was covered with a thick crust of hard, glittering snow, and every tree was encased in ice. The oaks and elms and chestnuts and beeches from their trunks upward and outward to their minutest twigs, and the pines and firs with their greenness shining through, sparkled like diamonds and emeralds in the brightness of the sun.

O, it was a glorious morning, and we have seldom since been so young in feeling as never we are sure in years, as when we walked forth into its bracing air. And Aunt Rachel—she enjoyed it; the broad icy fields, the difficult ascent of the steep slippery hills and the "duckies" down them, and the crackling of the icicles as we thrust our way through the bristling underbrush of those diamond-cressed woods. We loved even to eat the icicles that hung from the pines with their pungent flavour, strong as though their pointed leaves had been steeped in boiling water. It was a pleasure to taste as well as see the trees.

As we entered the "Main Road" and were passing along by the "Asylum for the Insane," a clear, pleasant voice from one of the cells in the upper story, accosted us: "Good morning, ladies." We looked up and bowed in reply to the salutation. "It is a beautiful morning," he continued, "and I should like myself to take a walk down on 'Main Street,' but my folks have sent me here to be shut up because they say I am crazy, but I am sure I am not crazy, and I can't see why they should think so." And we thought the same as we listened to the calm, pleasant tones of his voice, till he added, "It will soon make me beside myself to be with this wild, screaming set; and it doesn't do them any good either to shut them up here. What they want is the Grace of God, and I'll put the Grace of God into them."

His voice grew wild and excited, but we knew that a whole volume of truth had been uttered in those simple words: "What they want is the Grace of God."

The Grace of God. How many has it saved—rescued—from madness! how have prayer and watchfulness been blest in conquering self, in subduing rampant passion and the wild, disorderly vagaries of the brain!

As we listen, the low whispered prayer of a Hall when he felt the billows of angry passion about to sweep over his soul, "O, Lamb of God, calm my perturbed spirit," we feel that but for such interceding prayer and that watchfulness which accompanied it, the insanity to which he was temporarily subject would have won the same mastery over the mighty powers of his mind as over those of Swift, and the glory of his "wide fame" as well as the peace of his "humble hope," would have been exchanged for the vagaries of the madman or the drivellings of the idiot.

The Grace of God. We thought of John Randolph, with his sway over the minds of others, with a "wit and eloquence that recalled the splendours of ancient oratory," yet with so little command over himself that his weak frame sometimes sank beneath the excitement of his temper, and gusts of passion were succeeded by fainting-fits; and when the one desire of his heart was denied, when a love mighty as every other passion of his soul failed him, his grief, ungovernable and frenzied as his rage, overwhelmed him, and the "taint of madness which ran in his line," flooded his brain. But when the atheist became a Christian; when, in his own words, he felt "the Spirit of God was not the chimera of heated brains, nor a device of artful men to frighten and cajole the credulous, but an existence to be felt and understood as the whisperings of one's own heart;" his prayer of, "Lord! I believe, help thou my unbelief," was answered in calm and peace to his soul.

"The saddest thought," said Aunt Rachel, as we turned away from that gloomy edifice, "the saddest thought connected with that building is, that so large a number of its unhappy inmates have brought their misery upon themselves, are the victims of their own irregular and indulged passions."

As we turned and looked upon her smooth brow, her serious and serene eyes and her sweet, calm mouth, we marked a look of subdued suffering mingled with an expression of Christian triumph; and we knew that she had felt "the ploughings of grief;" that she had learned "how sublime a thing it is to suffer and grow strong;" but, though we wondered deeply, we never knew in what form she had been called "to pass under the rod;" but we heard a voice that said,

"Fear not; when thou passest through the waters, I will be with thee; and through the rivers, they shall not overflow thee."

> Nay, fear not, weak and fainting soul,
> Though the wild waters round thee roll,
> He will sustain thy faltering way,
> Will be thy sure, unfailing stay.

> And though it were the fabled stream
> Whose waves were fire of fearful gleam,
> He still would bear thee safely through
> The fire, but cleanse thy soul anew.

COMETH A BLESSING DOWN

NOT to the man of dollars,
    Not to the man of deeds,
Not to the man of cunning,
    Not to the man of creeds,
Not to the one whose passion
    Is for a world's renown,
Not in a form of fashion,
    Cometh a blessing down.

Not unto land's expansion,
    Not to the miser's chest,
Not to the princely mansion,
    Not to the blazoned crest,
Not to the sordid worldling,
    Not to the knavish clown,
Not to the haughty tyrant,
    Cometh a blessing down.

Not to the folly-blinded,
    Not to the steeped in shame,
Not to the carnal-minded,
    Not to unholy fame;
Not in neglect of duty,
    Not in the monarch's crown,
Not at the smile of beauty,
    Cometh a blessing down.

But to the one whose spirit
    Yearns for the great and good;
Unto the one whose storehouse
    Yieldeth the hungry food;
Unto the one who labours,
    Fearless of foe or frown;
Unto the kindly-hearted,
    Cometh a blessing down.

THE DARKENED PATHWAY

"TO some the sky is always bright, while to others it is never free from clouds. There is to me a mystery in this—something that looks like a partial Providence—for those who grope sadly through life in darkened paths are, so far as human judgment can determine, often purer and less selfish than those who move gayly along in perpetual sunshine. Look at Mrs. Adair. It always gives me the heart-ache to think of what she has endured in life, and still endures. Once she was surrounded by all that wealth could furnish of external good; now she is in poverty, with five children, clinging to her for support, her health feeble, and few friends to counsel or lend her their aid. No woman could have loved a husband more tenderly than she loved hers, and few wives were ever more beloved in return; but she has gathered the widow's weeds around her, and is sitting in the darkness of an inconsolable grief. What a sweet character was hers! Always loving and unselfish—a very angel on the earth from childhood upwards, and yet her doom to tread this darkened pathway! If Heaven smiles on the good—if the righteous are never forsaken, why this strange, hard, harsh Providence in the case of Mrs. Adair? I cannot understand it! God is goodness itself, they say, and loves His creatures with a love surpassing the love of a mother; but would any mother condemn beloved child to such a cruel fate? No, no, no! From the very depths of my spirit I answer—No! I am only a weak, erring, selfish creature, but—"

Mrs. Endicott checked the utterance of what was in her thought, for at the instant another thought, rebuking her for an impious comparison of herself with her Maker, flitted across her mind. Yes, she was about drawing a Parallel between herself and a Being of infinite wisdom and love, unfavourable to the latter!

The sky of Mrs. Endicott had not always been free from clouds. Many times had she walked in darkness; and why this was so ever appeared as one of the mysteries of life, for her self-explorations had never gone far enough to discover those natural evils, the existence of which only a state of intense mental suffering would manifest to her deeper consciousness. But all she had yet been called to endure, was, she freely acknowledged, light in comparison to what poor Mrs. Adair had suffered, and was suffering daily—and the case of this friend gave her a strong argument against the wisdom and justice of that Power in the hands of which the children of men are as clay in the hands of the potter.

Even while Mrs. Endicott thus questioned and doubted, a domestic opened the door of the room in which she was sitting, and said,

"Mrs. Adair is in the parlour."

"Is she? Say that I will be down in a moment."

Mrs. Endicott felt a little surprised at the coincidence of her thought of her friend and that friend's appearance. It was another of those life-mysteries into which her dull eyes could not penetrate, and gave new occasion for dark surmises in regard to the Power above all, in all, and ruling all. With a sober face, as was befitting an interview with one so deeply burdened as Mrs. Adair, she went down to the parlour.

"My dear friend!" she said, tenderly, almost sadly, as she took the hand of her visiter.

Into the eyes of Mrs. Adair she looked earnestly for the glittering tear-veil, and upon her lips for the grief curve. To her surprise neither were there; but a cheerful light in the former and a gentle smile on the latter.

"How are you this morning?"

Mrs. Endicott's voice was low and sympathizing.

"I feel a little stronger, to-day, thank you," answered Mrs. Adair, smiling as she spoke.

"How is your breast?"

"Still very tender."

"And the pain in your side."

"I am not free from that a moment."

Still she smiled as she answered. There was not even a touch of sadness or despondency in her voice.

"Not free a moment! How do you bear it?"

"Happily—as I often say to myself—I have no time to think about the pain," replied Mrs. Adair, cheerfully. "It is wonderful how mental activity lifts us above the consciousness of bodily suffering. For my part, I am sure that if I had nothing to do but to sit down and brood over my ailments, I would be one of the most miserable, complaining creatures alive. But a kind Providence, even in the sending of poverty to his afflicted one, has but tempered the winds to the shorn lamb."

Mrs. Endicott was astonished to hear these words, falling, as they did, with such a confiding earnestness from the pale lips of her much-enduring friend.

"How can you speak so cheerfully?" she said. "How can you feel so thankful to Him who has shrouded your sky in darkness, and left you to grope in strange paths, on which falls not a single ray of light?"

"Even though the sky is clouded," was answered, "I know that the sun is shining there as clear and as beautiful as ever. The paths in which a wise and good Providence has called me to walk, may be strange, and are, at times, rough-and toilsome; but you err in saying that no light falls upon them."

"But the sky is dark—whence comes the light, Mrs. Adair?"

"Don't you remember the beautiful hymn written by Moore? It is to me worth all he ever penned besides. How often do I say it over to myself, lingering with a warming heart and a quickening pulse, on every word of consolation!"

And in the glow of her fine enthusiasm, Mrs. Adair repeated—

"Oh, Thou, who dry'st the mourner's tear,
   How dark this world would be,
If, when deceived and wounded here,
   We could not fly to Thee!
The friends, who in our sunshine live,
   When winter comes, are flown;
And he who has but tears to give,
   Must weep those tears alone.
But Thou wilt heal that broken heart,
   Which, like the plants that throw
Their fragrance from the wounded part,
   Breathes sweetness out of woe.

"When joy no longer soothes or cheers,
   And e'en the hope that threw
A moment's sparkle o'er our tears
   Is dimmed and vanished, too,
Oh, who would bear life's stormy doom,
   Did not Thy wing of Love
Come, brightly wafting through the gloom
   Our Peace-branch from above?
Then sorrow, touched by Thee, grows bright
   With more than rapture's ray

> As darkness shows us worlds of light
> We never saw by day."

"None," said Mrs. Adair, "but those who have had the sky of their earthly affections shrouded in darkness, can fully understand the closing words of this consolatory hymn. Need I now answer your question, 'Whence comes the light?' There is an inner world Mrs. Endicott—a world full of light, and joy, and consolation—a world whose sky is never darkened, whose sun is never hidden by clouds. When we turn from all in this life that we vainly trusted, and lift our eyes upward towards the sky, bending over our sad spirits, an unexpected light breaks in upon us, and we see a new firmament, glittering with myriads of stairs, whose light is fed from that inner world where the sun shines for ever undimmed. Oh, no, I do not tread a darkened pathway, Mrs. Endicott. There is light upon it from the Sun of heaven, and I am walking forward, weary at times, it may be, but with unwavering footsteps. I have been tried sorely, it is true—I have suffered, oh how deeply! and yet I can say, and do say, it is good for me that I was afflicted. But I meant not to speak so much of myself, and you must forgive the intrusion. Self, you know, is ever an attractive theme. I have called this morning to try and interest you in a poor woman who lives next door to me. She is very ill, and I am afraid will die. She has two children, almost babes—sweet little things—and if the mother is taken they will be left without a home or a friend, unless God puts it into the heart of some one to give them both. I have been awake half the night, thinking about them, and debating the difficult question of my duty in the case. I might make room for one of them—"

"You!" Mrs. Endicott interrupted her in a voice of unfeigned astonishment. "You! How can you give place a moment to such a thought, broken down in health as you are and with five children of your own clinging to you for support? It would be unjust to yourself and to them. Don't think of such a thing."

"That makes the difficulty in the case," replied Mrs. Adair. "The spirit is willing, but the flesh is weak. My heart is large enough to take both of them in; but I have not strength enough to bear the added burden. And so I have come around this morning to see if I cannot awaken your interest. They are dear, sweet children, and will carry sunshine and a blessing into any home that opens to receive them."

"But why, my friend," said Mrs. Endicott, "do you, whose time is so precious—who have cares, and interests, and anxieties of your own, far more than enough for one poor, weak woman to bear, burden yourself with a duty like this? Leave the task to others more fitted for the work."

"There are but few who can rightly sympathize with that mother and her babes; and I am one of the few. Ah! my kind friend, none but the mother, who like me has been brought to the verge of eternity, can truly feel for one in like circumstances. I have looked at my own precious ones, as I felt the waves of time sweeping my feet from their earthly resting place, and wept bitter tears as no answer came to the earnest question, 'Who will love them, who will care for the when I am taken?' You cannot know, Mrs. Endicott, how profoundly thankful to God I am, that He spares my life, and yet gives me strength to do for my children. I bless His name for this tender mercy towards me when I lie down at night, and when I rise up in the morning, I bear every burden, I endure every pain cheerfully, hopefully, even thankfully. It is because I can understand the heart of this dying mother, and feel for her in her mortal extremity, that I undertake her cause. You have only one child, my friend, and she is partly grown. 'A babe in the house is a well-spring of pleasure.' Is it not so? Take one, or even both of these children, if the mother dies. They are the little ones who are born upon the earth, in order that they may become angels in Heaven. They are of God's kingdom, and precious in His eyes. Nurture and raise them up for Him. Come! oh, come with me to the bedside of this dying mother, and say to her, 'Give me your babes, and I will shelter them in my heart.' So doing, you will open for yourself a perennial fountain of delight. The picture of that poor mother's joyful face, painted instantly by love's bright sunbeams on your memory, will be a source of pleasure lasting as eternity. Do not neglect this golden opportunity, nor leave other hands to gather the blessings which lie about your feet."

That earnest plea was echoed from the heart of Mrs. Endicott. The beautiful enthusiasm, so full of a convincing eloquence, prevailed; and the woman in whose heart the waters of benevolence were growing stagnant, and already sending up exhalations that were hiding the Sun of heaven, felt a yearning pity for the dying mother, and was moved by an unselfish impulse toward her and her babes. Half an hour afterwards she was in the sick-chamber; and ere leaving had received from the happy mother the solemn gift of her children, and seen her eyes close gently as her spirit took its tranquil departure for its better home.

"God will bless you, madame!"

All the dying mother's thankfulness was compressed into these words, and her full heart spent itself in their utterance.

Far away, in the inner depths of Mrs. Endicott's spirit—very far away—the words found an echo; and as this echo came back to her ears, she felt a new thrill of pleasure that ran deeper down the electric chain of feelings than emotion had ever, until now, penetrated. There were depths and capacities in her being unknown before; and of this she had now a dim perception. Her action was unselfish, and to be unselfish is to be God-like—for God acts from a love of blessing others. To be God-like in her action brought her nearer the Infinite Source of what is pure and holy; and all proximity in this direction gives its measure of interior delight—as all retrocession gives its measure of darkness and disquietude.

"God will bless you!"

Mrs. Endicott never ceased hearing these words, and she felt them to be a prophecy. And God did bless her. In bestowing love and care upon the motherless little ones, she received from above double for all she gave. In blessing, she was twice blessed. About them her heart entwined daily new tendrils, until her own life beat with theirs in even pulses, and to seek their good was the highest joy of her existence.

Still there were times when Mrs. Endicott felt that to some God was not just in his dispensations, and the closer she observed Mrs. Adair, the less satisfied was she that one so pure-minded, so unselfish, so earnest to impart good to others, should be so hardly dealt by—should be compelled to grope through life with painful steps along a darkened way.

"There is a mystery in all this which my dim vision fails to penetrate," she said one day, to Mrs. Adair. "But we see here only in part—I must force myself into the belief that all is right. I say *force*, for it is indeed force-work."

"To me," was answered, "there is no longer a mystery here. I have been led by at way that I knew not. For a time I moved along this way, doubting, fearing trembling—but now I see that it is the right way, and though toilsome at times, yet it is winding steadily upwards, and I begin to see the sunshine resting calmly on the mountain-tops. Flowers, too, are springing by the wayside—few they are, as yet, but very fragrant."

Mrs. Adair paused for a moment, and then resumed,

"It may sound strange to you, but I am really happier than when all was bright and prosperous around me."

Mrs. Endicott looked surprised.

"I am a better woman, and therefore happier. I do not say this boastfully, but only to meet your question. I am a more useful woman, and therefore happier, for, as I have learned, inward peace is the sure reward of benefits conferred. The doing of good to another, from an unselfish end, brings to the heart its purest pleasure; and is not that the kindest Providence which leads us, no matter by what hard experiences, into a state of willingness to live for others instead of for ourselves alone? The dying mother, whose gift to you has proved so great—a good, might have passed away, though her humble abode stood beside the elegant residence I called my home, without exciting more than a passing wave of sympathy—certainly without filling my heart with the yearning desire to make truly peaceful her last moments, which led to the happy results that followed her efforts in my behalf. My children, too; you have often lamented that it is not so well with them as it would have been had misfortune not overshadowed us,—but I am not so sure of that. I believe that all external disadvantages will be more than counterbalanced by the higher regard I have been led to take in the development of what is good and true in their characters. I now see them as future men and women, for whose usefulness and happiness I am in a great measure responsible; and as my views of life have become clearer, and I trust wiser, through suffering, I am far better able, under all the disadvantages of my position, to secure this great end than I was before."

"But the way is hard for you—very hard," said Mrs. Endicott.

"It is my preparation for Heaven," replied the patient sufferer, while a smile, not caught from earth, made beautiful her countenance. "If my Heavenly Father could have made the way smoother, He would have done so. As it is, I thank Him daily for the roughness, and would not ask to have a stone removed or a rough place made even."

LOOK ON THIS PICTURE

O, IT is life! departed days
Fling back their brightness while I gaze—
'Tis Emma's self—this brow so fair,
Half-curtained in this glossy hair,
These eyes, the very home of love,
The dark thin arches traced above,
These red-ripe lips that almost speak,
The fainter blush of this pure cheek,
The rose and lily's beauteous strife—
It is—ah, no! 'tis all *but* life.

'Tis all *but* life—art could not save
Thy graces, Emma, from the grave;
Thy cheek is pale, thy smile is past,
Thy love-lit eyes have looked their last,
Mouldering beneath the coffin's lid,
All we adored of thee is hid;
Thy heart, where goodness loved to dwell,
Is throbless in the narrow cell:
Thy gentle voice shall charm no more,
Its last, last joyful note is o'er.

Oft, oft, indeed, it hath been sung,
The requiem of the fair and young;
The theme is old, alas! how old,
Of grief that will not be controlled,
Of sighs that speak a father's woe,
Of pangs that none but mothers know,
Of friendship with its bursting heart,
Doomed from the idol-one to part—
Still its sad debt must feeling pay,
Till feeling, too, shall pass away.

O say, why age, and grief, and pain,
Shall long to go, but long in vain?
Why vice is left to mock at time,
And gray in years, grow gray in crime;

While youth, that every eye makes glad,
And beauty, all in radiance clad,
And goodness, cheering every heart,
Come, but come only to depart;
Sunbeams, to cheer life's wintry day,
Sunbeams, to flash, then fade away?

'Tis darkness all! black banners wave
Round the cold borders of the grave;
Then when in agony we bend
O'er the fresh sod that hides a friend,
One only comfort then we know—
We, too, shall quit this world of woe;
We, too, shall find a quiet place
With the dear lost ones of our race;
Our crumbling bones with theirs shall blend,
And life's sad story find an end.

And *is* this all—this mournful doom?
Beams no glad light beyond the tomb?
Mark how yon clouds in darkness ride;
They do not quench the orb they hide;
Still there it wheels—the tempest o'er,
In a bright sky to burn once more;
So, far above the clouds of time,
Faith can behold a world sublime—
There, when the storms of life are past,
The light beyond shall break at last.

THE POWER OF KINDNESS

HOW much comprised in the simple word, *kindness!* One kind word, or even one mild look, will oftentimes dispel thick gathering gloom from the countenance of an affectionate husband, or wife. When the temper is tried by some inconvenience or trifling vexation, and marks of displeasure are depicted upon the countenances and perhaps, too, that most "unruly of all members" is ready to vent its spleen upon the innocent husband or wife, what will a kind mien, a pleasant reply, accomplish? Almost invariably perfect harmony and peace are thus restored.

These thoughts were suggested by the recollection of a little domestic incident, to which I was a silent, though not uninterested spectator. During the summer months of 1834, I was spending several weeks with a happy married pair, who had tasted the good and ills of life together only a twelvemonth. Both possessed many amiable qualities, and were well calculated to promote each other's happiness. My second visit to my friends was of a week's duration, in the month of December. One cold evening the husband returned home at his usual hour at nine o'clock, expecting to find a warm fire for his reception, but, instead, he found a cheerless, comfortless room. His first thought, no doubt, was, that it was owing to the negligence of his wife, and, under this impression, in rather a severe tone, he said,

"This is too bad; to come in from the office cold, and find no fire; I really should have thought you might have kept it."

I sat almost breathless, trembling for the reply. I well knew it was no fault of hers, for she had wasted nearly all the evening, and almost exhausted her patience, in attempting to kindle a fire. She in a moment replied, with great kindness,

"Why my dear, I wonder what is the matter with our stove! We must have something done to-morrow, for I have spent a great deal of time in vain to make a fire."

This was said in such a mild, pleasant tone, that it had the most happy effect. If she had replied at that moment, when his feelings were alive to supposed neglect, "I don't know who is to blame; I have done my part, and have been freezing all the evening for my pains. If the stove had been put up as it should have been, all would have been well enough." This, said in an unamiable, peevish tone, might have added "fuel to the fire," and this little breeze might have led to more serious consequences; but fortunately, her mild reply restored perfect serenity. The next day the stove was taken down, and the difficulty, owing to some defect in the flue, was removed. What will not a kind word accomplish?

SPEAK KINDLY

SPEAK kindly, speak kindly! ye know not the power
   Of a kind and gentle word,
As its tones in a sad and weary hour
   By the trouble heart are heard.
    Ye know not how often it falls to bless
    The stranger in his weariness;
    How many a blessing is round thee thrown
    By the magic spell, of a soft, low tone.
Speak kindly, then, kindly; there's nothing lost
   By gentle words—to the heart and ear
Of the sad and lonely, they're dear, how dear,
   And they nothing cost.

Speak kindly to childhood. Oh, do not fling
   A cloud o'er life's troubled sky;
But cherish it well—a holy thing
   Is the heart in its purity.
    Enough of sorrow the cold world hath,
    Enough of care in its later path,
    And ye do a wrong if ye seek to throw
    O'er the fresh young spirit a shade of woe.
Speak kindly, then, kindly; there's nothing lost
   By gentle words—to the heart and ear
Of joyous childhood, they're dear, how dear—
   And they nothing cost.

Speak gently to age—a weary way
   Is the rough and toilsome road of life,
As one by one its joys decay,
   And its hopes go out 'mid its lengthened strife.
   How often the word that is kindly spoken,
   Will bind up the heart that is well nigh broken,
   Then pass not the feeble and aged one
   With a cold, and careless, and slighting tone;
But kindly, speak kindly; there's nothing lost
   By gentle words—to the heart and ear

Of the care-worn and weary, they're dear, how dear—
    And they nothing cost.

Speak kindly to those who are haughty and cold,
    Ye know not the thoughts that are dwelling there;
Ye know not the feelings that struggle untold—
    Oh, every heart hath its burden of care.
And the curl of the lip, and the scorn of the eye
    Are often a bitter mockery,
    When a bursting heart its grief would hide
    From the eye of the world 'neath a veil of pride.
Speak kindly, then, kindly; there's nothing lost
    By gentle words—to the heart and ear
Of the proud and haughty they're often dear,
    And they nothing cost.

Speak kindly ever—oh, cherish well
    The light of a gentle tone;
It will fling round thy pathway a magic spell,
    A charm that is all its own.
    But see that it springs from a gentle heart,
    That it need not the hollow aid of art;
    Let it gush in its joyous purity,
    From its home in the heart all glad and free.
Speak kindly, then, kindly; there's nothing lost
    By gentle words—to the heart and ear
Of all who hear them they're dear, how dear—
    And they nothing cost.

HAVE PATIENCE

IT was Saturday evening, about eight o clock. Mary Gray had finished mangling, and had sent home the last basket of clothes. She had swept up her little room, stirred the fire, and placed upon it a saucepan of water. She had brought out the bag of oatmeal, a basin, and a spoon, and laid them upon the round deal table. The place, though very scantily furnished, looked altogether neat and comfortable. Mary now sat idle by the fire. She was not often idle.' She was a pale, delicate-looking woman, of about five-and-thirty. She looked like ones who had worked beyond her strength, and her thin face had a very anxious, careworn expression. Her dress showed signs of poverty, but it was scrupulously clean and neat. As it grew later, she seemed to be listening attentively for the approach of some one; she was ready to start up every time a step came near her door. At length a light step approached, and did not go by it; it stopped, and there was a gentle tap at the door. Mary's pallid face brightened, and in a moment she had let in a fine, intelligent-looking lad, about thirteen years of age, whom she welcomed with evident delight.

"You are later than usual to-night, Stephen," she said.

Stephen did not reply; but he threw off his cap, and placed himself in the seat Mary had quitted.

"You do not look well to-night, dear," said Mary anxiously; "is anything the matter?"

"I am quite well, mother," replied the boy. "Let me have my supper. I am quite ready for it."

As he spoke, he turned away his eyes from Mary's inquiring look. Mary, without another word, set herself about preparing the supper, of oatmeal porridge. She saw that something was wrong with Stephen, and that he did not wish to be questioned, so she remained silent. In the mean time Stephen had placed his feet on the fender, rested his elbows on his knees, and his head on his hands. His hands covered his face; and, by and by, a few large tears began to trickle down his fingers. Then suddenly dashing off his tears, as though he were ashamed of them, he showed his pale, agitated face, and said, in a tone of indignation and resolve,

"Mother, I am determined I will bear it no longer."

Mary was not surprised. She finished pouring out the porridge; then, taking a stool, she seated herself beside him.

"Why, Stephen," she said, trying to speak cheerfully, "how many hundred times before have you made that resolution! But what's the matter now? Have you any new trouble to tell me of?"

Stephen answered by silently removing with his hand some of his thick curly hair, and showing beneath it an ear bearing the too evident marks of cruel usage.

"My poor boy!" exclaimed Mary, her tears starting forth. "Could he be so cruel?"

"It is nothing, mother," replied the boy, sorry to have called forth his mother's tears. "I don't care for it. It was done in a passion, and he was sorry for it after."

"But what could you have done, Stephen, to make him so angry with you?"

"I was selling half a quire of writing paper to a lady: he counted the sheets after me, and found thirteen instead of only twelve; they had stuck together so that I took two for one. I tried to explain, but he was in a passion, and gave me a blow. The lady said something to him about his improper conduct, and he said that I was such a *careless little rascal*, that he lost all patience with me. That hurt me a great deal more than the blow. It was a falsehood, and he knew it; but he wanted to excuse himself. I felt that I was going into a passion, too, but I thought of what you are always telling me about patience and forbearance, and I kept down my passion; I know he was sorry for it after, from the way he spoke to me, though he didn't say so."

"I have no doubt he suffered more than you, Stephen," said Mary; "he would be vexed that he, had shown his temper before the lady, vexed that he had told a lie, and vexed that he had hurt you when you bore it so patiently."

"Yes, mother, but that doesn't make it easier for me to bear his ill temper; I've borne it now for more than a year for your sake, and I can bear it no longer. Surely I can get something to do; I'm sturdy and healthy, and willing to do any kind of work."

Mary shook her head, and remained for a long time silent and thoughtful. At length she said, with a solemn earnestness of manner that almost made poor Stephen cry,

"You say that, for my sake, you have borne your master's unkind treatment for more than a year; for my sake, bear it longer, Stephen. Your patience must, and will be rewarded in the end. You know how I have worked, day and night, ever since your poor father died, when you were only a little infant in the cradle, to feed and clothe you, and to pay for your schooling, for I was determined that you should have schooling; you know how I have been cheered in all my toil by the hope of seeing you, one day, getting on in the world, And I know, Stephen, that you will get on. You are good, honest lad, and kind to your poor mother, and God will reward you. But not if you are hasty; not if you are impatient. You know how hard it was for me to get you this situation; you might not get another; you must not leave; you must not break your indentures; you must be patient and industrious still; you have a hard master, and, God knows, it costs me many at heartache to think of what you have to suffer; but bear with him, Stephen; bear with him, for my sake, a few years longer."

Stephen was now fairly crying and his mother kissed off his tears, while her own flowed freely. Her appeal to his affection was not in vain. He soon smiled through his tears, as he said,

"Well, mother, you always know how to talk me over, When I came in to-night I did think that I would never go the shop again. But I will promise you to be patient and industrious still. Considering all that you have, done for me, this is little enough for me to do for you. When I have a shop of my own, you shall live like a lady. I'll trust to your word that I shall be sure to get on, if I am patient and industrious, though I don't see how it's to be.— It's not so very bad to bear after all; and, bad as my master is, there's one comfort, he lets me have my Saturday nights and blessed Sundays with you. Well, I feel happier now, and I think I can eat my supper. We forgot that my porridge was getting cold all this time."

Stephen kept his word; day after day, and month after month, his patience and industry never flagged. And plenty of trials, poor fellow, he had for his fortitude. His master, a small stationer in a small country town, to whom Stephen was bound apprentice for five years, with a salary barely sufficient to keep him in clothes, was a little, spare, sharp-faced man, who seemed to have worn himself away with continual fretfulness and vexation. He was perpetually fretting, perpetually finding fault with something or other, perpetually thinking that everything was going wrong. Though he did cease to go into a passion with, and to strike Stephen, the poor lad was an object always at hand, on which to vent his ill-humour, Many, many times was Stephen on the point of losing heart and temper; but he was always able to control himself by thinking of his mother. And, as he said, there was always comfort in those Saturday nights and blessed Sundays. A long walk in the country on those blessed Sundays, and the Testament readings to his mother, would always strengthen his often wavering faith in her prophecies of good in the end, would cheer his spirits, and nerve him with a fresh resolution for the coming week. And what was it that the widow hoped would result from this painful bondage? She did not know; she only had faith in her doctrine—that patience and industry would some time be rewarded. *How* the reward was to come in her son's case, she could not see. It seemed likely, indeed, from all appearances, that the doctrine in this case would prove false. But still she had faith.

It was now nearly four years since the conversation between mother and son before detailed. They were together again on the Saturday evening. Stephen had grown into a tall, manly youth, with a gentle, kind, and thoughtful expression of countenance. Mary looked much older, thinner, paler, and more anxious. Both were at this moment looking very downcast.

"I do not see that anything can be hoped from him," said Stephen, with a sigh. "I have now served him faithfully for five years; I have borne patiently all his ill-humour; I have never been absent a moment from my post; and during all that time, notwithstanding all this, he has never thanked me, he has never so much as given me a single kind word, nor even a kind look. He must know that apprenticeships will be out on Tuesday, yet he never says a word to me about it, and I suppose I must just go without a word."

"You must speak to him," said Mary; "you cannot leave without saying something; and tell him exactly how you are situated; he cannot refuse to do something to help you."

"It is easy to talk of speaking to him, mother, but not so easy to do it. I have often before thought of speaking to him, of telling him how very, very poor we are, and begging a little more salary. But I never could do it when I came before him. I seemed to feel that he would refuse me, and I felt somehow too proud to ask a favour that would most likely be refused. But it shall be done now, mother; I will not be a burthen upon you, if I can help it. I'd sooner do anything than that. He *ought* to do something for me, and there's no one else that I know of that can. I will speak to him on Monday."

Monday evening was come; all day Stephen had been screwing up his courage for the task he had to do; of course it could not be done when his master and he were in the shop together, for there they were liable at any moment to be interrupted. At dinner-time they separated; for they took the meal alternately, that the post in the shop might never be deserted. But now the day's work was over: everything was put away, and master and apprentice had retired into the little back parlour a to take their tea. As usual, they were alone, for the stationer was a single man (which might account for the sourness of his temper), and the meal was usually taken in silence, and soon after it was over they would both retire to bed, still in silence. Stephen's master had poured out for him his first cup of tea, handed it to him without looking at him, and begun to swallow his own potion. Stephen allowed his cup to remain before him untouched; he glanced timidly towards his master, drew a deep breath, coloured slightly, and then began:—

"If you please, sir, I wish to speak to you."

His master looked up with a sudden jerk of the head, and fixed his keen gray eyes on poor Stephen's face. He did not seem at all surprised, but said sharply (and he had a very sharp voice), "Well, sir, speak on."

Stephen was determined not to be discouraged, so he began to tell his little tale. His voice faltered at first, but as he went on he became quite eloquent. He spoke with a boldness which astonished himself. He forgot his master, and thought only of his mother. He told all about her poverty, and struggles to get a living. He dwelt strongly, but modestly, on his own conduct during his apprenticeship, and finished by entreating his master now to help him to do something, for he had nothing in the world to turn to, no friends, no money, no influence.

His master heard him to an end. He had soon withdrawn his eyes from Stephen's agitated face, then partially averted his own face, then left his seat, and advanced to a side table, where he began to rummage among some papers, with his back to Stephen.

Stephen had ceased speaking some time before he made any reply. Then still without turning round, he spoke, beginning with a sort of grunting ejaculation—"Humph! so your mother gets her living by mangling, does she? and she thought that if she got you some schooling, and taught you to behave yourself, your fortune would be made. Well, you will be free tomorrow; you may go to her and tell her she is a fool for her pains. Here are your indentures, and here's the salary that's due to you. Now you may go to bed."

As he spoke the last words, he had taken the indentures from a desk, and the money from his purse. Stephen felt a choking sensation in his throat as he took from his hands the paper and the money; he would even have uttered the indignation he felt, but, before he could speak, his master left the room. Disappointed and heart-sick, and feeling humiliated that he should have asked a favour of such a man, the poor lad retired to his garret, and it was almost time to get up in the morning before he could fall asleep. On the Tuesday, when the day's work was over, Stephen packed up his bundle of clothes;—should he say good-bye to his master? Yes; he would not be ungracious at the last. He opened the door of the back parlour, and stood just within the door-way, his bundle in his hand. His master was sitting, solitary, at the tea-table.

"I am going, sir, good-bye," said Stephen.

"Good-bye, sir," returned his master, without, looking at him. And so they parted.

The result of the application told, the mother and the son sat together that night in silence; their hearts were too full for words. Mary sorrowed most, because she had hoped most. Bitter tears rolled down her cheeks, as she sat brooding over her disappointment. Stephen looked more cheerful, for his mind was busy trying to form plans for the future—how he should go about to seek for another situation, &c. Bed-time came; both rose to retire to rest. Stephen had pressed his mother's hand, and was retiring, saying as he went, "Never mind, mother, it'll all be right yet," when they were startled by a loud rap at the door.

"Who's there?" shouted Stephen.

"A letter for you," was the reply.

Stephen thought there was some mistake, but he opened the door. A letter was put into his hand, and the bearer disappeared. Surprised, Stephen held the letter close to the rush-light Mary was carrying. He became still more surprised; it was addressed to Mrs. Gray, that was his mother, and he thought he knew the handwriting; it was very like his master's. Mary's look of wonder became suddenly brightened by a flash of hope; she could not read writing—Stephen must read it for her. He opened the letter, something like a banknote was the first thing he saw—he examined it—it was actually a ten pound Bank of England note; his heart beat rapidly, and so did his mother's; what could this mean? But there was a little note which would perhaps explain. Stephen's fingers trembled sadly as he opened it. There were not many words, but they were to the purpose. Stephen read them to himself before he read them aloud. And as he was reading, his face turned very red, and how it did burn! But what was the meaning of tears, and he looking so pleased? Mary could not understand it.

"Do read up, Stephen," she exclaimed.

With a voice broken by the effort he had to make all the time to keep from crying, Stephen read,

"MADAM—Put away your mangle-that son of yours is worth mangling for; but it is time to rest now. The note is for your present wants; in future your son may supply you. I let him go to-night; but I did not mean him to stay away, if he chooses to come back. I don't see that I can do well without him. But I don't want him back if he would rather go anywhere else; I know plenty that would be glad to have him. He has been seen in the shop, and noticed, and such lads are not always to be got. If he chooses to come back to me, he won't repent. I've no sons of my own, thank God. He knows what I am; I am better than I was, and I may be better still. I've a queer way of doing things, but it is my way, and can't be helped. Tell him I'll be glad to have him back to-morrow, if he likes. Yours,

"J. W."

"I knew it!" exclaimed Mary, triumphantly; "I always said so! I knew you would get on!"

Stephen did go back to his eccentric master, and he never had any reason to repent. He *got on* even beyond his mother's most soaring hopes. The shop eventually became his own, and he lived a flourishing and respected tradesman. We need scarcely add that his mother had no further use for her mangle, and that she was a very proud and a very happy woman.

DO THEY MISS ME?

Do they miss me at home? Do they miss me?
   'Twould be an assurance most dear,
To know at this moment some loved one
   Was saying, "I wish he was here!"
To feel that the group at the fireside
   Were thinking of me as I roam!
Oh, yes! 'twould be joy beyond measure,
   To know that they missed me at home.

When twilight approaches—the season
   That ever was sacred to song—
Does some one repeat my name over,
   And sigh that I tarry so long?
And is there a chord in the music,
   That's missed when my voice is away?
And a chord in each glad heart that waketh
   Regret at my wearisome stay?

Do they place me a chair at the table,
   When evening's home pleasures are nigh!
And lamps are lit up in the parlour,
   And stars in the calm azure sky?
And when the "Good Nights" are repeated,
   And each lays them calmly to sleep,
Do they think of the absent, and waft me
   A whispered "Good-Night" o'er the deep?

Do they miss me at home? do they miss me?
   At morning, at noon, or at night,
And lingers one gloomy shade round them,
   That only my presence can light?
Are joys less invitingly welcomed,
   Are pleasures less hailed than before,

Because one is missed from the circle?
Because I am with them no more?

Oh, yes! they do miss me! kind voices
Are calling me back as I roam,
And eyes are grown weary with weeping,
And watch but to welcome me home.
Kind friends, ye shall wait me no longer,
I'll hurry me back from the seas;
For how can I tarry when followed
By watchings and prayers such as these?